A BIRD IN THE HOUSE

BRONWEN GRIFFITHS

Three Hares Publishing

Published by Three Hares Publishing 2014

First published in Great Britain in 2014
www.threeharespublishing.com

Three Hares Publishing Ltd Reg. No 8531198
Registered address: Suite 201, Berkshire House,
39-51 High Street,
Ascot, Berkshire, SL5 7HY

ISBN-13: 9781910153062

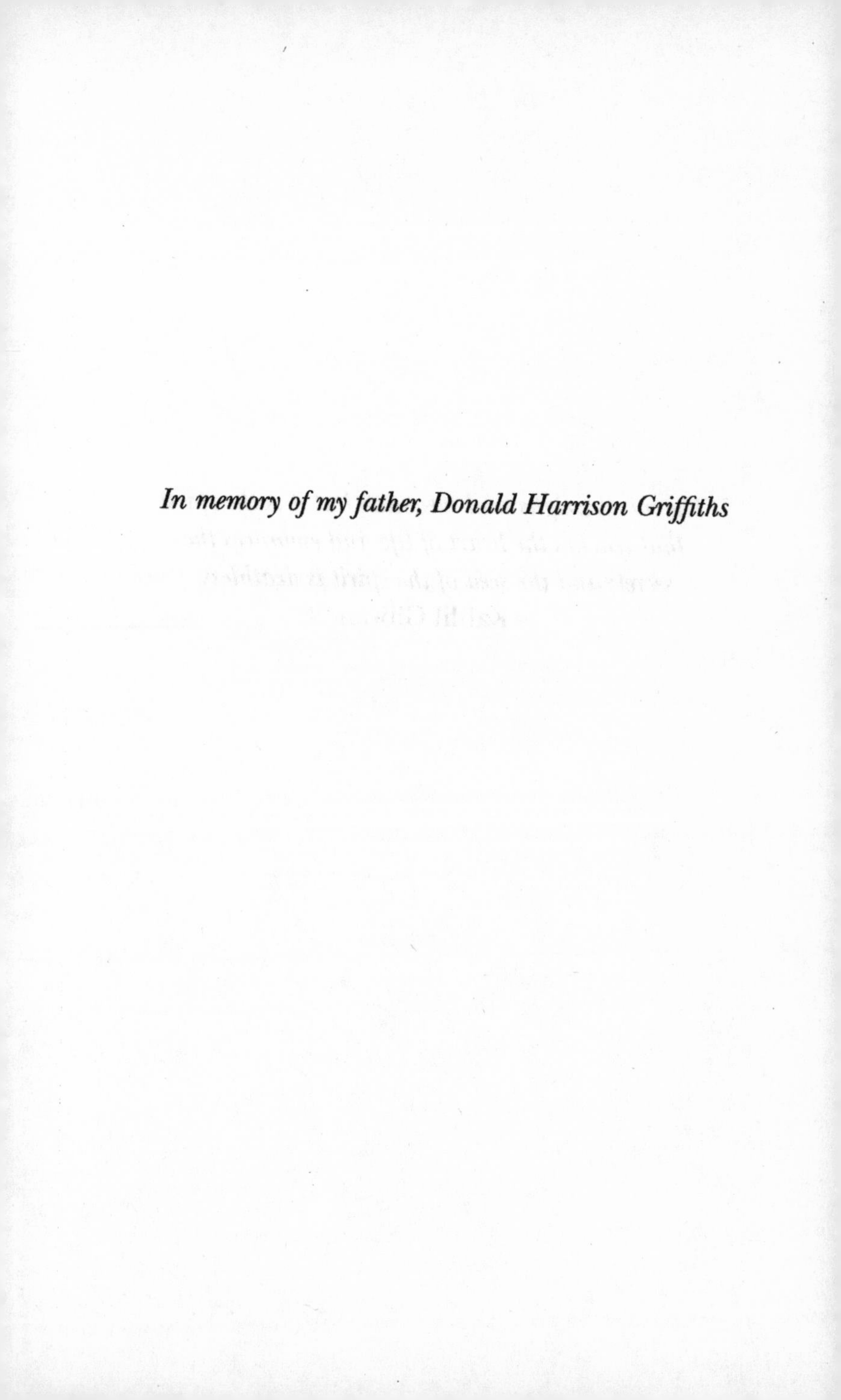

In memory of my father, Donald Harrison Griffiths

The mind weighs and measures but it is the spirit that reaches the heart of life and embraces the secret; and the seed of the spirit is deathless.
~ Kahlil Gibran

PART 1

Chapter One

Ahmed tips his dirty football kit out of his sports bag and places it in the washing machine. The blue bag is emblazoned with the Chelsea club logo. He persuaded his father to buy it last year. When his father asked why he should want such a thing, Ahmed shrugged. How can he ever explain? He cannot say to his father that he often feels like a stranger, that a sports bag isn't just a bag but a badge of belonging. But he doesn't belong. He is not sure where he belongs. And today the bag only reminds him of London, and whenever he thinks of London he feels muddled inside.

He can't remember that family trip to London. He was just a baby. But his sister, Safia, was ten at the time and she talked of it so often it was as if Ahmed remembered the fleets of red buses, the tall column set in a square where so many pigeons flew they darkened the sky, the girls walking the streets dressed in tiny skirts, their father not knowing where to put his eyes, and men, their pale hairy arms tattooed with mermaids, hearts and snakes.

But it must have been a happy time because when his father spoke of it he laughed. 'How it rained!' he said. 'Your mother couldn't stand the rain and I bought her an umbrella in all the colours of the rainbow.' He sighed and stared out of the open window, down onto the noisy street, his laughter blown away like dust.

'Do we still have the umbrella?' Safia asked.

His father shook his head. 'I think it got lost in the move.'

Ahmed pours a measure of washing powder into the drawer and presses the red button.

London, yes, London.

Three years ago Ahmed and his father returned to the city, but this time they arrived alone and Ahmed's heart felt as heavy as his suitcase. Safia had stayed behind in Tripoli but his mother was gone forever.

There is much Ahmed does not understand concerning his mother. The Colonel sent her to prison for a year because she said something he disapproved of – just a little something it was, his father whispered, but there is to be no talk of it, none at all – but that doesn't explain what happened later or why his mother was so unhappy.

Once upon a time.

Once upon a time his mother taught part-time at the local school. She loved working there she said, it's a real privilege to see children grow. 'Children are like seeds. They need water and sunlight and if you trample on the new shoots, they wither and die.'

Once upon a time his mother cooked *bazin* – stew and dumpling – and *mb'atten* – fried potato wedges stuffed with mince – and the house was filled with the scent of spices and the sound of her laughter. Once upon a time she sat with Ahmed every night and told stories, and every Friday she took him and Safia to the Italian ice-cream parlour or the café in Green Square.

After she came back from the prison she was not allowed to return to her job. 'I'm an outcast now,' she said. 'No one wants to see my face.' She stayed in bed all day and sometimes even for days at a time.

After she came back she turned into a stranger who grabbed Ahmed's hand and looked at him as if he were someone she did not know. And after came the unexplained move from their beautiful house by the sea to a cramped and dirty apartment in a different part of the city. And after came that terrible day, the last in the month of May and the beginning of a long, suffocating summer.

When Ahmed returned from school he crept into the bedroom where his mother was lying in bed. As usual the blinds were drawn and nothing stirred but the overhead fan ticking like a clock.

'Mama,' he called, softly. 'Mama.' He tiptoed to the bed, stretched out his hand and brushed her cheek with his fingers. He would often find her asleep when he arrived home, but that day her face was as pale as paper and her skin felt clammy and cold. 'Mama,' he repeated, his voice ringing out in the silence. 'Mama!'

The bird she'd insisted his father buy, a small grey and white creature, its beak orange like the tangerines that grew in their old garden, stood on its perch by the window – although it too was silent. He looked at his mother again. Her mouth hung open and her left arm lay across the bed-cover, the skin almost white and her fingernails, once neat and manicured, now bitten and ragged.

He lent over, his face close to hers. Whoosh, whoosh went the fan, and a call came from the street, a woman's voice.

'Mama, Mama.'

He remembers this: a sound exploding from deep inside him like a bomb, Safia running, the door bursting open, the bird suddenly shrill. He remembers the empty glass of water on his mother's dresser, an open bottle fallen on its side, a strange and sickly smell, and he remembers Safia calling their father, her voice echoing through the apartment. But no more remains, only something closed and dark like the inside of a well.

After their mother was buried, their father said, 'Your mother's heart gave out. She had a weakness there.' His father would know: he was a doctor. But they never spoke of his mother's illness: the days she would not eat a single juicy date or a ripe pomegranate, the weeks she would jump at her own shadow and turn her face to the wall. Ahmed wanted to ask his sister what she thought, but Safia sat silent and withdrawn so he kept his questions to himself.

Eight years old and his mother dead, the weight of it on his shoulders heavy as a mountain.

The key turns in the lock: his father, home from work, a happy sound.

'How was your day?' his father calls. The same question every day, the same answer.

'Fine, Father. It was fine.'

His father hangs up his coat by the door and goes to the bathroom to wash. First they will say their prayers and then they will prepare their evening meal. The same every day, always the same.

After prayers, Ahmed carries the cutlery and plates into the living room and sets them on the low coffee table. What will he and his father eat tonight? In Libya they always ate well, but in England they live on rice and couscous. On special occasions they have pizza or fish and chips from the takeaway.

A low singing from the kitchen. His father? This is not usual. Ahmed does not move. He listens, his ears straining to catch the words. It is an old Libyan song from the desert, a song his father learned from Ahmed's grandmother who grew up there. But this is the first time his father has sung a note in all the time they've been in England. 'Why should I sing?' his father said, whenever Ahmed asked. 'What is there to sing for? I lost almost everything.'

A few months after their mother died, their father arrived home early from work.

'What are you doing back at this time?' Safia asked, fanning her face with a sheet of paper.

Though it was late October, the air in the apartment hung heavy like a blanket they could not shake off. 'Is something wrong?'

Their father slumped down onto the sofa and closed his eyes.

'Are you unwell?' When his father did not answer, Ahmed turned to Safia, who stood in the doorway, her head framed against the light.

'I'll fetch him a glass of water,' Safia said. 'It's so hot in this place. I don't remember heat like this in our old house.'

She placed the glass on the table and Ahmed moved over to the window. The blinds were closed against the heat and the whirr of the fan blades overhead spun round with the muffled sounds of the city traffic.

His father gulped the water but said nothing. He just sat there, his eyes vacant, threading his fingers in and out, back and forth. Ahmed and Safia waited. The fan whirred. The traffic passed. The shadows moved on the walls. When their father finally spoke, his words sounded thin and stretched.

'I am afraid I have more bad news for you.' He picked at something on his shirt, coughed and stared up at the ceiling. When his gaze fell back on them, Ahmed saw that his face was grey and tired. 'My job, my life's work, it is gone, lost.'

'What? You've been sacked? Is it because of mother?' The words shot out of Safia's mouth and winded Ahmed like a punch to the belly.

Their father wiped a bead of sweat from his brow with the handkerchief he always kept in his pocket. 'Leave the room, Ahmed, will you, please?'

Ahmed hesitated. He glanced at his father and Safia but their expressions were as blank as the walls of the apartment. Then, from the gloomy kitchen where it had been moved, his mother's bird cheeped miserably. For a moment he hated that bird, he wished it would fall off its perch and die.

'He's old enough to hear,' Safia said. 'He'll only listen in through the keyhole anyway.'

'Sit down and turn on the radio,' their father ordered.

Ahmed sat on the rug at his father's feet and Safia switched on the set before settling into one of the few chairs they'd managed to rescue from the old house. Their father wiped away the sweat from his brow again and cleared his throat. He spoke quietly but his voice did not waver.

'A few days ago a baby under my care died. She was premature and very sick. I did everything I could to save her but in the end there was nothing more I could do, nothing anyone could have done. But now I stand accused of misconduct, of allowing the baby to die. As if I would do such thing!' He beat his chest with his hand. 'They wanted rid of me when your mother was sent to prison but I had a powerful ally. Now he has disappeared and no one knows what has happened to him, or where he has gone.'

He reached for the empty glass, drew his hand away. Neither Ahmed nor his sister moved to refill it. 'To be frank, I am surprised my dismissal has taken so long.'

'This is an outrage!' Safia said, her voice spilling over the sound of the radio. 'You can't allow them to get away with this.'

'You know as well as I that there is nothing to be done. I am powerless. We are all powerless here.'

'Powerless,' Safia muttered. 'Why does everyone bow down to that man? Are we so weak? Is no one willing to take him on?'

Their father held up his hands. 'Shhh, that is enough. We must not speak of these things. Do you want to end up in prison like your mother? Think what that would do to Ahmed, to our family.'

The fan continued to whirr and a car honked its horn loudly in the street below. But Ahmed had drifted far from the apartment and the fan and the cars and his father's work. His was thinking of ice-cream – tutti-frutti ice-cream, his favourite, the one his mother liked too. Mmm – its creamy, icy sweetness, that irresistible crunch of candied fruits and nuts. His mouth watered. Oh, what he would do for an ice-cream right now.

'We must leave Libya,' their father said, his voice strong again. 'It is imperative that we do so.'

The ice-cream vanished like a cheap trick and Ahmed's mouth turned dry.

'I'm not going,' Safia said, twisting her dark hair in her fingers. 'I have my studies. My life is here. I will not go.'

'It is no longer safe for us. His spies are everywhere.'

'I'm not afraid. It's what he wants for us to fear him.'

Ahmed understood that they were talking about the Colonel, the man who had ruled the country for years. His face was everywhere in the city, beaming down on them like a god. That's what his mother had said, but his father had hushed her saying that it was dangerous to speak like that. Ahmed fidgeted on the chair. Didn't they hide tiny microphones behind the lights or under the tables where you would never find them? Perhaps the Colonel and his men were listening right now, even over the sound of the radio.

'You should be afraid, Safia,' his father continued. 'Without fear you will forget to be vigilant.'

Safia frowned and tugged on the twist of hair she had created. 'We must build a new future. Surely that is what mother would have wanted.'

Their father, who rarely lost his temper, leapt to his feet. His skin flushed and his expression turned thunderous. 'Don't tell me what your mother would have wanted.'

Before Ahmed and his father left Tripoli there were more disagreements, though the subject of the Colonel was not mentioned again. But Safia would not budge and his father gave in. He agreed that she should move in with their Aunt Nafissa – their mother's sister – to continue her studies at the university. Ahmed was surprised that Safia got what she wanted. Perhaps he was even a little envious. Now he is not so sure.

His father clatters a plate in the kitchen and an aeroplane flies over the apartment. Ahmed peers through the living room window but he is unable to see the plane through the thick cloud. On the day he and his father flew to England, he didn't understand what he was going to, or why the danger was so great it made their leaving necessary and hurried, but he remembers how his stomach fluttered with excitement, although underneath the sadness lay like an unmoveable boulder.

Safia had flung her arms around his neck. 'I will miss you, little brother. Don't cry. We'll see each other soon, *insha'Allah*.'

Soon? Three years has gone by and their only contact has been their weekly telephone calls. His father has warned him not to speak too much of their life in England and he has forbidden certain questions. As a consequence, when Ahmed talks to Safia, their conversations are often stilted and awkward. Safia was supposed to have visited last summer but at the last minute she was unable to obtain the correct papers. His father said perhaps they would go back to Tripoli instead, but they did not.

And now? Now a war is raging across Libya and despite his father's promises that Safia and Aunt Nafissa are OK, they can no longer be reached.

His father has tried to shield him from the events in Libya but the news is full of it. 'This is our fight for freedom,' his father has said. 'The noose is tightening.'

Ahmed does not know what noose his father speaks of and he does not like to ask.

Mohamed peels the onions and picks up the chopping knife. How he misses Nour, his wife. This knife in his chest would be as nothing compared to the pain he feels. He has tried to protect Safia and Ahmed, but it is like pushing back a wall of sand. And now he is stuck here in this wet, grey country with almost nothing to fall back on: his daughter left behind, his son slowly forgetting his country and his religion, the news filtering out of Libya worsening hour by hour. He should have insisted that Safia accompany them to England but he has never been a man to lay down the law. Perhaps that weakness is what has brought them to this situation.

He slices the onions and throws them into the pan. He ought not to be ungrateful. It is a crime to complain when others suffer and, all told, he and Ahmed have not done badly. They have a pleasant rented apartment on the edge of town, Ahmed is succeeding at school and he, Mohamed, has a full-time job. There are many people worse off even here in England. He shakes the pan and turns down the gas. What would Nour have said if she had seen him cooking? She would have probably laughed and teased him because he never cooked back home in Tripoli – he never needed to. There is so much he and Ahmed have had to learn.

With a soft sigh he peers out of the kitchen window to the grass scattered with daisies and empty crisp packets, and then across to the horizon where a bank of clouds is massing, threatening rain. Where will it all end? The war in Libya is entering a dangerous phase. Should he return? To do what exactly? And he has Ahmed to consider.

The smell of the cooking onions brings him back to the present. 'I could do with some help,' he calls.

Ahmed comes running in. With his hair damp and curly from the shower, he looks like one of the Roman portraits from the Villa Sileen, close to Tripoli.

'Do you think Safia will call tonight?' Ahmed asks.

'I do not know. Remind me to buy chillies when we're next at the shop, will you? We're quite out of them. Now, perhaps you could put the kettle on for the couscous?'

Once the meal is ready, Mohamed sits at the low table, opposite his son. Ahmed is no longer a small, shy boy with only a few words of English. He has grown up, adapted to his new life. The three years has passed quickly, more quickly than Mohamed imagined it would. He is even beginning to get used to this country and is no longer surprised by the greenness of the grass or the wintry lace of trees, although he still shivers in the cold and his bones ache on damp days.

The drunken youths roaming the estate, the cold rain, the way the mist hugs the landscape in the early mornings when he goes to work, these things are a part of him now. But his heart is not here and never will be, not when his wife is buried a thousand miles away in the cemetery by the old Turkish mosque, under the blue skies of Tripoli.

There are days in Tripoli when the wind whips in from the Mediterranean and the rain pours down, blocking the drains and flooding the streets with dirty water. Here the drains rarely block although people still complain: they moan about the lateness of trains, the cost of food and the state of the government. But in this country no one has to look behind him, wondering if he is being stalked for no good reason. No one has to fear men arriving in the night, heavy boots stamping on the stairs, their eyes like tombs. They have peace while his country is in turmoil, its towns blackened and ruined. Tanks roll along the streets, snipers fire from rooftops. Young men and old, women and children are dying and lying wounded in the hospitals. Blood flows and the cemeteries fill up. People weep. They pray. All this, for freedom.

'One day, *insha'Allah,* we will have a different life.' His wife spoke those words before she died. One day.

'Why hasn't Safia called?' Ahmed says, forking up his couscous. 'It's been ages.'

'I expect the phone is out of order. You know how it is in Tripoli. The phones never work. Nothing works properly in Libya.'

Ahmed looks at him. There is an expression on his face Mohamed has not seen before, a slight frown, even a scepticism in his son's eyes. How much longer can Mohamed pretend that all is well? But perhaps it is. All he can do is hope.

Chapter Two

Betty and George bought Orchard House in 1957, the year they married. The place is large and ramshackle, too large for one person alone. It was built in the 1920s on a substantial plot of land, the name of the house given for the orchard – but few fruit trees remain from that time and those that are left have limbs arthritic with age.

In spring white blossoms fizz from the branches like bubbles of champagne, but come autumn, hard, wizened apples and worm-eaten pears drop into the long grass and are eaten by the birds. The house too is showing its years. Flakes of paint curl along windowsills, the verandah sags and, here and there, a roof tile has slipped. Moss and ferns grow in the cracks, and pigeons nest in the unused chimneys.

When Betty and George first moved in, the house stood alone, but over time other buildings have sidled up like unwelcome guests. However, the new estate is scarcely visible from the house for she and George planted hedges, now grown thick and dark, and a large stand of bamboo. After she and George retired Betty imagined they would have years to spend in the garden. They had plans to redevelop the pond, to build a pagoda where the rotting wooden shed lies, but that was not to be.

She taps her stick on the tiled floors and clicks her tongue, convinced she has forgotten something. How irritating it is to have things slip one's mind. Fragments drop into her head at inappropriate times – the fragrance of lilacs, a rock engraving of two antelopes, George's rust-coloured beard – and yet fewer of her memories hang together.

But some images remain as clear as day: her daughter Eva heaving her rucksack onto her back before she left for Gaza; the city of Ghadames in the Libyan desert, its whitewashed clay walls bright under an indelible blue sky; George diving off the boat in the Red Sea, forgetting that his straw hat was still on his head. Oh, no more of this. She must concentrate on finding her spectacles.

Small pieces of yellow paper are stuck to the fridge in the kitchen – these days such reminders are a necessity. *Monday: paper and cans. Thursday: dentist.* But she's fine, really, she is. Everyone forgets a little when they are old. It's normal. All the same, it concerns her that the past is clearer than the present, that once people sought her opinions. Nowadays no one seeks her opinion on anything. And people don't drop by either. Not like they used to.

Annette says there's nothing wrong with Betty's memory. 'You're not over the hill yet, my dear friend.'

Ah, the spectacles. Here they are on the kitchen table next to the fruit bowl. Betty slips them on and picks up an apple. She can still eat apples; her teeth are good, not a single false one. The clock in the hall chimes three and a police car sounds its siren on the road. It used to be a quiet road. The whole area was peaceful until the estate was built. George liked to complain about that, though when he and Eva were here, the house was always noisy: the radio boomed out all day long, the phone rang constantly and a stream of people visited – Betty could rarely hear the tick of the clocks. Now she can hear them all the time, counting her days. She tuts. There are far too many clocks in the house – the grandfather clock in the hall, the carriage clock in the living room, this one on the kitchen wall. What on earth is she going to do with them all?

Abandoning the apple, she cuts a slice of fruit cake and sits down at the heavy oak table she bought forty years ago for a song. The china dinner service, the battered sea chest in the hall, the knick-knacks and objects crammed on shelves, all were picked up for a few pounds. She supposes she ought to begin to get rid of some of the stuff, but she has no one to give it to and without George here to help her sort through everything the task feels insurmountable. She yawns. How tired she feels. But if she sleeps now, she'll be awake half the night.

A sudden knock at the door startles her. The slice of cake is lying on the table in front of her. She takes a bite. It is a good cake, she made it herself only yesterday. The knocking stops. Now all she can hear is the tick of the clock and her own chewing. Her hearing is still acute although she sometimes wonders for how much longer. When Annette visits, Betty is forced to shout. It is so exhausting.

The knocking resumes, louder than before. She hopes it isn't one of those Bible thumpers come to remind her of the sins of the world, or some young man trying to sell her expensive cleaning materials. She peers at the clock. She must have fallen asleep for a while. Of course: Savannah and her mother. She hadn't realised the time had sped on so.

She shuffles into the hall and sees two blurry figures swimming at her through the stained glass in the door.

Betty turns the lock.

'Are we early?' Savannah's mother asks in her bird-like voice. Betty notices her hair has been dyed again; this time it is so blonde it is almost white.

'Of course you're not,' Betty says, more roughly than she means to. Savannah's mother calls herself Dee-Dee but Betty cannot bring herself to call the woman anything but Delia, so she often calls her nothing at all.

'Hello, Betty,' Savannah says and she rushes into Betty's arms. She is dressed in pink and today her fair hair is tied back with a satin ribbon while another circles her waist. She looks like a birthday present. Betty never dressed Eva in fluffs and frills, but then Eva would not have stood for it and neither would George. He always hated women fussing about their appearance. 'You're beautiful as you are,' he would always say, and he meant it.

'How are you?' Betty asks, addressing the child. Savannah is jiggling about as if plagued by a swarm of ants. She is as thin as a blade of grass, although that's hardly surprising as she's such a fussy eater. Now that Betty is going to have Savannah for the whole summer, she will have to persuade the girl to be less picky.

'You can manage your bag, can't you darling?' Delia says to her daughter before turning to Betty. 'It's so good of you. I don't know what I'd have done otherwise.'

Though she is immensely fond of Savannah, Betty now wonders why she ever agreed to the plan. What on earth will they do all summer together? But it's far too late to back out now. 'Come on in.'

Delia strides into the hallway, her high heels clicking on the chequered tiles. 'I've always admired that photo of you and your husband,' she says, flicking her eyes at the pictures in the hall. 'He's very handsome, isn't he? Oh, and how young you look there, Betty.'

Betty grits her teeth. I was young once, she wants to say. I wasn't always so grey and slow.

Delia turns her attention to the black and white photograph of Eva that Betty had recently placed in the hall. Betty hopes she will not be required to explain Eva because explaining always results in questions – questions followed by an inevitable bout of sentiment –something she abhors. She is lucky: a loud and insistent buzzing diverts Savannah's mother and puts a stop to further conversation.

A gleaming pink mobile phone is fished out of Delia's white patent shoulder bag. 'Oh, Scott, darling! Hi. Yes. I won't be long.' She signals to Betty and Savannah and disappears into the kitchen, the mobile glued to her ear.

We don't know the meaning of silence any more, Betty thinks. *Nothing is so good for an ignorant man as silence; and if he was sensible of this he would not be ignorant.*

'She's always talking on her mobile,' Savannah says, tapping her pink ballet-style shoes on the tiles. She raises her eyebrows and flashes Betty a smile.

'Indeed,' Betty says.

Chapter Three

Ahmed stares at the ticking clock. The room is small but it is, at least, his. When they arrived in London, he and his father stayed with his father's younger brother Hashim and Ahmed shared a room with two of his younger cousins. They were always shouting and sometimes they made rude noises. Ahmed was not used to sharing. It did not suit him. Nor did he like London. It was so big and strange.

Uncle Hashim had moved to London when Ahmed was a baby – but why, Ahmed does not know. His uncle later married a Scottish woman, Marie. She was kind to Ahmed but Ahmed felt homesick: he missed Safia, he missed Tripoli and his school friends. He would not say that he missed his mother because her loss was a deep wound, something no word could really describe. But he and his father only stayed a few weeks with Uncle Hashim and the family. They moved instead to a town in the south of England, a place of tumbledown houses, red-roofed estates and a castle with broken walls.

His father did not like London either, he said the place gave him a headache. In Libya they had always lived in Tripoli though Tripoli never made his father's head bad.

Ahmed reaches for the blind and pulls the cord. A pale light filters into the room. The apartment block where they live is on the edge of this town; a huddle of yellow brick buildings like Lego. Spindly trees line the roadsides and poke up from the grassy areas, but some of the tree branches are broken and dangle like fractured bones. The borders of the estate are planted with rose bushes. In the summer they smell so sweet. He opens the window to try and catch their scent but the roses are past their best and the cool air dampens their perfume.

How his mother had loved roses! Every Friday his father would buy her a large bouquet from the florists and she would say, 'You shouldn't have bothered, *habibi,*' but she always smiled and gave his father a kiss.

Today the sky is polished and grey. For the past few weeks there has hardly been a glimmer of sun. But Ahmed likes this damp weather, the quietness of rain, the clouds drifting across the sky like great puffs of smoke and he smiles as he remembers his mother's words, 'Your head is always filled with clouds, Ahmed.' The summers in Tripoli were boiling hot and he used to long for the cool winter nights, but then the time arrived when all he wished for was their old life back and his mother to be well again.

He puts his head to the open window. The apartment faces away from the coast, inland to the low hills. Each block contains six apartments, though Ahmed and his father don't really know their neighbours, with the exception of Mrs Preston who lives alone in the flat next door. The very first Saturday they were here, Mrs Preston rang the doorbell and handed them a plate of homemade biscuits. Ahmed's father invited her in but after polite introductions, she ran her hands through her black spiky hair and said, 'Thank you, Mr Masrata, but really I must be going.'

When Ahmed bit into one of the biscuits he almost broke a tooth. He no longer eats them but his father continues to accept Mrs Preston's gifts graciously and remonstrates with his son for his lack of humility. 'We are guests in this country. We must never forget that.' Ahmed doesn't feel like a guest and he doesn't believe, like his father, they should be grateful for everything England has to offer.

'Perhaps we will return home soon, my son, *Insha'Allah,*' his father used to say. He never speaks those words now.

Ahmed leaves the window and walks into the windowless bathroom. In the mirror, his dark brown eyes stare out at him and it is as if another boy stands there, someone he does not know. His mother said, 'Eyes are the windows to the soul. Always look at people's eyes, Ahmed. You can learn all you need from there.'

He stares at his eyes in the mirror until his sight turns blurry with the effort. Is that true? Can't people also lie with their eyes? He wishes he could ask her.

Now he cannot even remember what she sounded like because her voice is lost in a babble of other voices and the phrases of his new language.

He splashes his face, rinses his hands and turns off the taps. Water continues to trickle from the cold. He screws the tap tight but the dripping continues. His father has been promising to mend the tap for weeks. Drip, drip.

'Someone will come and fix it,' Ahmed said. This is how things work here.

'I will deal with the problem,' his father said, his face serious. 'We must not expect this country to provide everything.' His father may have been a doctor in Libya but he has little knowledge of spanners, wrenches and screwdrivers. In any case, his father has already left for work. When he's on the early shift he leaves before Ahmed wakes. When they first arrived, his father took a job in an electrical place but that closed after six months. Now he works in a supermarket warehouse two bus rides away.

'I'm lucky to have work,' his father said when he was offered the new position. 'Many of our people can't get jobs in this country because they don't have the right papers.'

'What papers?'

'Everyone who comes here must have a paper to allow them to stay. Without the right papers you can be sent back to where you came from.'

Ahmed felt sick to his heart. 'Do we have the papers, Father?'

His father ruffled Ahmed's hair. 'Don't worry. Everything is in order.'

Ahmed did not understand. It was not as if they moved to England by choice. Now he understands a little more. He and his father are refugees, weeds in a garden. In Libya his father was a person of standing, but here he is a nobody.

Only last week, as they were walking along the path in the estate minding their own business, a man cursed and spat at Ahmed's father. Afterwards the man walked away, one finger stuck in the air. His father took out his handkerchief, wiped away the spittle from his coat and carried on as if nothing had happened.

'Why did he do that?' Ahmed felt like crying.

'He is afraid. He thinks we are terrorists because of the way we look. You must never feel afraid, Ahmed.'

Ahmed stared miserably at his father. With his faltering English and his shabby clothes he suddenly seemed diminished and old. 'Why aren't you a doctor any more?' Ahmed knows there are foreign doctors in all the hospitals; he has seen them on television. 'Uncle Hashim works in a hospital in London.'

'London is different,' his father said, the tone of his voice warning against further discussion. 'Now hurry or we will be late.'

Ahmed has no ambition to be a doctor. His father is always urging him to study, 'So that you can obtain good position,' but Ahmed wants to work as an artist.

'An artist?' his father said. 'This is not a proper profession for a young man. You will never earn living as an artist. In this country, artists are like pop stars. It has nothing to do with talent. When we return, Libya will need engineers and doctors to rebuild the country. It will not need artists.' His father has no idea that Ahmed has seen caricatures of the Colonel painted on walls all over Libya, or that he too has drawn a picture of the Colonel with the body of a snake and his tongue forked like the devil. Nor does his father know that Ahmed has looked at pictures of the war on the internet at school when the teacher has been occupied elsewhere, that he has seen the things his father has tried to hide – the city of Misrata destroyed, its buildings black like rotten teeth, two babies covered in dust on the tiled floor of their home, eyes closed, their clothes stained with blood, a man bleeding to death on the street.

He stands back from the mirror. He is not tall like some of the boys in his year, but he is not the smallest either. He turns sideways and flexes his arms. Last month he beat Max in the cross-country race. Max had never been beaten before. He smiles and his mirror image smiles back at him. Maybe next year he'll win again. Except that next year he won't be at St Barnaby's. He'll be moving to the Academy. If he was bigger and older he'd go back to Libya and fight. But there is no possibility of that.

He goes back to his room and flings himself on the bed. The trees are green and leafy now but in a few months they will be just black sticks. Perhaps there will be snow again. Last winter Ahmed lay for hours watching the snowflakes dance in the pale sky. How envious his friend Kadeen would be if he knew Ahmed had seen snow. He and Kadeen used to dream of the Arctic on hot summer days in Tripoli: they talked of icebergs, polar bears and blizzards. Ahmed wonders what his friend is doing now, but the truth is that after almost three years he can scarcely remember Kadeen's face.

The days are long when there is no school. It will be hours and hours before his father returns and Ahmed cannot stay in the apartment all day. He picks up his rucksack from the floor, searches for a pencil and his book, *Mosses of the British Isles,* and drops the items inside. From the tin in the kitchen, he grabs a handful of ginger biscuits – proper biscuits, not the hard ones Mrs Preston brings – and stuffs them into the side pocket. As he leaves the apartment he glances at the scuffed pink walls and the carpet in the living room, a mass of undistinguished flowers, and walks out of the door.

A group of boys is lolling about on the rough patch of grass outside, bicycles slung down. Ahmed recognises Billy from his class but Ahmed's friend Rob isn't with them: he is in Spain with his family. The other boys in the group are older: they must already be at the Academy.

The boys are laughing, joking and punching each other in a friendly way. Billy says, 'All right,' as Ahmed passes but Ahmed only nods his head and continues towards the field that lies on the boundary of a small wood. Nine horses inhabit the field, docile creatures with sturdy legs and patches of grey on their white coats. They are not magnificent and proud like the Arab horses Ahmed remembers from his childhood picture book, but he likes them all the same.

Halfway along the road that runs between the estate and the field, hidden from view by a thick dark hedge and a line of trees, stands a large, white house. Ahmed didn't notice the house until last autumn when a gale sent a huge tree crashing through the fence, creating a gap. Who lives there? Someone must. When he passes, he sometimes hears a car on the gravel drive or sees smoke rising from one of the chimneys, but he has never set eyes on anyone.

He is almost at the wooden stile when the sound of a bicycle tyre skidding across the road makes him turn sharply. Behind him are two of the boys he passed earlier. The boy nearest is short and scrawny, his face obscured by the peak of his red baseball cap.

The boy jumps off his bike and stands less than a foot away, arms folded across his narrow chest. 'Got any fags?' he says, his voice hard like a punch against a wall.

Ahmed shakes his head. 'I don't like smoking.'

'You don't like smoking,' the boy mimics.

The second boy is pink-faced and as plump as a wood pigeon. This boy remains seated on his bike. 'What's in the bag?'

'Nothing.'

The fat boy leaps off his bike surprisingly fast, dumping it on the edge of the road, wheels spinning. 'Give it me,' he says, pointing to Ahmed's rucksack.

'I said there's nothing in it,' Ahmed says, but he takes the bag off his shoulders and hands it over.

'Liar,' the fat boy says, shaking the rucksack. 'Fucking liar.'

The scrawny boy snatches the rucksack from his fat friend and tips it upside down. Out drops the notebook, the pencil and the book, and a clump of dried moss Ahmed had forgotten about. The boy scowls, then laughs. 'What's this green stuff? You sure that's not weed?'

'Weed? No, it's moss.' Ahmed takes a step back, stinging his hand on a nettle. In the field a horse snorts and a bird makes a shrill noise like an alarm clock, and the sun eases out from behind a cloud. Steam rises off the wet road. A car passes by, an old car, dark green, a sticker of a dragon on its rear end. The car vanishes, leaving nothing but the faint noise of its engine. The scrawny boy unzips the pocket of the rucksack.

'Nothing else. Just a few old biscuits.' He sounds disappointed.

'You're lucky,' the fat boy says, picking up *Mosses of the British Isles* and slinging it across the road. The book falls with a slap into the gutter, spine open, pages face down in the dirt. 'You might not be so lucky next time, Paki.'

The boys get back on their bikes and pedal off, taking the track that leads down into the wood.

Ahmed grabs the rucksack, crosses the road, picks up his book and turns back towards the estate. He does not quite know what he feels but whatever it is, it is not good.

Chapter Four

'I hope you'll be happy here,' Betty says to Savannah.

'She's happy, all right, aren't you?' Delia says, smoothing her daughter's hair. 'There might be some news when we get back.' Delia's cheeks turn a dark shade of pink.

Betty wonders what news, although she has her suspicions. 'Best not to count your chickens before they hatch,' she says.

Delia turns a shade pinker, before bending down and gathering Savannah in her arms. 'You won't miss me, will you?'

'I don't think so,' Savannah says. 'I've got Betty and the cats and the chickens...'

Delia frowns and steps back, the pink wiped from her cheeks. 'Well. I did ask.' She kisses Savannah on the cheek. 'Must dash. Be good, won't you, darling?'

After Delia has left, Betty picks up a cushion in the sitting room and bangs the dust out of it so hard she has a sneezing fit.

'What are you doing?' Savannah asks, dumping her Barbie doll on the sofa.

'Banging a cushion.'

'Are you cross?'

'Of course not. Why should I be cross?'

Savannah wrinkles up her nose and rushes off into the garden. Betty follows, though rather more slowly. However, the moment Savannah reaches the pond, she turns and runs back up the path. 'Mummy says I've got to be careful of the pond in case I fall in,' she says, grasping Betty's hand.

'Your mother is a worrier. You won't fall in. Anyway, the water's not deep. It's all clogged up with mud.'

'Why does she worry?'

'She cares for you. Mothers always worry. ' The truth is, Betty was never a worrier. She let Eva do whatever she wanted. Maybe if she had been the worrying type events would have turned out differently. But they didn't. A tiny silver moth flies out of the long grass. It reminds Betty of the sequins on a dress she once owned, one she left in that hotel in Tripoli. She sighs. The memory is so painful. She must not think of it.

'Can I collect eggs today or have you collected them already?'

'I was waiting for you. We'll go together, shall we? If you'd just fetch an egg carton from the kitchen. You know where they are.'

The egg box is fetched and she and Savannah walk through the garden – past the walled area planted with old roses, past the disused greenhouse and the vegetable patch which is now mostly weeds, down the sloping lawn with its clover and daisies, its vetches, mallows and dandelions, and on to the hen coop. Betty keeps six hens, although once there were seven. The hens are called Un, Deux, Trois, Quatre, Cinque and Six-Six.

'Those are the numbers one to six in French,' Betty explained when Savannah first came to the house.

'Oh yes. We learn French at school. But why Six-Six? Shouldn't it be Seez?'

Betty tapped her walking stick on the dusty gravel. 'I'm not sure. I suppose I thought it sounded good.' She didn't say that her daughter Eva named the hens, that she has continued to keep the same names even though the hens Eva once loved are long since gone. She and George bought their first hens soon after Eva was born. The hens delighted Eva. Even during a difficult adolescence when getting Eva to do anything became a battle, she continued to feed and care for them.

Savannah throws a handful of grain and collects the eggs, six in all.

From the coop, the remaining garden tumbles down to the boundary hedge and the bamboo patch. Savannah has always been afraid of the bamboo patch. She claims that a horrible, creeping monster lives there. Sometimes Savannah is brave enough to edge up to the nettles which grow close but then she will run up to the house, shouting and waving her arms. Betty always hugs her tight and tells her there is nothing to be scared of.

'I'm going to write on this,' Savannah says, picking up a bamboo leaf that has drifted over to the coop.

Betty runs her hands through her hair. It feels dry and brittle. She ought to take more care of it. These days though, she finds she can't be bothered. After all, there is no one to be bothered for. 'What will you write?'

'*Panda bears love bamboo.*'

'We could get two pandas to come and live here.' Betty looks at Savannah. The ribbon on her hair has already come undone. 'They can have our bamboo.'

Savannah rolls her eyes. 'Pandas eat tons and tons of bamboo and anyway they prefer living in China.'

'I suppose they do,' Betty says. 'But they might scare away the monster.'

'*Pfft*,' Savannah says. 'I don't believe in monsters any more.'

Chapter Five

The supervisor nods at Mohamed. She is followed by Doreen, an older woman who works in the office. Doreen waves and beams at him. She always waves and smiles. This is a friendly place, not like the previous workplace where one of his fellow workmen called him all sorts of names when no one was around. Mohamed ignored the taunts, though to do so was not easy. He did not want to cause trouble.

He finishes his sandwich and wipes his hands. In five minutes the lunch break will be over. There is little enough time to pray and eat during lunchtime, let alone chat to people, even if he wished to talk. He supposes he ought to make more of an effort – it would help his English, but he has learned that it is best to keep one's head low and the years of practice in Libya have become a habit he cannot easily give up.

After Nour disappeared into that black hole of a prison, he no longer knew whom he could trust. Anyone might betray you: a colleague, even a cousin or a brother. People would disappear and never be heard from again.

Once he was, if not a happy-go-lucky person, contented with his lot. He had a wife and a family and a respected job, but all that has vanished and in its place rests a cloud of worry and guilt. He wishes he did not have to leave Ahmed alone at home all day. In Tripoli, Ahmed was never alone: there was always Safia and Nafissa, and various cousins. Now the long school holidays have begun and they are always a concern. Ahmed claims he doesn't mind being by himself but that is beside the point: Mohamed trusts his son but a child can land in all sorts of trouble in this country, especially a child who does not belong. But if they had stayed in Tripoli, life might have taken a more difficult turn. Mohamed's heart contracts. It's been almost two weeks since he last heard either from his sister-in-law or Safia, and the news from Tripoli is troubling.

He checks his watch again. His wife gave him this watch a year after they married. It's a good watch. Reliable. Lasting. There are some things that should last and others that should not, but in the end that is for Allah to decide and Mohamed must accept what is.

It is time to get back to work. He gets to his feet and walks out into the warehouse where the crates of apples and bananas lie stacked on the floor.

Ahmed pauses at the gap in the hedge. From here he can see a stand of bamboo and beyond a sea of tall grass that almost obscures the house. He hesitates but then he hears the sound of the boys again – the tyres on the road, the click of pedals, their harsh voices – and he slips into the overgrown garden.

He is not sure how long he should stay hidden. The boys might come back at any time. But he's sure they didn't see where he went. He lies in the damp grass and watches a spider spin its web between two stalks of grass. When he is tired of the spider he turns to gaze at the sky. The clouds, earlier so dense, are now small and white and within no time they become nothing more than puffs, like his breath on a cold morning. After a while he grows bored and restless and the temptation to explore the garden becomes more than he can bear.

Keeping to his knees, he creeps up the slope towards a stand of fruit trees. Every now and again he checks the house but there is no sign of any movement. He is startled by the cluck of a hen, although he cannot see it.

Beyond the fruit trees is a small pond, fringed with clumps of reeds and spiky, green plants. Ahmed shuffles up to the edge and, lying on his belly, trails his hands through the cool water. Long-legged insects race up and down between the floating lily pads, sometimes bumping into each other like the kids in the playground at school, and a tiny fish darts in the gloom, its movement creating a small shudder on the water's surface. In the distance he can hear cars on the road and sometimes a shout from the estate, and, nearby, the buzz of bees in the flowers. Other than that, everything is quiet.

He flips over and stares up through the tracery of apple branches which overhang the pond, the fragments of sky a clear blue between the leaves like a mosaic. He thinks of the patterned tiles of the old city mosque. A wave of sadness washes over him. How long ago that seems, a different life.

Through the sitting room window Betty can see Savannah over by the hen coop but she is almost certain that something else is moving in the garden. Perhaps it is a fox or, more likely, Stealth, out on the hunt again. She ought to ask Fred Marsden to come by and cut the grass. It has grown so long. She looks again. Yes, there is definitely something there.

She and George never kept the garden immaculate but when George was alive it was managed to a degree. He used to cut the lawns and hedges, and rake the leaves in winter, while she planted and weeded. But now the weeds are poking up through the stones, and daisies, plantains and dandelions are laying claim to the lawn. The thought of George stabs at her heart. How she misses his company, even if she did not always appreciate it at the time.

George. Dear George. But to think of George is also to think of Eva. And to think of Eva brings her to a dark place.

A sudden breeze sweeps through the garden, fluttering the leaves. A cat appears on the path. Betty eases herself out of the chintz-covered sofa, dislodging a cushion, and walks to the open door. The cat is not Stealth, but a tabby with a torn ear, a large tom. She has never seen it before. It glares at her with its cold eyes, before vanishing back into one of the overgrown flowerbeds. Well, that explains it.

To the left of the back door, Betty keeps a small herb garden. Leaning on her stick, she bends down and picks a few salad greens for supper. Perhaps she will persuade Savannah to try them. She places the leaves in her apron pocket and proceeds to pull out a few stalks of stray grass and weeds. Then she walks down the brick path and sits on the wooden bench that George placed close to the old fruit trees. A pigeon flies overhead, wings whirring and a moth skims over the beaded grass, followed by a faint thud as another pinecone falls to the ground.

'I'm going inside,' Savannah says, marching up from the hen coop. Her face is ruddy and her hair is tangled, the ribbon gone. 'Can I have some paper and scissors?'

'You know where they are,' Betty says. 'In the right hand drawer of my desk.'

'Are you tired?' Savannah makes a plopping sound with her mouth as if she were eating a plum.

'A little,' Betty says, closing her eyes. Only a little, she thinks.

She is woken from her short slumber by a loud rustle. Blinking against the sunlight, she leans forward on the bench and focuses her eyes on the pond. There *is* something lurking there, hidden behind the reeds. 'Stealth? Is that you?' she calls. 'Bad cat,' she mutters to herself.

Savannah comes running out of the house, waving a long line of paper dolls. She comes to an abrupt halt halfway down the path. The dolls drop from her hand and lie on the ground, white and fluttering like small birds.

'What is it?'

'There's a boy in the garden.'

There is indeed a boy in the garden, standing near the pond, dark-haired and thin, his arms like sticks. He is wearing a red T-shirt and muddy shorts that cover his knees and a pair of old-fashioned sandals. He begins to walk slowly towards them, his eyes turned to the ground.

'I think he's from my school,' Savannah says, picking up the paper dolls and folding them.

'Is he?' Betty whispers. She has no idea why she is whispering.

'Yes,' Savannah whispers back.

The boy stops on the path.

'Who are you?' Betty says, waving her stick. She is not afraid, of course she is not.

'Ahmed,' the boy answers uncertainly.

'You do know this is private property, don't you?' She doesn't intend to sound grumpy but the words come out that way. Well, she doesn't care for strange people in her garden, whatever age they are.

'I am sorry,' the boy mumbles in slightly accented English.

'Is there a reason for you to be trespassing on my property?'

He points towards the hedge that borders the road. 'I came in through the gap in the hedge.'

'What gap?'

He trembles and his brown face pales. 'The gap where the tree has fallen.'

'Ah, that.' Betty ought to have got Fred to fix the fence, but for now it is more important she gets a fix on the boy. 'Ahmed.' She rolls the name around her tongue. 'Where are you from, Ahmed?'

He waves towards the estate. 'Over there.'

That's not what she meant. All the same, she still feels uneasy. How she hates getting old, this weakness in her limbs, the lapses of memory, the constant fuzz of anxiety. If George were still here she would not feel like this.

'I'm sorry,' the boy says. 'I will leave.'

She looks at him again. He must be about ten or eleven years old, but how frightened he looks and she is not an ogre, is she? 'I suppose now you're here, I could offer you a drink. I'm sure you meant no harm. Would you like a drink?'

'Yes, please,' he says and his face brightens.

'I'm Betty and this is Savannah. She's staying with me over the summer holidays.'

'I'm pleased to meet you.' Ahmed bows his head as if he were an old man.

Savannah peers at him through narrowed eyes and when Betty goes inside to fetch the drinks, she follows. 'Why is he really here?'

'Go and ask him.' Betty looks through the kitchen window. Ahmed is still standing in the middle of the path, his arms hanging loosely at his sides. There is a long and bloody scratch on his ankle, most likely he got that from the brambles. 'I expect he was just curious.'

The old woman gestures for him to sit down on the wooden bench. Her right arm is covered in bracelets, the skin underneath spattered with brown patches. A few minutes ago he was almost scared of her but now she's smiling and offering him a drink. He takes the glass of squash. It is good and he's thirsty, but he doesn't gulp it down; that would impolite. The fair-haired girl sits cross-legged on the grass and drinks hers in one go, and when she has finished she burps loudly. His sister would never burp in public.

'Betty says to ask why you came into her garden,' the girl says, gazing up at him. Her eyes are the colour of the sky and she has a mole on her chin like a tiny dark star.

He hesitates. He wants to tell the truth but he doesn't want to appear small and cowardly in front of these people he's never met before.

'It's not important,' the old woman says.

If he should lie, will Allah forgive him? He wonders what his father would think. He would hate Ahmed to lie unless his life depended on it. Cradling the glass in his hands he says, 'A boy threw my book into the road. There were two boys. I thought they might come back so I came here.' He takes another sip of the squash. How dry his throat is.

'Boys are horrid,' the girl says.

Miss Betty – he can't call her Betty – smiles again and waves her arm, making the bracelets jangle. She sits back on the bench and smooths her grey hair with her hand. 'Savannah doesn't really think that. The other day, she was singing their praises.'

'You're at my school, aren't you?' the girl says, frowning. 'I'm sure I've seen you there.'

'St Barnaby's?'

She nods and makes a sucking noise with her lips. 'Yes.'

'I'm in Year 6, Mrs Bradley's class.'

'Oh, I'm a Year 4. Have you seen me at school?'

He shrugs. He can't remember if he has or not. 'Maybe.' He drinks the last of the squash. He's been lucky but he should go. 'Thank you,' he says to Miss Betty. 'I won't come into your garden again.'

'Don't go yet.' The girl's voice is plaintive. 'Can he stay a little longer, Betty?'

'That's up to Ahmed.'

She looks at him and now she reminds him of someone, although he cannot think who it is. Her eyes are grey like rain clouds, her lips are pale and cracked and her skin is a mesh of lines. But she has a kind face. It isn't like those boys' faces, cruel and tormenting, or like the Colonel who rules his country. The Colonel always wears a smiling mask, but that is to hide the monster underneath. His mother said so once but she made him swear never to repeat it.

'You are welcome to stay, Ahmed, if you'd like to. We'll be having tea soon. Savannah gets very bored with my company. I'm too old, she says.'

'You are old.' The girl turns back to Ahmed. 'But Betty was on a boat once and she travelled to lots of exciting places.'

Miss Betty laughs. Ahmed feels himself blush. He would never say those things to an older person.

'Please stay, Ahmed.' Savannah jumps up and hops around in the grass like a kangaroo, her golden hair flying around her face. It's a surprising colour. When he first came to England he was astonished to see people with hair like the sun, although now he understands that the colour sometimes comes out of a bottle.

'She is nothing if not persistent,' Miss Betty says.

Betty cuts a slice of fruit cake. That accent of his, she cannot quite catch it. 'How long have you lived in England, Ahmed?'

He wriggles on the bench. 'Nearly three years.'

'Where do you come from?'

'Libya.'

'Libya,' she repeats. The word explodes like a firework in her heart. 'My husband and I did research there, though that was a long time ago. Before you were born.'

'Where's Libya?' Savannah asks, cramming a piece of cake into her mouth.

'North Africa.'

Ahmed takes a tiny, polite bite of cake.

'We worked in the desert, as archaeologists,' Betty continues. 'We were surveying the rock art in the far south-west of Libya, the Fezzan.'

'I've never been there. We lived in the city, in Tripoli,' Ahmed says, half closing his eyes.

'Ah, Tripoli, I know it well – the ancient city of Oea, mermaid of the Mediterranean.' What wonderful times Betty had in Tripoli all those years ago. In the late 1960s it was quite the place to be. Cosmopolitan, fun, exciting. The cinemas showed Western films and there were parties, sometimes quite outrageous parties. You wouldn't get that now. But Tripoli holds other memories too, ones she has tried to put aside.

'How ancient?' Savannah asks, licking her fingers.

'It was there before the Romans.' Betty turns back to Ahmed. 'Your English is very good. I presume you're with your family here?'

Ahmed's eyes travel to his plate. 'Only my father.'

'Ah,' Betty says, not knowing quite what else to say.

But Ahmed smiles and says, 'Thank you. This is a very good cake, Miss Betty. Can you tell me, is it five o'clock?'

'I think so, thereabout. Do you have to be home?'

He nods and, placing the empty plate on the tray, gets to his feet. His shoulders are hunched and he is tapping his fingers on the side of his face. Perhaps she shouldn't have detained him so long. She hopes he won't be in trouble. 'Of course. You need to be home. But do come back, Ahmed. We'd love to see you again.' All the same, she wonders if he will.

She and Savannah clear away the plates and glasses and when Savannah is settled in front of the television, Betty goes into the kitchen, sits at the table and weeps. It has been a long time since she wept like this. When the weeping is over she dries her eyes and pours herself a glass of wine. But perhaps she has no need of wine for she feels suddenly light, as if some weight had been lifted from her.

Chapter Six

Mohamed dumps the two shopping bags. He will sort them later. He is about to pick up the telephone when Ahmed comes rushing up the stairs and into the cramped hallway.

'You'd better shower and change,' Mohamed says, seeing the mud on his son's short trousers, the scratches on his legs. 'Did you fall?'

Ahmed nods but he does not move.

'You're not in trouble, are you?'

'No,' Ahmed replies. 'No trouble. I was playing football.'

'I thought you said you fell.'

'I fell playing football.'

Mohamed examines his son's face. Nothing in his expression says that he is lying but Mohamed is suspicious.

'Do you want me to help you unpack the shopping?'

'I'll do it. You shower. I've got meat, vegetables and a bag of barley flour. The barley flour was difficult to find, I had to ask for it. We will have *bazin* tonight, after our prayers.'

'*Bazin*? We haven't had that since we left Tripoli.'

'I have found a recipe. Maybe it will not be as delicious as your mother's but we will do our best.'

The bathroom door closes and Mohamed lifts the receiver. There are two messages. The first is from Hashim: 'Have you heard from Nafissa?' It would be pleasant to have a, '*How are you, brother?*' but Mohamed has learned not to expect that. His younger brother is not heartless and, if it had not been for him, Mohamed would never have managed in England. But Hashim has his own life in London and it is as different to the one Mohamed lives as the desert is to the ocean.

The second message is from his sister-in-law Nafissa in Tripoli. That is a relief. 'Call me as soon as you can,' she says. However, something in the tone of her voice troubles him and when he calls the apartment in Tripoli there is no answer. She ought to be home now. There, it is eight in the evening. After he has checked Ahmed's shower is still running, Mohamed dials Safia's mobile.

He rarely calls her mobile because of the expense and because she has asked him not to. The mobile is not safe, she claims. But the phone is dead: he cannot even leave a message. For a moment he considers telephoning Hashim and asking him what they should do, but if there is a problem what, realistically, can Hashim do? What can either of them do? Anyway, it is probably just a technical glitch. The regime has cut the phones before.

He ought to begin preparing the *bazin* but he feels tired, more than he ought. He takes the bags into the kitchen, then sits down on the shabby old sofa and turns on the early evening news. Libya. The country is always in the news now, and yet not so long ago no one here had even heard of the place. Even if they had, they remembered the policewoman shot and killed outside the Embassy in London and the terrible tragedy of Lockerbie – and if the person knew Mohamed's origins he would get a raised eyebrow, a frown. It used to make him feel bad, as if he was somehow responsible for the policewoman's death and the deaths of the passengers on the plane.

He concentrates on the news. The Libyan rebels – how he dislikes that term – claim they are in control of the town of Brega but, as normal, the regime is denying any rebel gains. In the early days of the Revolution the mood in the media was positive, but now the BBC and the other news channels talk of stalemate, the war continuing for months, years even. It won't take much for the public mood to change. And now there is Tripoli to consider. Allah only knows what Gaddafi will do to secure the capital.

Why oh why did he allow his daughter to stay in Libya?

If Allah brings you to it, He will bring you through it.

A noise. Ahmed is in the room. 'What's the matter, Father?'

'It is nothing. I have a headache, that is all.' He looks up at Ahmed and smiles. Ahmed is a good boy.

He has never been any real trouble, not like some boys he knows.

'Was that Safia on the phone?'

'No, Nafissa. Everything is fine.' How he hates to lie to his son.

'The Americans and the others are bombing Tripoli, aren't they?'

A drop of water splashes onto Mohamed's trouser leg. For one awful moment he thinks that Ahmed is weeping but it is only his son's wet hair. 'Yes,' he says wearily. 'But the targets are military ones. They will be careful.' That much is true but it still makes him uncomfortable.

Ahmed rubs his hair with the towel. 'That's good, isn't it?'

Mohamed smiles at his son again. 'Yes. It is.' He picks up the controller and switches off the television. 'I must go and prepare the *bazin*.'

'Won't that take a long time? Can't we have it tomorrow? We could have fish and chips tonight.'

'That is a treat for the weekend, Ahmed.'

'Please, Father, and you do have a headache.'

Mohamed taps his fingers on the table, a cheap and old thing, like the sofa, like everything in this place. 'All right, but only this once.' He is relieved not to be cooking tonight but is reluctant to allow his son an easy victory.

A grin spreads across Ahmed's face. Sometimes, when his son smiles, Mohamed catches a trace of Nour's smile. She used to smile often; it was one of her charms that so attracted him. 'Your smile is the rain in the desert,' he used to say to her. But in those last few months she did not smile once. Not once. That was something else they took away from Nour, from all of them.

'Fish and chips, eh? But you must never forget our Libyan food.' Mohamed is glad that his son has settled into English life, but he does not want him to become too English. Integration is one thing. Assimilation is quite another.

Savannah is sitting at the kitchen table drawing a picture of a girl with long, yellow hair and a large, red mouth.

'How about an egg for tea?'

'I hope Ahmed will come back,' Savannah says, drawing a fish next to the girl's face. 'He seemed nice.'

'I hope so too.' Betty turns to the kitchen window. The evening is grey and cool, the light muted. But Betty turns inside herself and sees nothing of the evening. Instead she sees a landscape of rolling sand dunes, sliced by dark, curved shadows and a sky as deep blue as the tanzanite ring she wears on her finger. The ring was a present from George for her thirtieth birthday. But she does not think of George.

There is another man at her side, a tall man with eyes the colour of sea glass and skin the colour of the late shadows. This man's name is Omar and the year is 1969 and, though they do not know it yet, in a month the King will leave Libya and the country will be changed forever.

The dunes surround Omar's home town of Ghadames, a long way from Tripoli. From the top of the sand dune the town reveals itself. From this distance, the mud brick walls and whitewashed finials resemble a thousand origami geese settled on the desert floor.

As they walk together Omar quotes lines of Arabic poetry and Betty slips the tanzanite ring into the pocket of her long trousers. The heat of the late afternoon sun burns through her hat and grains of Saharan sand drift into her shoes. She stumbles and Omar reaches out and takes her hand. She looks into his eyes and he into hers and her heart leap-frogs in her chest.

A girl's voice carries across the sand. 'I want to show Ahmed the bamboo patch.'

'What?'

'Weren't you listening?'

A spot of rain hits the window. The desert has vanished. 'I'm sorry. I was miles away.'

'Where?'

'A desert somewhere.'

Savannah makes a funny face but she doesn't ask any more, and now the cat flap opens and Napoleon ambles in, his tail in the air. It is a relief to think of the cat. Thinking of the desert turns Betty maudlin and sometimes even angry for what she has lost. It does not do.

Betty took in Napoleon, a rescue cat, soon after George died. Napoleon is a friendly, round creature with paint-dipped paws and a purr like the vacuum cleaner. Betty's other cat is a stray, almost feral, and as thin and grey as a column of smoke. Stealth spends his nights stalking through the bamboo and his days sunning his stringy body on the patch of grass behind the shed where Betty keeps her compost bin. He also hunts mice and birds.

'You were going to cook an egg,' Savannah says, stroking Napoleon.

'So I was.' Betty checks the egg carton but it is empty. 'Go and fetch a couple for me, will you?'

Savannah runs off outside, taking the carton with her. Betty watches her zigzag down the path and skip off through the grass. Savannah doesn't resemble Eva at that age – Eva wasn't such a skinny little creature – but at times like this she reminds Betty so much of her daughter it is painful to watch. Eva used to run like that – a dash, then a sudden halt and a hop on one leg – as though she was bored with only one way of doing things.

When she returns with the eggs, Savannah's face is pale. 'Maurice and Holly have disappeared.' Maurice and Holly are the names she has given to the pair of doves who frequent the garden.

'They must have gone to roost.'

'It's too early.'

'We'll have another look when we've had our tea.' Betty pours water into the pan, sets it on the stove and pops in two eggs – one each for both of them. Then she glances at the clock on the wall. It is exactly six, time for the news but perhaps it is better not to think of the news right now.

Halfway through her egg, Savannah says, 'Do you think you could make me a dove out of wood?'

Betty started making sculptures out of scrap wood and metal a few years ago, though it's only a hobby, not like the serious work she once undertook. It is also something to pass the time and ease the loneliness that can descend on her with the weight of a juggernaut. 'I can try, though I'm not very good at making things appear realistic. It might end up quite abstract.'

'What's abstract?'

'An approximation, an idea.' Savannah smashes the empty eggshell with her spoon. 'Like a shadow,' Betty continues. 'You know what it is but you can't quite grasp it.' Betty knows she is not explaining it well. She is thinking of love instead.

Betty has a chilled glass of Chardonnay in her hand when Savannah comes barging into the sitting room, almost knocking over the vase of flowers. 'Something is wrong with Holly. She's stuck in the grass.'

Savannah is right. There is something wrong with the dove. She is lying near the hen coop, her eye glassy. Betty reaches out with her walking stick and carefully turns the bird over. Its stomach is slit almost from throat to tail.

Savannah lets out a loud shriek and bursts into tears.

'I tell you what,' Betty says, pulling a handkerchief out of her pocket for Savannah. 'We'll bury her under the holly tree. Then Maurice can mourn her properly.'

Savannah wipes her eyes. 'Yes,' she says, her voice small and quiet.

Betty fetches the spade from the shed and digs a small, shallow grave close to the bamboo patch. It's a long time since she last did any digging. From time to time she has to stop and rest against the wall of the shed, but she manages. When the hole is large enough, she picks up the dove with the blade of the shovel and drops it into the hole.

Savannah shivers but she watches all the same. 'Is your husband buried in the garden?'

'No,' Betty says. 'He's at sea.'

'Is he buried there?'

Betty nods. She always promised George she'd give him a sea burial and that was one promise she did keep, difficult as it was to arrange.

They say a prayer for Holly and walk up the garden. When they are almost at the back door, Savannah screams again: a grey and bloody shape is lying in the middle of the path. 'That's Maurice!'

'Stealth,' Betty says darkly.

'Stealth is a murderer. I hate him!' Savannah throws herself down on the grass, sobbing bitterly.

'It's possible that Stealth killed Maurice,' Betty says, when Savannah's sobs have subsided. 'But I don't think he killed Holly. Cats don't kill in that way.'

'What was it then?' Savannah asks, her face grim.

'Perhaps it was a sparrow hawk.' Betty has never seen a hawk in the garden. Perhaps she should get that fence fixed.

Delia telephones an hour after Savannah has gone to bed. Right in the middle of an interesting documentary. 'I'm sorry it's so late,' she says. 'I couldn't get to the phone earlier.'

Her news doesn't amount to much. They've been here and there. Scott's talk at the conference went well. It's so terribly hot and gosh, isn't America vast. And the food, Betty. You should see the food. Oh, and everyone is so friendly.

Betty listens with half an ear.

When she gets back to the documentary it is almost finished. She will watch the news and then she will go to bed.

The shouting wakes her. Eva? Betty struggles between sleeping and waking. Eva must be in danger. Yes, of course she is. She remembers now. Betty must get help. It is imperative she gets help. Where is everyone? My daughter needs help. What are you doing? Why have you left her there? She sits bolt upright, her heart hammering so hard she can scarcely catch her breath.

It is not Eva.

She switches off the television and climbs the stairs.

Savannah is sitting up in bed, whimpering.

'You must have had a bad dream.' Betty sits on the edge of the bed and takes Savannah's shaking hand.

'I was dreaming about Stealth,' Savannah says. 'He had grown very, very big and he was in the bamboo patch and he was scaring me.' She rubs her eyes. 'Can you be born wicked?'

'Not in my opinion.' Betty strokes Savannah's hair. Just as she did with Eva. 'Now try and go back to sleep. It's the middle of the night.'

Before long Savannah's eyes close. Betty continues to sit a while longer, her hand still in the girl's own. Then she lets go and quietly leaves the room.

Chapter Seven

It is half past eight and his father has already been gone for over an hour. Ahmed sits down cross-legged on the rug and opens a book but he doesn't feel like reading. Not right now. Perhaps he could return to the big, white house. Miss Betty said he was welcome at any time but Ahmed is not sure what that really means. And he hasn't yet said anything to his father.

He switches on the television. There is a discussion about Libya, two men talking about a serious situation, the concerns for Tripoli. His father usually waits to watch the late news after Ahmed has gone to bed but the news is everywhere and when his father is at work, Ahmed often checks.

It has been a while since they heard from his sister and aunt. His father says they are all right. But how does he know? Ahmed turns off the news, goes into the hall and dials the number in Tripoli. The telephone clicks and goes silent. He dials again. Nothing. Maybe the phone is cut. Or something dreadful has occurred. His heart pitter-patters in his chest like heavy raindrops falling on the roof and he closes his eyes and says a *dua* for his sister to keep her safe.

His father says Safia is strong-minded. Ahmed's mother was strong-minded too, his father said but it was because of that she was sent her to prison. What if Safia and Nafissa are in prison? And his mother wasn't strong when she came back. No! She had become thin and pale, her thick black hair gone almost all grey. Sometimes she would weep silently and Ahmed would go and comfort her, and still she cried.

When they had to move out of the house into that horrid apartment, his father did not explain. He said they had been 're-allocated.' Safia whispered in his ear, 'It's a punishment for mother's behaviour.' Ahmed still didn't quite understand. Now maybe he understands a little more.

Once he overheard Safia saying to his mother, 'Why do you put yourself through this?'

'I cannot fight any more,' came his mother's reply. Ahmed pressed his ear to the keyhole. 'I'm too tired. One day change will come.'

'I'm not going to wait,' his sister said. 'Waiting is like death.'

Ahmed picks up the receiver and dials again but it is useless. Not a crackle. Just the beep beep of the numbers he punches in and then nothing. He walks into his room and lies down on his bed. The sky is as blue as in Tripoli, and from time to time a swallow flutters high up above the trees before disappearing out of view. But he feels miserable and lonely. If only his father were here, or Safia, or anyone.

He washes the breakfast bowls and plates. Then he makes his bed and tidies his room. It is important to keep everything in order. After that, he gathers a few items together and leaves.

The bus into town comes at quarter past every hour. He wants to buy a new notebook with the pocket money he's saved – and it's something to do, something to pass the long hours. The bus ride takes fifteen minutes and from the stop he goes straight to the bookshop. He likes this shop, although he can't afford to buy books. For books there is the library. But the shop has comfortable seats and sometimes he sits in the corner and reads and no one ever bothers him.

'Is that really mole's skin?' he asks, picking up a smart notebook with a black cover.

'Rest easy,' the shop assistant answers. She smiles. 'It's never seen a mole.'

'Why is it called mole's skin?'

'Moleskine. That's a brand name.' This time the assistant shrugs and raises her eyes. 'Like Pepsi or Coca-Cola.'

'Oh,' he says.

'You've been in here before, haven't you?' The assistant is young. Her eyes are lined with dark make-up and she has pink streaks in her hair and a ring in her nose. No one in Libya ever looked like this.

'Yes,' he says, nodding.

'What's your name?'

'Ahmed.'

'That's a nice name. So, do you want the note-book?' She leans over the counter towards him. He can smell mint and a faint whiff of tobacco. 'I can give you a discount, if you like.'

He is not sure how to answer. 'Yes,' he says again. 'Thank you.' He wants the book for his notes and drawings. Last year he wrote an essay about moss for a school project and his teacher, Mrs Bradley, awarded him five gold stars. 'Well done, Ahmed,' she said in front of the whole class. 'That's quite the best project I've ever seen.'

Ahmed felt himself redden. Later some of the kids teased him and called him 'The Prof'. When Ahmed recounted the incident, his father said, 'People don't want to learn, Ahmed. There is much ignorance in this country. They prefer football and that lager beer.'

'Come back, won't you?' the assistant says, as he leaves.

Betty places the cafetiere of coffee and her favourite Denby cup on a tray and carries it into the sitting room. On the lawn a blackbird pulls on a worm and the trees cast dappled shadows as a single cloud, long and wispy like the tail of a scraggy, old cat, drifts lazily across the sky. The cloud reminds her of Stealth, and Stealth reminds her of Savannah's nightmare. She hopes the girl will be all right. It's a long time for her mother to be away.

She sips the hot coffee and waits for the caffeine to rouse her from sleepiness. The clock in the hall chimes nine. She pours a second cup and picks up a small-egged shaped stone from the windowsill. The stone is covered in tiny, dark crackle marks. She can no longer remember where it came from.

The clock strikes the quarter and then the half hour. She is about to call Savannah when she hears the girl on the stairs.

'Oh there you are,' Savannah says, padding into the room in her bare feet. 'I had a bad dream last night, didn't I?'

'You did. By the way, your mother rang after you'd gone to sleep. It's a different time zone there. I think she'd forgotten that. She said she would try again later today.'

'Right,' Savannah says with a shrug. She wanders to the bookshelf and picks up a large pinecone.

Betty's shelves groan under the weight of a lifetime's reading and every other space is crammed higgledy-piggledy with objects. A beaded handbag from the 1930s that once belonged to Betty's mother. A small, rusted tin of her father's and a collection of her grandfather's magnifying glasses. Everything gathering dust.

The walls of the sitting room, which Betty had painted yellow, are, like the hallway, jammed with pictures, photos and textiles – a watercolour of a misty landscape, a photo of a single red dune, an aboriginal bark painting, a rug from Iran, an African mask. The mask always reminds Betty of George in a bad mood, though, to be fair, he was rarely bad-tempered. A museum of objects, years of collecting. She never tires of this room: she can't imagine how people live in big, empty spaces with nothing but blank, white walls and chrome lights like a hospital wards. Sometimes George complained about her collecting, but he tolerated her foibles. He tolerated a great deal, not that she considered it at the time. She is not sure she could have been so forgiving.

'What's that?' Savannah asks, pointing.

'A sea urchin.'

'Aren't sea urchins prickly? My teacher says they're the hedgehogs of the sea.'

'The spines fall off when they die and then you just get the shell. It's beautiful, isn't it?'

'Can I pick it up?'

'Yes. But treat it gently. It's terribly fragile.'

'Did you find it?'

'Yes, I did. I dived into the sea and brought it up.' Betty used to love free diving. She liked to watch the sun's ripples crisscross the sand under the water, the seaweed swaying, the shoals of tiny fish flying by. She was good at it once: she could hold her breath for a full two minutes. Now she'd be lucky to hold her breath for thirty seconds.

Savannah tilts her head and a puzzled expression crosses her face. 'The sea's very, very deep. If you put the tallest skyscraper in the world in the middle you still wouldn't be able to see it.'

'The sea urchin was in shallower water. You'd need a special craft to dive at that depth. Because of the water pressure.'

Savannah looks a little disappointed. 'How old were you?'

Betty laughs. 'I was twenty-seven. I can remember it well.'

The past is a clear sea, the present sometimes a muddy channel. And how could she not remember that day? She and George had been married seven years and she'd recently discovered she was expecting a child. How excited she and George were. What plans they had. But the excitement did not last. She miscarried at fourteen weeks.

'Mummy's twenty-seven.'

'That's a good age.'

'Do you think nine is a good age?'

'Every age is a good age, although it's nice to be young. When you get to my age you aren't so fast on your feet.'

'How old are you?'

'Seventy-three.'

'Seventy-three,' Savannah echoes and her mouth drops open. 'That is old.'

'It's not that old,' Betty says, laughing again. 'People live to ninety these days.' Not George, she thinks. Dear, old George.

⚜ ⚜ ⚜

Annette visits every other Friday afternoon. She always arrives on the dot of two-thirty. 'How are you?' she asks, kissing Betty on the cheek.

'Fine,' Betty says, as always. After George died Betty admitted to Annette that she was depressed and lonely, but Annette fussed so much it drove Betty almost crazy.

'You mustn't suffer in silence,' Annette said more times than Betty would care to count. 'Go and see the doctor.'

'I don't need a doctor.'

'Everyone's on happy pills these days. There's no shame in it, Betty.'

Betty avoided the doctor's surgery because she did not, and does not, believe loneliness could be cured with pills. All she wanted was to be left alone.

'I've had an awful week,' Annette is saying. 'They've had to take so much blood out of my arm I'm surprised there's any left.' She laughs and Betty tries to laugh with her but she ends up choking on a piece of cake. It is a warm day and they ought to be sitting outside but Annette doesn't like to be outside, it gives her the chills. Goodness, is this what she and Annette are coming to? Old age, loneliness and nothing to talk about but their aches and pains? They used to have such interesting times together.

'Where's the girl you're looking after? I'm dying to meet her.'

'Here I am!' Savannah shouts, marching into the sitting room. There is a grass stain on her embroidered pink T-shirt and a smear of mud on her trousers.

'Ah, hello.' Annette takes a sip of tea and picks a piece of fluff off her skirt with the other hand. 'What a pretty blouse.'

'It's a T-shirt,' Savannah says. She turns and grins at Betty, before stepping back outside.

'I don't know how you cope at your age,' Annette says. 'Children are so unpredictable. I rarely see my grandchildren.'

Betty knows better than to ask why. 'It's nice to have a child in the house again.' She glances out of the window. Savannah is skipping close to the herb garden, the rope swirling round and round. It is good to see a child skipping. She thought that perhaps children had forgotten such games.

'I suppose. How long is she staying?'

Savannah throws down the rope and runs off through the long grass, waving her arms in the air.

'Savannah? For the summer holidays. Her mother has gone to America.'

'I can't imagine why anyone would want to go to Antarctica. Isn't it rather expensive? I've heard they run cruises there.'

'It's America!' Betty says loudly.

Annette fiddles with her hearing aid. 'Oh, America? I thought you said Antarctica. Silly me. I've got an appointment with the audiologist in a week or two. I don't think this is working properly.'

'That's good,' Betty says. 'About the audiologist.'

'What's the girl's mother doing in America?'

'She's accompanying her fiancé, my nephew, Scott, on a business trip.'

'Scott? Oh, she's with Scott. You didn't tell me. Is she divorced? Well, I must say.' Annette lifts her spectacles as if this will somehow give her an understanding of the situation.

The clock chimes in the hall and Betty opens her mouth and closes it again.

Annette clanks her cup down on the tray. 'I know what you're thinking. I'm a hypocrite. Well, maybe I am. But honestly, Betty, my situation was a little different. *Our* situation was different. Divorce is too easy these days. People divorce at the drop of a hat. I mean you didn't, did you?' She reaches over and cuts another slice of cake. 'You shouldn't be put in this position, looking after a child who's not your own, and at your age. You're not exactly a spring chicken.'

'They're planning on getting married. Well, that's what I understand. I'm not exactly in the picture.'

'Married in America?' Annette shakes her head. 'Whatever next.'

Savannah bursts back into the room. 'Stealth isn't in the garden. Where is he?'

'I don't know.'

'Holly and Maurice were murdered!'

Annette's hands fly to her throat and she makes a bleating sound.

'It's all right,' Betty says. 'Holly and Maurice are doves.'

'Oh,' Annette says. 'Did you say doves?'

'Betty's cat killed them, or maybe a hawk.'

'Yes, it was very sad.' Betty knows how important these things are to children. 'We loved those two doves. They were an item.' She glances at Annette but perhaps she has not heard.

'Betty's going to make me a dove out of a piece of wood.' Savannah gives the sofa a soft kick and a thousand particles of dust rise into the air and dance in the sunlight. Annette doesn't have dust. She has a cleaner.

'That's nice,' Annette says, cleaning her fingers on the napkin.

Annette never brings me anything, Betty thinks. And she's so greedy. That's the second piece of cake she's taken.

'It's going to have a slit in its stomach and Betty is going to use wire wool to show its insides coming out,' Savannah says loudly.

'Goodness,' Annette exclaims, 'that doesn't sound nice at all.'

'It will be!' Savannah yells, dashing outside.

'What a peculiar child.' Annette brushes the last of the crumbs off her immaculate linen skirt. Then she sits back and crosses her legs. She still has good legs, Betty notices. But knowing Annette, she's probably had her varicose veins seen to.

'Like Eva, you mean?'

Annette pales. 'I know my hearing is bad, Betty, but I did hear that.' Her face is a mixture of pain and indignation. 'That isn't fair. Eva was unconventional but I would never have called her peculiar.'

'I'm sorry,' Betty says. Why did she say that? It was unforgivable. She twists the bracelets on her wrist and closes her eyes. When she opens them again Annette is smiling. Goodness. She must get a grip on herself. Annette is a dear friend. Yet Eva has always come between them.

There is a knock on the door but before she can get to her feet, Savannah has run in from the garden and is hurtling down the hall, skidding on the tiles. 'It's Ahmed!'

'Who's Ahmed?'

'A friend of Savannah's from school. He's Libyan.'

Annette raises her perfectly plucked eyebrows but says nothing. For that, at least, Betty is thankful.

Savannah grabs Ahmed's hand before he can protest and almost drags him into the room. Miss Betty is with another old woman, a thin, bony person with bright hair. She lowers her spectacles and peers at him until he begins to feel like a specimen in a museum.

'This is my old friend, Annette,' Miss Betty says.

'Pleased to meet you,' the old woman says in a loud voice, extending her hand with its long, red fingernails. 'Betty says you're from Libya. Has she told you about all the times she spent there?' She turns to Miss Betty and shakes her head. 'She had quite a run.'

'Annette,' Miss Betty says. She sounds almost cross.

'Don't worry. I'm on my way out.' The old woman winks. He has no idea why but the wink makes him feel uncomfortable, as if she has let him into a secret he should not know. She gets to her feet. 'It's nice to meet you, Ahmed. Perhaps we'll meet again.'

'She's rather deaf,' Miss Betty says when the friend has gone.

'She's got funny hair,' Savannah says, falling into a fit of giggling. 'It's like a Christmas tree decoration.'

'That's not very nice,' Miss Betty says but she smiles all the same.

'Her hair *is* funny.' Savannah bounces up and down on the small sofa. 'What shall we do?' she says, settling down and tucking her hair behind her ears. 'What *shall* we do?'

'I could do with some help to scare away the moles,' Miss Betty says. 'I don't have anything against moles but they're ruining the lawn with their digging.'

'Moles?' Ahmed is not sure if Miss Betty is being serious, but then she disappears and returns carrying a small blue and yellow flag.

'What's that for?' Savannah asks.

'Wait and see.' Miss Betty taps her nose.

The grass on the lawn nearest the house has been cut short and a large number of molehills have formed. The remainder of the lawn is uncut and filled with flowers, like the edges of the meadow.

'This is what we do,' Miss Betty says, waving the flag and marching across the grass, trampling the molehills as she goes. 'Aren't you going to join us?'

'We're scaring away the moles,' Savannah sings, jumping on a molehill. 'Scaring them away.'

Ahmed can't imagine a mole being scared by an old woman waving a flag and a girl stamping her feet. 'Please,' he says, feeling suddenly brave. 'I'm making a study of moss. Can I take some mosses from your garden?'

'Be my guest,' Miss Betty says, flapping at another molehill. 'It's good to have an interest. The secret of a long and happy life is never to stop learning, Ahmed.'

'Can I help?' Savannah has dirt on her face. 'I'm fed up with scaring moles.'

'All right,' Ahmed says, though he would prefer to search for the moss alone.

'I know where there's heaps of it.'

Savannah leads him through an ivy-coloured arch and into a walled garden. Here the brick paths creep with moss. But there are also roses, flowerbeds overrun with weeds and, in the centre, a statue of a woman. Ahmed is amazed that anyone could have a garden with so many parts to it.

'I bet you don't have moss in that country you come from,' Savannah announces. 'Betty says it's terribly hot and sandy there.'

'Moss is strong. It grows everywhere. There's moss in the Antarctic that is five thousand years old. It grows in deserts too.' Ahmed squeezes a clump of moss in his hand. 'When it's dry you think it is dead but it can return to life with water. Like magic.'

He thinks of his mother and how nothing would bring her back to life, not even his father wailing and beating his chest like a woman.

'Why do you want to study moss?'

Ahmed wipes his face with the back of his hand. Where did that tear spring from? He hopes Savannah didn't see. 'Moss is interesting.'

The moss is silky to touch: cat's fur and velvet. He brings a piece close to his nose. It smells like an old, closed-up room. His mother's room. Yet he doesn't mind that; he finds it strangely comforting.

'This is fun,' Savannah says, crawling on her hands and knees. 'I've never looked at moss before, not properly. It's like a tiny forest, isn't it?'

He searches around some broken pots. The moss is everywhere: on the trunks of trees, hiding between the cracks in the stone paths, creeping up the walls and along the roof of Betty's garden shed, clinging to the broken greenhouse.

'Do you have brothers and sisters?'

He peels away a strip of moss from a flowerpot and places it in between two empty pages of his notebook. 'I have one sister.'

'Does she live on the estate?'

'No. She's in Tripoli with my aunt.'

'Trip-oh-lee. That's your city, isn't it?'

'Yes,' he says. 'We can't go back now because there's a war.'

Savannah sits up and looks at him with her big, round eyes. 'Isn't that dangerous?'

'I suppose so.'

'Is your mother in Tripoli as well?'

He pinches the clump of moss between his fingers. 'My mother is dead.'

'That's sad,' Savannah says. She frowns. 'What did she die of? Was she ill?'

'She was in prison. When she came back she got sick and then she died. My father says there was something wrong with her heart.'

'Prison? Did she do something bad?' Savannah sounds puzzled. But how can he explain – even if he wanted to?

A shout from Miss Betty. 'Savannah! Your mother is on the phone.'

'I've got to go. My mother is in America.' Before she runs off, Savannah glances at him again and he notices she is biting her lip hard, like Safia when she wants to know the answer to something and cannot find it.

Ahmed sits on the edge of the path. Savannah's questions about his mother have unsettled him. He stares at the clump of moss in his hand. It is like a tiny green forest, just as Savannah described it. White hairs are caught there, and ants too, scurrying along, a whole tiny world. As he places the moss in his bag, something blue and shiny catches his eye, a child's marble hidden in the grass. He picks it up. The glass is chipped and dirty but when he polishes it clean with spit the inside looks as blue and clear as the sea. He wouldn't like to ask but he wonders if Miss Betty has children. But they'd be grown up now, wouldn't they?

Miss Betty calls again. 'We're having tea, Ahmed. Do come in.'

'Mummy saw a shark,' Savannah says. She looks small, sitting at the large kitchen table.

'Well that's something,' Miss Betty answers.

'I wish I could see one.' Savannah picks up a spoon and turns it over and over in her hand. 'I wish I could have gone to America.'

Miss Betty pours tea into her cup. 'You'll see a shark one day, Savannah.'

'Do you think so?' She sighs and blows air through her lips, then lifts her arms in the air. 'Mummy says America is HUGE. She says you can go to a canyon that's so deep it takes a whole day to walk to the bottom and when you get there it's almost as hot as fire. And there's a white house in the city that's a hundred times bigger than your white house, Betty.'

'Did your mother tell you all that?' Miss Betty laughs. Ahmed likes to hear her laugh.

Savannah twists her mouth into a strange shape. 'Some.'

'Do you like parkin?' Miss Betty asks.

'It's a type of cake. Betty cooked it this morning.' Savannah takes a slice from the plate. 'Try it. It's really yummy but it's quite hot because there's ginger in it.'

Ahmed takes a bite. It is good.

'You must ask your father to visit,' Miss Betty says. 'It would be my pleasure to meet him. *Sayakoun min dawa'i sUrourian ubuabiluhu.'*

'You speak Arabic?' Ahmed has never met an English person who speaks his language.

'I'm a little rusty. I haven't used it for a while. You forget.' Her face falls and for a moment she looks rather sad.

'What's Arabic?' Savannah asks, her mouth half full of cake.

'Arabic is the language they speak in Libya, and in many other countries too.' Miss Betty cups her hand under her chin and stares out of the kitchen window.

'Is it like French?'

'No,' Miss Betty says. 'Not at all. It's quite difficult to learn.'

'French is hard to learn.' Savannah rests her head on one elbow. 'Do you know, Ahmed has an older sister but his mother is dead. His sister lives in that place... What is it called, Ahmed? I've forgotten.'

Ahmed swallows a morsel of cake. The taste has turned to paper. 'Tripoli.' He should never have told Savannah. His father says it is not something they should speak of outside the family. Now he really is in trouble.

'Your father?' Miss Betty says again. 'Do you think I could call him?'

Ahmed wonders how he will explain. He writes down the number anyway.

⚜ ⚜ ⚜

As Betty watches Ahmed walk away in his loose cotton trousers and those old fashioned sandals, the questions she wanted to ask him niggle in her mind like mosquito bites.

'I'm glad Mummy has gone to America and not Ahmed's country,' Savannah says, breaking into her thoughts. 'They don't have wars over there. They have Britney Spears and doughnuts instead.'

'That's one way of putting it.' The news about Ahmed's mother has disturbed her. Even so, Savannah's words make her smile. Eva was often serious. Too serious, perhaps. Betty can't imagine Savannah growing up to be an activist like Eva. But who knows?

'I wish she'd taken me with her,' Savannah adds, wistfully.

'But then you wouldn't have met Ahmed.'

Savannah sucks her little finger and thinks on that a while. And Napoleon walks in, his tail in the air. Like an Emperor.

CHAPTER EIGHT

Mohamed lifts the box of bananas from the wooden pallet. This job is not so bad. It does not carry the weight of responsibility that was a necessary part of his work in the hospital in Tripoli. Here he has time to think, he can even go home at the end of the day without the worry of a patient on his mind. But today he *is* worried and there can be no getting away from it. Just after Ahmed went to bed last night, Nafissa telephoned. No one calls at that time.

'Is something wrong?' he asked. There was a long pause, long enough to make his heart jump. 'Are you still there?'

'Safia's been gone two days,' Nafissa said.

'What?'

'You heard.'

'Does she have a boyfriend?' A stupid question, as though Safia would disgrace them like that. His daughter is headstrong, yes, but she would never let them down in that way.

'Perhaps it would be better if she did.'

He took the phone into the living room, closing the door behind him. 'What do you know? Can you talk?'

'I know very little, I'm afraid.' Nafissa's voice was curt.

The door downstairs banged in the wind and Mohamed flinched, then everything went quiet. Too quiet. A quiet that demands questions. And there was a sudden homesickness for Tripoli: for the noise of traffic, the people in the streets, the heat and fumes and dust. 'It's time I returned,' he said, without thinking.

'What about your son?'

'I shall find a way. There is always a way.' He hesitated. 'Nafissa?'

'I'm sorry, I must go.'

A click and the line dead, and a crowding of terrible thoughts entered his mind. Perhaps the woman on the phone was not Nafissa but someone impersonating her. They could do that. They could do anything. He spent the night sleepless. Was it Nafissa or not? Why was she so abrupt? Perhaps there was someone in the room with her? Questions and questions but never answers, his mind circling like an eagle after its prey. Should he have stayed in Tripoli? Was it cowardice or bravery to leave? He does not know. All he knows is that after Nour died something died in him too: he became a stranger in his own land. He suspected that others knew the truth, though he and Nafissa took every precaution, but at the hospital he felt as if he was being constantly watched. It was likely that he had always been under surveillance. But after he began to sense it more keenly.

'Careful, Mo!'

Mohamed almost drops the box of bananas. 'Sorry. I am not looking properly.'

'That's a fact, for sure.' Fred, his co-worker, shakes his head. 'You all right, Mo? You look like you've seen a ghost, mate.'

'I have not sleep so well.'

Fred scratches his chin. 'Happens to all of us. It's age, Mo, age. About time we retired, eh?'

For the first time in the day, a half smile creeps across Mohamed's face. 'Indeed,' he says. 'Indeed.'

He wishes he could talk to Fred but he cannot.

⚜ ⚜ ⚜

There is a slow patter of rain on the leaves. It is only a shower.

'You go on ahead,' Betty says.

Savannah runs off and Betty follows through the wood. It is damp and gloomy under the canopy. Birds twitter in the undergrowth and a pale light filters through the silent trees. The path is slippery in places and tree roots poke through the earth. She stops and rests against the rough bark of an oak, listening to the brook singing to itself down in the hollow. She and George used to walk here almost every day when they were home. In the year before he died he would get a little breathless, just as she does now, but he never complained of any other difficulty and he did not see the doctor. Perhaps she should have insisted.

At the bridge – which isn't a bridge at all but a plank of knobbly wood – Betty takes another rest. Savannah is already clambering up the trunk of the half-fallen oak. Eva liked climbing. She was fearless in that way.

'I'm at the top,' Savannah calls.

'What can you see?'

'The grass a hundred miles down.'

'It sounds fun.'

'Oh, yes,' Savannah shouts. 'But it's too hard for old people.'

'I expect it is,' Betty shouts back.

Close to the brook there is a patch of flat ground where three cherry trees grow, their bark ringed with age and blotched with lichen. In spring their branches sink under an abundance of white and pink blossom but they rarely produce fruit. Betty throws down the blanket under one of the trees and takes out the sandwiches and the slices of pizza she has packed. When she peers into the bottom of the rucksack she realises she's forgotten the biscuits.

Savannah climbs down from the tree and takes a slice of pizza. Then her eyes wander to the stream. 'It's dangerous being near water, Mummy says.'

'Goodness me.' Betty bites into her fish paste sandwich. 'First the pond, now the brook. What's dangerous about it?'

'I could fall in and drown.'

'I think that's rather unlikely.' Betty holds up her gnarled right thumb. 'The brook's no deeper than this. It would be difficult to drown, unless you were knocked unconscious of course. Now, will you have a sandwich as well?' Savannah has already gobbled the pizza. She must have been hungry.

Savannah shakes her head. 'They smell yukky.'

'It's fish paste. Won't you try it?'

'I don't like fish. I like fish fingers and ketchup.'

Betty smiles. 'I'll try and remember that.'

When Betty opens her eyes, Savannah is drying her feet with a sock.

'I went paddling. You were asleep.'

'So you didn't drown?'

'Of course I didn't.' Savannah rolls her eyes and wriggles her bare, muddy toes.

That's a relief, Betty thinks, imagining headlines. These days everything is a danger. No one worries about what really matters. You look at the dangers but you don't see the real ones. She sighs and leans back on her elbows and looks up through the grass and the flowers. The creamy-white heads of the cow-parsley are like lace against the pale sky. She lets the sigh go and breathes in deeply. Everything smells earthy and clean after rain. It's a good smell: something to make you feel alive. Not like winter when loneliness sets in and the darkness seems never-ending.

She packs the remains of the picnic and folds the blanket while Savannah flies up the field, turns two cartwheels and disappears behind the hawthorn hedge. She's braver than she was. When Delia first asked Betty to look after Savannah a year ago, the girl was so timid she scarcely spoke.

Betty catches up with Savannah at the bench halfway up the slope.

'You were a long time,' Savannah says. There is a blackberry in her mouth. The juice has stained her lips a dark, wine colour.

'Are they good?'

Savannah wrinkles her nose. 'They're hard and the pips are stuck in my teeth.'

'That's the trouble with blackberries. They're not quite ripe yet. We need to give them another few weeks.' Betty takes out her handkerchief and wipes her damp forehead. Now that the sun has come out it is unexpectedly warm.

They walk further up the field, following the path that winds up to the ridge. Butterflies flit amongst the purple knapweed, and the pink and white clover. A grasshopper burrs and a woodpecker bobs up and down before disappearing into the line of trees.

'I'd like to live there,' Savannah says, pointing to the small gabled house that sits at the summit. 'It looks like a fairy house.'

'It is pretty, isn't it? And it has a marvellous view. You never know, perhaps one day you will live there.' Betty has always liked the house, although it needs more than Fred Marsden with his hammer and nails to put it to rights.

'Do you think so?' Savannah sounds doubtful.

'You'd need a job to buy the place and pay the bills. Houses aren't cheap.'

'I don't want to be a hairdresser like Mummy. That's a silly job.'

The comment is unexpected, but all the same Betty feels the need to come to Delia's defence. 'Someone needs to cut hair, don't they? So, what do you want to be?'

'A deep-sea diver. Divers can look at all the fish. I bet that's fun.' Savannah tilts her head one way and then the other. 'Or maybe an astronaut because I can float up into space and wave to people and look at the stars.'

There's nothing like having ambition, Betty thinks.

'Are we going to walk up to the fairy house?'

'Another day, if you don't mind. I think it's time we got back.'

Savannah tumbles off down the hill, arms outstretched, and disappears into the long grass. Betty catches up with her at the brook. From here there are a series of wooden steps which lead back up to the stile. Halfway there, Betty has to rest on the stick again. She is quite out of breath.

'Did Mummy tell you that she took me to Market Street before she went away? She tried on a wedding dress.'

Perhaps that's what Delia meant.

Savannah chews on a fingernail. 'The dress was white and shiny with a long trail at the back. When Mummy came out of the changing room the shop lady said she looked like a princess and she asked Mummy when she was getting married and Mummy said she was waiting for a ring. Do you have to have a ring to get married?'

'It's usual but there's no law to say you have to.'

In the corner of the field the horses whinny and flick their tails against the flies. 'If Mummy gets married again, Scott will be my daddy. I don't think I want a new daddy.' Her voice drops to a whisper. 'I wish my daddy would come back.'

'Life can't always stay the same, Savannah.'

A breeze moves through the line of trees that line the edge of the field and five magpies fly up, making an unholy racket. 'Five for a wish,' Betty says.

'A wish? What wish?'

'Don't you know the saying? *One for sorrow, two for joy, three for a letter, four for a boy, five for a wish, six for a kiss, seven for silver, eight for gold, nine for a secret never to be told.*'

'Should I make a wish?'

'Of course. But don't tell anyone or it won't come true.'

Betty sets the plate of biscuits and two glasses on the tray: homemade lemonade for Savannah and a chilled rosé for herself and she and Savannah decamp to the wooden bench in the shade of the fruit trees. Savannah takes a gulp of lemonade, sticks out her tongue and makes a terrible croaking noise.

'Don't you like it?'

'It's not like the lemonade Mummy buys.' Savannah brings the glass back to her mouth but this time she takes a tiny sip. 'Sorry, Betty, but it's very sour.'

'Put another spoonful of sugar in it.'

Savannah stirs in the sugar. 'Is that wine?' she asks, staring at Betty's glass.

'It is, yes.'

'I've never seen pink wine. Why is it that colour?'

'It depends on the grapes and the process.' Betty drinks her wine and sits back on the bench. The garden is past its best; the blossom is long gone and the roses are mostly overblown and faded. May and June are the best months for gardens. But the garden looks beautiful, whatever the season. There is always something new and unexpected: a few stalks of barley and a group of pink mallows that have appeared out of nowhere, or a butterfly she does not recognise, a slow-worm under the compost. Eva used to like helping in the garden but she always preferred to work with George. Fathers and their daughters. When she thinks of that she's not sure if she wants to cry again or laugh.

Savannah pokes Betty in the arm. 'Mummy giggles when she drinks wine. She drinks it when Scott comes round. He doesn't like wine. He likes beer. Afterwards Mummy kisses Scott and she goes all silly.'

'That's quite normal.'

'Is shouting and banging on doors normal?'

'Who shouts?'

Savannah blows on a greenfly that has landed on her arm. 'Mummy and Scott shout and Mummy runs out of the room and bangs the door. Oh, but it's not dangerous fighting. Not like lions or the boys at school.'

'Those boys sound terrible,' Betty says. That's a relief. She was worried for a moment.

The bamboo rustles and a shadow emerges from the darkness. 'Stealth,' Savannah whispers.

It is Stealth, but for a moment Betty wondered what it was.

⚜ ⚜ ⚜

Ahmed is lying on the carpet drawing a picture of a fox. He has captured all the lines of the animal so that it appears to move across the page. Perhaps Mohamed has been too harsh on his son, discouraging his talent.

'How was your day?' he asks.

'OK.'

He bends down and tousles Ahmed's hair. 'Did you see this fox?'

'I see her every day. She lives near the dustbins. I think she has cubs.'

Mohamed hangs up his jacket and wanders into the kitchen. 'Did you remember to buy bread, Ahmed?'

Ahmed comes running in. 'I'm sorry, Father, I forgot.'

'Never mind. We need rice too, and tomatoes. I will make a list.' He opens the cupboards and checks the fridge and writes down what they need on a scrap of paper. He writes in Arabic. He hopes that Ahmed will not forget the beauty of the Arabic script. But Ahmed does not study Arabic at school. 'You may have an ice-cream,' he says, handing Ahmed the list. 'Or a packet of sweets.'

As soon as the door closes at the bottom of the stairs he picks up the phone and dials Hashim's number. 'You worry too much, brother,' Hashim says. 'No one would pretend to be Nafissa. You are not thinking right.'

Why is it that his younger brother always makes him feel so inadequate? 'She says Safia has been gone two whole days. Two days, Hashim.'

Hashim sighs loudly. 'Don't assume the worst. Maybe Safia has a boyfriend.'

'A boyfriend?' Mohamed splutters, even though the thought occurred to him too. 'She does not have a boyfriend.'

'Let's look at this rationally, Mohamed. Perhaps she visited a friend and was unable to get home. The phone lines do not always work in Libya and these are far from normal times.'

'Even so. She's always been reliable.' His stomach tightens.

'All right. Phone me as soon as you have news. I will do all I can to help, you know I will.' Hashim's voice has softened.

'If I were to go to Libya...'

'Seriously?' There is surprise in Hashim's voice and perhaps, if Mohamed is hearing it right, a tone of disapproval.

'I am thinking of it.'

'How would you get there? And what about Ahmed? You can't possibly take him with you.'

'I said I'm thinking on it!' Mohamed shouts.

'Brother,' Hashim says, soft again. 'There's no need for anger.'

Mohamed puts his hand to his head and looks out of the window. An old newspaper is flapping about on the path below. 'I am sorry, Hashim. It is the worry. You cannot imagine how worried I am.'

'So what will you do?'

'I am not yet sure.'

Mohamed puts down the receiver. His hands are shaking.

When Ahmed returns with the shopping, he is surprised to see his father changed out of his work clothes into traditional shirt and trousers.

'I'm going to the mosque,' his father says.

The mosque is a small red brick building, a twenty minute walk from the estate. It's not like the mosque Ahmed remembers from Tripoli, a grand place of tiles and domes. His father says there are large mosques in the cities here but this is not a city. It is just a small town.

'Today?' They always try to attend the mosque on Fridays but usually they pray at home during the week, except during the festivals. He glances at his father again. Beads of sweat line his forehead and he is playing with his fingers. He does that when he is worried.

'Am I to come with you?'

'Of course.'

Ahmed wants to ask why. Why today? But he knows such a question will be met with a frown and a shake of the head. However, when he takes his father's hand on the path outside, he feels it tremble like the leaves on the trees and that makes him afraid and his fear prompts him to ask, 'Is something wrong, Father?'

'Not at all,' his father says, smiling. 'You should remember that silence is the language of Allah, all else is poor translation. Now let us go and forget our worldly concerns.'

As they walk into the mosque a wind whips down the street, turning the leaves and scattering the litter, and a cold shiver makes its way down Ahmed's spine.

CHAPTER NINE

The wind is blowing the leaves inside out and clouds scud across the sky like sheep running down a track. It is Monday but there is no school uniform, no lunch to pack, just another day alone. Until his father returns from work. Last night Ahmed heard his father talking on the phone. But his father has said nothing about that.

He opens his book and reads a few pages. It is a good book but he just can't concentrate. The words keep jumping and turning inside out like the leaves. Idly, he picks at the scab on his knee that he got when he tripped over on the concrete stairs last night. A trickle of blood runs down his leg, and he gets scared because he thinks of the blood that marks the pavements and houses of Libya, and he thinks of Safia and how she might be dead, and Nafissa with her.

Picking up his rucksack, he locks the door and runs down the stairs.

The usual gang of boys is on the grass outside but Ahmed walks on, his hands balled into fists; no one bothers him.

'Ahmed,' Miss Betty says, opening the door. 'How pleased we are to see you. I hope you had a good weekend. Is your father well?'

'Yes, thank you, Miss Betty.'

She grins. 'Do call me Betty.' She lowers her voice. 'I know Savannah is a little younger than you are, Ahmed, but she does get rather fed up being with me all the time. I hope you can try and be friends. She's out in the garden.'

'It's OK,' Ahmed says. He likes Savannah.

Savannah is by the fruit trees, practising handstands. 'Hello, Ahmed,' she says. Her face is pink from the exertion.

'Hello.'

'Did Betty tell you about the doves?'

He shakes his head.

'It was horrible. I think Betty's cat killed them both but she says cats don't kill like that.' Savannah's lip wobbles. 'Their bellies were slit right open.'

'I'm sorry,' Ahmed says. He fishes around for something more to say but he can't think of anything.

'You don't think someone came in the garden, do you?' She gives him such a hard stare that he has to look away.

'No one followed me,' he says. Perhaps she thinks he did it. 'It wasn't me. I wouldn't hurt a cat, or anything.'

'I don't think that. Maybe it was a hawk.' Savannah reaches for a branch of the apple tree. 'Let's do some climbing,' she says and she pulls herself up, releasing several small green apples which tumble down into the long grass. She grins at him through the shaking leaves. She appears to have forgotten she was sad only a moment before. 'Come on, Ahmed. It's not difficult. We can spy on people.'

He follows. The wind is almost gone and now a faint breeze plays in the garden. It is a little giddy up in the tree but it feels special too. The tree is not big, not like Betty's fir or the line of trees at the boundary, but he can still see over to the estate, to the red tiles and the wind vane that sits on top of their apartment block, and beyond that to the town itself – the huddle of roofs, the wind of streets and the gulls wheeling in the distance where the sea is.

They climb up and down all morning but no one sneaks into the garden, not even a cat. Then it grows hot and Betty calls them in to lunch.

⚜ ⚜ ⚜

His father's face is thunderous. If Ahmed hadn't been so greedy, his father would never have known.

Ahmed was on the point of leaving Betty's house when he spotted a globe set inside a box like fruit in jelly. 'Can I look at this?' he asked.

'Go ahead. It won't break. It may look like glass but it is not.'

He picked up the strange box and turned it over in his hands. He'd never seen anything like it and suddenly he wanted to own it, though he did not say so.

Now the box is sitting on their low coffee table in the apartment. Inside, the globe is coloured green and pale yellow, though the countries don't look like those in his atlas. The seas are filled with masted ships, giant serpents and weird fish, and right at the bottom, where Australia should be, a red winged horse strides across an empty plain.

'This is Libya,' he said to Betty, 'Here, where there are palm trees and camels.' He handed her the box and she took up a magnifying glass and peered through it.

'You must have it,' she said. He hesitated but she pressed it into his hand and he did not resist. 'I have far too many things, Ahmed. I'd like you to have it, really I would.'

'Where did you get his?' his father says angrily.

Ahmed glances at this father but his father is still glaring at the box. 'It's a present.'

'But who has given you this, and why? It looks of value.'

'A lady gave it to me.' He doesn't want to tell his father about Betty.

'What lady?'

Betty and Savannah prove hard to explain.

His father's face tightens. 'I don't need this trouble, Ahmed. Your deception pains me.' He bangs his fist on the table, rattling the cups. 'How do I know you are speaking the truth? Perhaps you stole it?'

Tears of anger and shame prickle Ahmed's eyes. His father rarely used to get angry. His father worries too: he worries about money and the food they eat. He worries about the news and how Ahmed is getting along at school and a hundred and one other things that Ahmed can hardly bear to think of.

His father puts his head in his hands. There is silence in the room broken only by the voices of the kids playing outside. 'Miss Betty would like to ask you for tea. She's been to Libya, Father. She even speaks Arabic.'

His father looks up, his face surprised. 'Is this really so?'

'I am telling the truth, yes.'

'You are lucky, Ahmed. What if this Miss Betty had been someone bad?'

'Will you go?'

His father sighs and runs his fingers through his greying hair. Perhaps Ahmed is going to get another telling off but instead his father says, 'If there is time.' He sighs again. 'You see, I may have to go to Tripoli soon.'

That is why is father has been so secretive. It occurs to Ahmed suddenly that it is not just children who keep secrets; he wonders what else his father has kept from him. 'Am I going too?'

'I do not know yet. I have many arrangements to make.'

'You've spoken to Safia and Auntie Nafissa?'

'Yes. They are all right, Ahmed. You must not worry.' Ahmed opens his mouth to ask another question but his father holds up his hand. 'We will talk on this matter later. Now I need you to go to the shop. I did not have time to pick up what we need for our evening meal.' He wipes his brow with a handkerchief before handing Ahmed a small purse. 'How hot it has grown today. It is most unusual. Perhaps we will have a storm.'

Ahmed hurries through the estate, past the emaciated trees and the dusty roses, their leaves hanging dull and heavy in the still air, and on past Charles Green House and the dustbins, and into the gloomy alley. As he walks, the purse grows damp in his hand and sweat trickles down his back.

A group of boys is hanging outside the shop, sprawled on the grass next to their BMX bikes, but there is no one he recognises. These are older boys. One, with shaven hair and pale eyes, is wearing a T-shirt printed with the English red cross flag, another has the hood of his sweatshirt pulled halfway down his face. When Ahmed gets close the shaven-headed boy shouts, 'Bloody Paki,' his mouth twisting like barbed wire. Ahmed grips the purse tight in his sweaty hand and walks on.

Mr Abdullah is standing behind the counter, his face a pasty grey in the strip lightning, his large hands resting on the counter near the packets of chewing gum. Mr Abdullah sells gum but he doesn't like the mess it makes on the pavements. 'Bad American habit come to this country,' he says. 'Too many bad American habit.'

'Good evening, Mr Abdullah.'

'Good evening, Ahmed. I think you grow tall even from last time I see you.' One of the boys outside curses and Ahmed hears the sound of an empty can hitting the wall. 'Every day I call police.' Mr Abdullah gestures towards the door. 'Those boys cause trouble, much trouble. But how your father? I not see him in long time.'

'He's busy. He has to work late sometimes.'

'Always busy, busy, me also. Those boys give you trouble tonight?'

'No,' Ahmed says, shaking his head.

A deep rumble echoes through the shop and rattles the shelves.

'Now storm,' Mr Abdullah says. 'That is good. Storm get rid of boys.' He clicks his fingers and grins. 'They not like storm and rain.'

Ahmed grins back.

'You can stay in shop for while, if you like. Wait for storm pass. Wait for boys go.'

'Thank you, Mr Abdullah, but my father is waiting for me.' He would like to stay awhile but if he doesn't get out of the shop soon the boys will think he's a coward, or worse.

'You say hello your father. He is good man. Maybe you soon go proper home, eh? Now this war is almost over.'

Is it nearly over? Perhaps that is why his father is planning to go back to Tripoli.

Before he leaves, Mr Abdullah hands him a packet of wine gums. 'You keep for yourself. Not good for teeth. But sometimes nice, eh?'

'Thank you,' Ahmed says and he steps out into the evening. The wind has blown up again and large spots of rain splash onto his face. But the boys are still there. Now two cans of beer are doing the rounds and there is laughter, swearing.

'Here comes girlie!' It is the boy with the twisted mouth. 'She sends you to the shops does she, your Paki mother?' An empty can flies in Ahmed's direction.

He grips the shopping bag and hurries away. The spots of rain are heavy and cold. Thunder rumbles and growls, and a crackle of white lightning spiders its way across the sky.

He doesn't hear the boy coming up behind. He just feels the force of the bag being torn from his hand, the surprise of it. Oranges roll into the grass, the packet of biscuits splits open on the concrete path. Ahmed lashes out: his fist hits nothing but air. The boy laughs, a hyena's laugh, and Ahmed's stomach knots in fear. What if the others come too?

A sudden blast and he is almost knocked to the ground. The blast is followed by a vivid flash that turns the darkness into an electric, dazzling daylight. And now the rain lashes down in columns, a deluge.

Ahmed looks round but the boy has vanished. He picks up two oranges and drops them into his coat pocket. The packet of biscuits is wet and trampled and the remaining oranges have rolled out of sight. Shivering, he ties up the ripped bag and runs.

The boy is at the corner. By the dustbins. Where the fox comes.

Mohamed checks his watch and stares out of the window. Ahmed should be home by now but perhaps the storm has delayed him. He paces up and down the room, checks the time again. The rain has almost stopped and a faint band of light is hanging on the horizon. There is no reason for Ahmed to be so late.

As if he doesn't have enough to worry about.

Go easy on yourself, for the outcome of all affairs is determined by Allah's decree. If something is meant to go elsewhere, it will never come your way, but if it is yours by destiny, from you it cannot flee.

How long should he wait before calling someone?

The shadows are inky dark, the path slippery with wet leaves. Wooden steps lead down to a brook, swollen and churning from the rain, the water sloshing up over the planks. Ahmed treads the makeshift bridge with care but just beyond, where the path has worn away, he loses his footing. Mud smears the knees of his trousers, the palms of his hands, his shirt. Tears spill down his cheeks. Stupid rain! Stupid country! Why couldn't things have stayed as they were?

His fist hurts from where he punched the boy next to the dustbins. He's never hit a boy before.

The rain beats down, soaking through his clothes. Lightning and thunder crackles overhead.

He's not afraid of the storm. Or the boy. Nothing matters any more but that his mother is gone forever and his father is going away.

Slowly the thunder fades until it is only a faint rumble like a distant aeroplane. Ahmed finds a log to sit on and he feels in his pocket for a tissue to wipe his muddy hands, finds one of the oranges. Still sniffing from the tears, he peels it and bites into the flesh. How sweet and good it is. Now a strip of pale blue appears in the sky and the rain becomes a soft patter.

The sound reminds Ahmed of the times his sister used to tap on the wall to wake him up and he cries a little, but not so bitterly as before. A bird opens its beak and starts to sing, a long and soothing melody. He closes his eyes. He is in the apartment in Tripoli. His mother is on the bed, the bird twittering in its cage nearby. She reaches out and strokes his forehead. 'Allah will take care of you when I am gone,' she says and she smiles at him but her eyes are sad and distant. 'Mama!' he calls softly. 'Mama!' The bird sings, oh how it sings!

Ahmed opens his eyes. Above the trees the clouds are a deep pink, the same colour as his mother's silk scarf. His father got rid of most of his mother's belongings but he kept that scarf. He must have it still.

Kicking the orange peel into a thicket of bramble, Ahmed walks out of the woods, along the road and back into the estate.

⚜ ⚜ ⚜

'*I see you ran from under the leaking roof and sat in the rain*,' his father says.

Ahmed smiles at the proverb, even though he's heard it a hundred times before.

'We must get you dry and cleaned up. But what happened? What took you so long?'

'A boy grabbed the bag and ripped it open and I fell.'

His father puts his head in his hands again and Ahmed thinks he might be crying. But when he looks up, his father's face is determined. 'You will be fine, *insha'Allah*. Be strong. Never allow those boys to see weakness in you. Now, get yourself dry and I will cook our supper. You must be hungry.'

Ahmed nods. He is hungry, hungrier than he thought. Then the warm shower, the dry clothes – these make him feel safe, as if nothing could ever touch him and his father again. And when they have eaten and cleared away his father says, 'Let's have a story, shall we?' He sits down on the sofa and Ahmed smells the cologne he always wears – a clear, bright smell like the stream in the woods.

'Solomon owned a carpet of green silk, embroidered with gold and silver, and studded with precious stones,' his father begins. 'The carpet was sixty miles long and sixty miles wide, large enough to take Solomon's throne and all his companions.'

Ahmed yawns.

'Are you too tired for this?'

'No, please go on, Father.'

'"Carry us," Solomon said to the wind and the wind took up the carpet and a flock of birds appeared. "Shade us," Solomon commanded and the birds flew overhead to form a canopy with which to shade everyone from the sun. The carpet flew so fast that Solomon was able to breakfast in Damascus and eat his evening meal in Medea.'

'Where's Medea?' Ahmed interrupts. 'Is it in Libya?'

'Medea is in Iran. What beautiful rugs they make there.'

'Have you been?'

His father nods. 'Once I had cause to visit but that was many years ago, before you and Safia were born.' At the mention of Safia, his father falls silent.

'Is this rug from Iran?' Ahmed says, pointing to the small rug on the floor, one of the few things, apart from their clothes, they bought with them from Tripoli.

'No, this is a Berber rug from Libya. The design is good.' His father taps his foot on the pattern. 'Do you remember your grandmother's house, Ahmed?'

'A little.'

'When we return to Libya we must visit Ghadames. It has been far too long.' His father pauses. How sad he looks. But he clears his throat and carries on. 'Your grandmother lived in one of the old houses. Few people live in those now because Gaddafi ordered a new town to be built.' His father's eyes flash with anger. 'The new houses are useless. They may have modern conveniences but they are far too hot in the summer. Why is it that our rulers think they have the answer to everything?'

Ahmed does not know what to say. Instead he tries to recall the house. He thinks there were red and green paintings and brass plates on white walls, but the image is faded and he cannot quite catch at it.

The telephone rings and his father answers it.

'Yes, it is,' Ahmed hears his father say. His voice sounds doubtful, suspicious.

There is a short silence.

'Yes, thank you,' his father continues. 'It is... Ah...you speak Arabic?' He walks out into the hallway, closing the door behind him.

Ahmed shifts uncomfortably on the sofa. The minutes tick by. From time to time he hears his father's voice rise and fall, and above that the sing-song of the dripping tap.

The door opens. 'That was Miss Betty.' His father fiddles with the buttons on his shirt. 'I am sorry if I doubted you, Ahmed. But I stand by my earlier words.'

'I'm sorry, Father.'

'Miss Betty has asked us to take tea with her next week and I have accepted. It is lucky that we are not yet in Ramadan because this is English tea at five o'clock. What would I have said then? Refused?' His father sighs. 'Perhaps next year you will fast with me? You will be old enough.'

'I'd like to fast this Ramadan. Can't I do that? I'm eleven.' He hasn't considered this before but now it feels important, essential even.

His father looks thoughtful. 'We will see, Ahmed, we will see.'

Ahmed picks up the boxed globe. 'Look,' he says, pointing to the palm trees and the camels. 'This is Libya.'

His father peers at the globe, then fetches his glasses. 'I do believe you are right.'

'Are we going to go back?'

His father closes his eyes and clasps his hands together. '*Insha'Allah*, my son. When calm returns.'

Chapter Ten

Betty wakes at dawn. The time is gone when she would sleep like a mountain. Now the sound of a fox barking in the garden or the wisteria creaking outside the window can startle her into hours of wakefulness. But it was not noise that kept her awake last night: she was thinking about Ahmed and his father. She unfolds the duck-blue blanket and the cotton sheet underneath, and eases her legs to the floor. The birds are calling through the open window and from the blue shadows at the bottom of the garden the bamboo leaves reach out like children waving.

As she stands there, watching, waiting, the sun illuminates the tips of the trees and slowly moves to the fiery sunflower heads. Perhaps she and Savannah will plant sunflower seeds together next year – that's if there is a next year. You have to think of these things. After all, her own mother was only sixty-six when she died and George a mere sixty-one, a heart attack, so sudden and unexpected.

She buttons up her blouse and slips on an old skirt. In the distance the traffic hums like a river.

⚜ ⚜ ⚜

Savannah charges down the stairs just as the grandfather clock in the hall chimes eight. 'We're going to the seaside!' She dances across the tiles in her bare feet, her hair flying out behind her like the sail on George's old boat. 'You haven't forgotten have you, Betty?'

Betty peers through the kitchen window. The sun has vanished and a fat layer of grey clouds has settled. 'I don't think it's a day for the beach,' she says, collecting the dishes from the table. 'That storm has quite turned the weather. What about a trip to the museum instead? And if we go to the beach another day, we might be able to take Ahmed with us.'

Savannah presses her head against the window as hard rain drives in. 'I want to go to the beach.'

Betty taps her fingers on the kitchen table. 'We could go to the aquarium. They have stingrays and basking sharks. It's almost like the beach.'

'I went there last month.'

A wave of fatigue washes over Betty. How difficult it is pleasing children these days, but perhaps she has forgotten how it was with Eva. 'Well, we'll have to stay here, won't we?'

'Can I phone Ahmed? Perhaps he can come over.'

'You can call him later. I'll fetch you some paper and pens. I'm going to work on my sculpture.'

The lunchtime forecast is not good. A large Atlantic depression has settled across the country and it doesn't seem like it's going to shift for a day or two.

'What do you want for lunch?' Betty shouts. She cuts a slice of bread and takes a piece of cheese and a tomato from the fridge. The news is not good either but that's no surprise: like the British weather, bad news blows in and blows out again. Today it's the phone hacking scandal and the stalemate in Libya. Tomorrow it could be a wildfire, a coup in some country she knows almost nothing about. 'I'll have a sandwich. You can have beans on toast.'

There is a short silence, followed by the sound of Savannah's bare feet padding along the hallway. 'All right,' Savannah says from the door. 'Can't I phone Ahmed now? I'm bored.' Her mouth is like an upside down boat.

'I'll do it.' Betty fetches the phone and dials the number. Ahmed answers in two rings. After a short conversation she puts the phone back down.

'What did he say? Will he come?'

'He can't come today. I'm sorry, Savannah.'

'Why not?'

'He didn't really explain. Come on, let's get that lunch.'

Betty keeps the radio on while they eat. The last item is a good-news tale about a teenage boy who slept in a tent in his garden for a year to raise money for charity. The boy gives her an idea. 'Let's get my tent. We'll put it up in the living room.'

'Is it a big tent?' A toast crumb is stuck to Savannah's chin.

'It's a two-man tent.'

Savannah sticks her neck out like a peacock. 'I'm a girl.'

'A two-girl tent. It amounts to the same.'

The crumb drops onto the quarry tiles and Savannah pushes her bare heel against the door jamb. 'All right,' she says and she helps Betty pull the tent out from the cupboard under the stairs.

Betty has to stop every now and again. The tent isn't particularly heavy but she is tired today and everything is an effort.

It isn't the tent that George and Betty used when they were first married. That has long since worn out. This is the tent Betty purchased for her trip to Arizona a year after George died. She thought the holiday would help her forget her loneliness and grief. It didn't. But it was a good trip nonetheless.

She sits on a stool and spreads the tent out on the dining room floor. They won't be able to use tent pegs: they will have to hold down the flysheet with books. Yet it is all quite simple; the procedure comes back to her in a jiffy. Savannah helps fix the poles and stands inside to hold the roof steady. When the tent is up, she tucks her hair behind her ears and crawls inside. 'It's very cosy. Come and have a look.'

Betty puts down her walking stick and, stretching out her stiff leg, manoeuvres herself to the floor. It is warm in the tent, much warmer than in the room outside. There is something calming and protective about an enclosed space like this, she thinks.

Savannah is sitting cross-legged in the corner. The pale light filtering through the fabric has turned her hair a mossy green colour and Betty remembers how George used to tease her about her own hair, in the days when it was dark, long and glossy; not like it is today, grey and thin, the skin of her scalp showing through in places. George said her hair reminded him of a horse's mane.

When they first met George's teasing irritated Betty, but over the years she came to accept and love that part of him. George was always a leg-puller and a practical man. Not like Omar. He was more serious and a real romantic; he swept her off her feet like a tidal wave. Oh, goodness, she sounds like a character in a bad novel. Anyway, you should never compare or look back to a life you've lost, a corner you could have turned and didn't.

'Why are you making that funny noise?'

'My leg is stiff. It hurts a little.'

'Will my leg go like that?'

'Not necessarily.'

A crease folds itself across Savannah's forehead. 'I won't ever be old,' she says.

'You can't ever know,' Betty says. 'None of us can know.'

'Who decides? Is it God?'

'I don't know.' Betty has never been particularly religious but she is reluctant to give up the idea of God completely.

'It's snowing outside,' Savannah says, peering through the door of the tent and forgetting old age and bad legs. 'I won't be able to come out for days.'

'When I was camping in Arizona, it was so cold the water froze in the taps and I couldn't sleep a wink all night, even though I was inside the sleeping bag with all my clothes on, and a woollen hat.' It was February, Betty remembers. But it could get cold in the Sahara too at that time of the year, so cold she would wake and not be able to sleep again.

'Where's Arizona?'

'In America. Most of it is desert. They have huge cacti there with prickles like the edges of a sword.'

'America? Where Mummy is?' Savannah snorts and wrinkles her nose again. The expression reminds Betty of an angry crab. 'Ahmed says that moss can grow in deserts. But deserts are burning hot.'

'Not always. You can get frost in the winter, especially at altitude.'

'This is the tundra. It never gets hot.'

The telephone rings in the hallway. But neither of them moves. They sit and listen to the insistent ringing. When it stops the house falls silent, a big and empty silence, like Betty imagines the tundra to be.

For a moment, Betty wonders where she is. Of course, she's in her own sitting room. She must have fallen asleep. Then she remembers Savannah in the tent but when she checks the dining room, she can hear Savannah breathing quietly from inside.

It is a relief to have a few moments of peace. Betty remembers how much she used to grab them in the days before Eva went to school. George was a good father in many ways but the day-to-day caring of Eva fell to Betty a great deal of the time. She is not sure she expected life to be any different, though it was supposed to be the era of women's liberation.

She returns to the kitchen and taps a row of nails into the wood but the sculpture isn't going well. The door, which she intended to be a mouth, is wrong and one of the nails has gone in crooked. Irritated, she abandons it and makes herself a cup of sweet, milky coffee and afterwards she feels a lot better. Sculptures can't be hurried. Sometimes they have to be left to mature like good cheese.

At last the rain has begun to ease off. Through the watery panes of glass the garden is blurred and green like something deep in the sea.

She is in the kitchen making sauce for macaroni cheese – though she does not like making cheese sauce because it is so temperamental – when Savannah walks in, her face covered in red creases like cat scratches.

'Is that a bird house?' she asks, turning to the sculpture.

'It's supposed to be a head but it looks more like Baba Yaga's hut.'

'Who's Baba Yaga?'

Betty is focused on the sculpture and does not answer.

'Betty!'

Betty jumps. 'Baba Yaga? Oh yes. She was a very scary witch who once lived deep in the dark forests of Russia in a hut that stood on chicken legs. Her hut span round and round like a top and made the most terrible screeching noises.'

Savannah claps her hands. 'Oooh! That's horrible. So, what did she do?'

Betty stirs the cooked pasta into the cheese sauce and places the dish in the hot oven. Then she sits down at the table with Savannah and relates the story of Baba Yaga: how she constructed a fence of human bones and topped each post with a human skull packed with fiery embers, how the girl Vasilissa was sent by her wicked stepmother to fetch fire from Baba Yaga's hut and was forced by Baba Yaga to undertake a series of impossible tasks and how Vasilissa was saved by a magic doll given by her mother. 'But in the end,' Betty says, 'the stepmother was burned to ash.'

Savannah asks lots of questions during the story. Children always ask questions. Eva was like that. Questions, questions, questions. She never ceased. But as Eva grew into a teenager she argued about anything and everything and certain questions made Betty anxious.

'The stepmother deserved to die,' Savannah leans her head to one side. 'I don't think Ahmed's mother deserved to die, even though she was in prison.'

Betty's heart falters. Prison? Is that why Ahmed and his father are here? 'Not everyone who goes to prison has done a bad thing, Savannah. In some countries you can be locked up for saying something against the government.'

Savannah kneels on the chair and leans forward, her elbows on the table top, her blue eyes round and fearful.

'The man who runs Ahmed's country won't accept anything against him,' Betty continues. 'He has to be right.'

'Like the Queen?'

Betty laughs a little. 'Libya doesn't have a queen, or king. It has a leader instead.' Dictator, more like, Betty thinks but she doesn't say. 'If I go outside now and paint on the wall, *I hate the Queen*, nothing will happen to me, although I don't suppose I'd be very popular.'

'You aren't allowed to paint on walls,' Savannah says rather piously.

'That's true, but if I paint on my own property, no one will worry. But if I painted words like *I hate the leader* in Ahmed's country even on my own wall, I might get put in prison.'

Savannah's nostrils flare. 'Do you think Ahmed's mother wrote on a wall? Ahmed said she was a teacher.'

'I don't know. Maybe. When the enemy is at the gates, you have to act.'

'What enemy?'

'Never mind. I was thinking out loud. Well, I expect our macaroni is cooked.'

A low sun is shining in through the kitchen window, revealing the smears on the glass and the drying raindrops. Betty takes the macaroni cheese out of the oven. It is bubbling nicely. After she has set it down on the table, she looks out onto the garden again: at the long expanse of lawn, the tumbling roses and the thick hedges, and the bamboo patch, now grown tall as the house.

Even with Fred Marsden to help, she wonders how on earth she will go on coping with it all. But she is lucky, it is peaceful here and no one will send her to prison – well, not unless she does something pretty awful. For a moment she feels desperately sad, for Ahmed and his father, for her beloved Libya, but then there is the macaroni cheese to eat, and Savannah at the table and none of it seems to matter any more.

Chapter Eleven

Mohamed pats his chin with the towel but as he splashes on the cologne, he clumsily knocks the bottle onto the floor. He is nervous. He has never been to anyone's house here in England, only to Hashim's place in London but Hashim is family and that is different.

He picks up the bottle, which has not broken, places it back in the bathroom cupboard and peers into the mirror. There seems to be a touch more grey in his hair and surely the lines of his forehead are deeper than before. He pats his face again, runs the comb through his hair and turns away from the mirror. He is no longer a young man: he must remember that.

'Are you ready?' he calls, opening the bathroom door. 'You have combed your hair and cleaned your teeth?'

'Yes, Father.' Ahmed is standing in the living room in a newly pressed white shirt and long trousers. Mohamed never imagined that one day he and Ahmed would have to iron clothes and do their own washing.

He rechecks his watch. 'I think we should go. You say it is only ten minutes to walk?'

He locks the door and they walk down the familiar concrete stairway, with its musty and unpleasant smell. As always, that rusty old bike is parked at the bottom. He wonders for how much longer it will be their home.

⚜ ⚜ ⚜

'Are we making a cake?' Savannah asks. 'You haven't forgotten Ahmed and his father are coming to tea, have you, Betty?'

'I haven't forgotten.' Betty stares up at the cobwebs in the kitchen. It isn't just the garden that needs attention, the house could do with sprucing up too. But people must take her as she comes. A few cobwebs and the odd piece of peeling wallpaper are nothing to fuss over. 'I'm going up to change.'

'Shall I wear my pink dress?' Savannah is sitting at the kitchen table, Napoleon purring on her lap.

'Why not?' Betty is not fond of pink, unless it's a dark shade, a fuchsia perhaps. But if Savannah likes the dress, then she should wear it.

Upstairs, Betty tries on a pair of black trousers, but she has not worn them in a while and they are tight around the waist. Next she tries on a beige linen suit but that looks dowdy and she tosses it back onto the bed. After pulling out several other skirts and dresses she opts for her trusted blue skirt and a cream silk blouse.

For jewellery, she hangs the pearl necklace George bought for her around her neck. But it just doesn't feel right. She never was a fan of pearls, not that she ever told George. How upset he would have been if he had known what she really thought of his generous gift. She puts the pearls back in a box and takes out her Tuareg necklace. She runs her finger along the coloured beads and incised silver cross, then she presses it against her lips and sighs.

The Tuareg necklace is her most treasured possession, though she rarely wears it.

'This will protect you,' Omar said when he fixed the necklace round her neck. 'Its patterns symbolise the desert and the tribe and the four points of the cross are the four directions of the world. You see here, this is the north. This is you, a woman from the north.' He kissed her and her heart fluttered under his gentle hands.

How happy she was that day. It was as if she were a bird, singing, as if she could fly forever. She told George she'd bought the necklace herself and he seemed to believe her. She hated deceiving him but the truth is she never wanted to lose George because, deep down, although she did not wish to think of it, she knew her relationship with Omar could not, and would not, last.

She stands back and examines herself in the full-length mirror. For a moment she is afraid, but the necklace is perfect. She *will* wear it.

The knock on the door comes at half past three. The man standing in the porch is serious-faced, with greying hair, a neatly trimmed beard and the same dark brown eyes as his son. His linen suit is slightly crumpled and his brown leather brogues, though polished like a mirror, are creased and old. He is older than Betty imagined, old enough to be the boy's grandfather, but he stands upright, if a little stiffly, like a soldier at attention.

'It is most kind for the invitation,' he says, bowing and pulling on his fingers.

So he too is nervous.

'*Marhaban. Kaifa haloka,*' Betty says.

'*Ana bekhair, shokran,*'Ahmed's father replies. He does not smile but turns to Ahmed and with a click of his fingers, says, 'Remember your manners, Ahmed.'

Betty takes a careful step back into the gloomy hallway. Is there not just a trace of the Omar she knew all those years ago in this man? Omar was taller and darker-skinned but something in the way Ahmed's father holds his hands and those long, slender fingers remind her of Omar. She must not keep looking at him: it will seem most improper. She turns to Ahmed. He has had his hair trimmed and he is carrying a large bunch of red roses wrapped in cellophane. 'These are for you, Miss Betty.'

'Why, thank you Ahmed. Now please do come in both of you. No need to stand on ceremony.' The flowers unsettle her. George was not a man who brought flowers and gifts; he wasn't like Omar who remembered every occasion and made one up if there was not. But flowers can mean many things, even the end of something. Betty gathers up the roses and Savannah bounces into the hall and there are more explanations and introductions to be made and the painful memory fades into the background.

She and Savannah have prepared tea in the sitting room. It is a bother to take everything outside and the grass is still damp from yesterday's rain.

'Ahmed says you still have family in Tripoli,' Betty says, pouring from the china pot.

Ahmed's father clears his throat. 'Yes, my daughter is in Tripoli.' His eyes alight on the necklace and she wonders if, after all, she has made a mistake, wearing it. 'This necklace. Forgive me, but I think this necklace is Tuareg.'

She touches the silver cross and nods. 'Yes, I bought it in...in Ghadames.' If he hears her hesitation, the slight stumble, he is too polite to draw attention to it.

'Ghadames, the Pearl of the Sahara. This is a big surprise.' He blinks and rubs his forehead as if wiping away an invisible drop of sweat. 'Because my mother is born in Ghadames, though later she comes to live with us in Tripoli. It is much years since I visit. But a beautiful place, is it not?'

'Indeed.' The tea cup shakes in her hand. He knows Ghadames? How old is he? He must be sixty or more. Perhaps he even knew Omar's family. She sets the cup down hard, slopping tea onto the saucer. 'I have been there, several times, although it was a long time ago.' Before Gaddafi too, Betty thinks, although she does not say so.

'I think it goes bad in Ghadames now. In Tripoli it goes bad too, though not so grave as the other cities.' He places his hand on his heart. 'Who knows our future? We can only wait and hope, *insha'Allah.*'

'Tripoli is a lovely city, as I remember it. I love the Sidi Salem mosque – it has such a pretty minaret. The red fort and the medina, how could one ever forget them?' She's babbling because she needs to keep away the memory of Ghadames, that splinter grown deep into her skin, or else she may be in danger of breaking down. And that will not do.

'What's a miniret?' Savannah interrupts, slurping her lemonade.

'It's a min-*a*-ret,' Ahmed corrects.

Savannah fiddles with the large pink bow she insisted Betty tie in her hair. That's her mother's influence, all fripperies and froth. Betty is so caught up in such thoughts that she misses Ahmed's father patiently explaining the purpose of minarets.

'Why don't we have minarets?' Savannah asks, swinging her legs, her need to be grown-up and sophisticated forgotten.

'Our churches have spires instead,' Betty says, relieved to be on a new topic. 'We have a different religion. Isn't that so, Mr...' She realises she does not know his name.

'Please call me Mohamed.'

Savannah places her empty glass on the table. 'Can we go outside? Ahmed would like to.'

'If that's OK with...Mohamed,' Betty says. If his name had been Omar, she would have been unable to utter it.

Mohamed nods. When the children have gone, he turns to Betty and says, sadly, 'You cannot visit Libya now. How can we imagine such a thing? When I am young I cannot imagine it. I am twenty-two when Gaddafi comes to power. We think to have a brilliant future but we do not. That man – he steals the happiness from our eyes.' A deep furrow appears on his forehead. 'Ah, the old times. To be old, Mrs Betty. This is when we look back.'

'The old days,' Betty echoes. 'You are not so old.'

He smiles again. 'I am old enough.'

She looks down at the carpet and the faded rug. Suddenly it seems as if the decades have flown by in the blink of an eye. Too often the present is grey and dull while much of her past seems illuminated, like the sun dancing on the mosque in the late afternoon. 'I am sure the war will soon be over,' she says, without conviction.

'Perhaps this is so.' He coughs and takes a sip of tea. A long silence follows. The clock ticks in the hall and the children's voices drift in from the garden. Betty would like to ask Mohamed what he really thinks about the situation in his country but the question seems perilous. An involuntary sigh escapes from her mouth. When she was young, how uncomplicated life seemed.

'My son is a good boy,' Mohamed says, breaking the awkwardness. 'But sometimes, like all boys, he is not so kind. I hope he is behaved here.'

'He's a good companion for Savannah. I'm looking after her while her mother is away.'

'That must be much work.' He raises his eyebrows a fraction. 'So, what is it that brings you to my country, to Libya?'

'I trained as an archaeologist. My husband, George and I worked in the Fezzan. We studied the rock art. We were very lucky to be there at that time.' She stops and grips the edge of the chair to steady herself. Those days full of purpose, the long discussions under the stars, the sense of companionship and shared effort are gone, just as Omar is gone and George and...

She looks at Mohamed. A smile flits across his face. 'Stealing all our treasures.' He is mocking her.

She feels herself blush but the discomfort she feels is nothing to the wrench of those memories. 'Luckily, it's very difficult to steal rock art, although I understand that there has been some vandalism in recent years.'

'This is bad. This I also hear. Yes, I visit Ghadames many times but I never see the rock carvings. It is long journeys from Ghadames.'

'You must go when this is all over.'

He nods politely.

She picks up the empty cup and turns it round in her hand. 'I had a number of friends in Libya. But you know how it is, one loses touch.'

'It is an interesting life,' he says.

An interesting life? Yes it was. But it is difficult to think of it now. 'You must be worried for your daughter.'

He does not answer right away but turns to look out of the window while he plays with his hands. 'It is worry. Great worry. If you have children, you understand this.'

The question will follow as it always does but Betty has her answer, practised over the years. This afternoon however she is saved by Savannah who dashes in through the door, shouting, 'Ahmed and I are looking for ants!' before rushing out again.

'Ah, children.' Mohamed is smiling, beaming almost. How much less severe he looks when he smiles.

Betty smiles back. 'Would you like to see the garden?'

'Yes, I like this very much.'

They walk side by side down the path. Creeping daisies and moss are growing up between the bricks, and brambles and clumps of grass poke out of the flowerbeds. A blackbird calls out in alarm and one of the chickens clucks from the coop.

'The garden is a little overgrown,' Betty apologises. 'George and I used to do all the work ourselves. I have help but it's never enough.'

'This does not matter,' Mohamed says gently. 'It makes me happy to see a garden. This is something I see in England. What is it they say?' He pauses and lifts a hand. 'Ah, yes. You are a country of gardens.'

'Indeed,' Betty replies. 'We can sit in the walled garden. It's always sheltered there.'

'This sounds most pleasant,' he says and for a moment she thinks he will take her arm but he does not. They move on down the path. The children's voices eddy around the lower garden and a blackbird clacks, alarmed perhaps by Stealth in the bushes, hunting again.

'Ah! What lovely and many roses,' Mohamed exclaims. '*The rose and the thorn, and sorrow and gladness are linked together*,' he adds, in the Arabic.

'Saadi,' Betty says. Just when she thought she was safe he comes up with Saadi.

Mohamed turns to look at her but she cannot quite read his expression. 'You know Saadi?'

The walled garden is still warm and the scent of the late roses is almost intoxicating. Oh, yes, she knows Saadi all right. '*Some are far distant, some are dead,*' she says. But as soon as the quote falls from her mouth she realises it is quite inappropriate.

'That is so.'

A swallow flutters like an ink-spot in the sky and a robin lands on the statue of Diana the huntress that George bought and had placed in the centre. Betty fishes in her mind for another quote but she cannot think of anything suitable and then Savannah comes running into the walled garden, shouting, 'Mummy's on the phone! She wants to talk to you.'

'I won't be long. Please do sit down.' She gestures to the bench. 'Or feel free to walk, whichever you would like. The garden is yours.'

He gestures for her to go and reluctantly she moves towards the house.

⚜ ⚜ ⚜

Mohamed settles onto the wooden bench and breathes in the spicy scent of the roses. It has been a long time since he sat in a garden like this, perhaps not since the day he and Nour took leave of their house in Tripoli and moved into that cheap and unpleasant apartment on the other side of the city. He can never think of his wife without pain. Her loss is like an old wound, one which never properly heals.

If only she had talked. But each time he asked about the prison she held up her hands and stopped him. 'This is my life now,' she said. 'We must move forward, Mohamed.'

He thought that meant she was getting better. He was wrong. As the weeks passed, her mental state grew increasingly fragile and, as a consequence, he felt side-lined, inadequate. At times he was even impatient with her but he had no one to turn to, only Nafissa who – like him – had no real idea how to deal with Nour's erratic behaviour, and a colleague who prescribed tranquillisers to help with Nour's nightmares. The drugs made little difference. Nour slept more but she began to refuse food and would hardly look at him, as if he were to blame.

He tried to shield Safia and Ahmed from Nour's illness; perhaps with Ahmed he was partially successful for he was still young, but Safia turned moody and argumentative.

'There you are, Father.'

Mohamed jumps. 'I am here, yes. Mrs Betty is on the telephone.'

'Where is Savannah?'

'The girl? I do not know.'

'Perhaps she's looking for the cat. It's nice here, isn't it, Father? And Miss Betty is very kind.'

Mohamed looks at his son. Ahmed's eyes are shining and he looks happier than at any time since they arrived in this country. But that too pulls at Mohamed's heart.

When Betty gets off the phone, she is so angry she has to go to the kitchen and pour herself a glass of water before she can face her guests. She finds Mohamed standing outside the back door, Ahmed at his side. There is no sign of Savannah. 'I'm sorry,' Betty says. 'That was more complicated than I anticipated.'

'Do not trouble,' Mohamed replies, with a wave his hand. 'It is very kind for your invitation but now we must leave you. It grows late.'

'Please do come again.' She hopes she doesn't sound desperate but oh, how she has missed talking to someone interesting, someone who understands a little of her past.

'Thank you, Mrs Betty. I hope this will be possible.' He smiles again. She has missed a man's smile too.

After Mohamed and Ahmed have left, Savannah says, 'Why were you so long on the phone? Was it something Mummy said?' She reaches for a mug from the rack. 'Can I have a hot chocolate?'

'Go ahead,' Betty says. She taps her fingers on the kitchen table. 'Your mother is in Las Vegas.' How on earth will she break this news? Really it's not fair.

'I know. Mummy says Las Vegas is really pretty. There are lights everywhere. She's going to send me a postcard.'

'How nice.'

Savannah opens the fridge door and takes out the carton of milk. 'You sound cross.'

Betty sighs. 'I'm not cross, Savannah. Your mother has some news.' She fiddles with a dirty cup on the table, pushes it away. She might as well tell the girl. If Delia can't, or won't, then why not? 'She's got married. She and Scott were married yesterday, in Las Vegas. I imagine that will come as a shock.'

'Mummy's married? Why has she got married there?'

'It's a popular place. Lots of people do.' How idiotic she sounds.

Savannah's face turns red and then pale like the milk, and a single tear falls down her cheek.

'I'm sorry.'

Another tear tracks its way down Savannah's face. 'Why didn't she tell me? Why?'

'She was going to tell you later, really she was.'

Savannah opens her mouth and gasps, as if she were drowning. Then she breaks into great, heaving sobs.

Betty gets up and takes the girl in her arms.

It is midnight when Betty opens the door to Savannah's room. Savannah is breathing steadily, her hair drifted across the pillow, the old teddy that once belonged to Eva dropped onto the carpet. She should have waited for Delia to phone back and explain, but it's done now and she can't change it. Savannah wouldn't be comforted, no matter what Betty tried. But things will seem better in the morning. They usually do.

Chapter Twelve

Ahmed's father is on the telephone to Aunt Nafissa in Tripoli. 'Do you have any more news?' he hears his father say. More news? What does he mean?

His father falls silent and Ahmed can hear his aunt's voice, small and thin down the telephone, all those miles away. It must be dark in Tripoli now; people strolling in the heat of the summer evening. He wonders what Safia is up to: perhaps she is eating an ice-cream or walking with her friends, maybe she's been picnicking on the beach today, although she's never learned to swim.

He remembers their early family outings to the beach. There was always more food than anyone could possibly eat. The adults would sit on plastic chairs under the shade of umbrellas, the women gossiping, the men smoking while he and his cousins splashed in the warm water or raced each other along the burning sand. But Safia won't have gone to the beach today. She's probably shut up inside the apartment, afraid to go out, because of the bombs.

His father claims the bombs are targeted at military buildings, that no one will be hurt, except the Colonel and his men. But how can he be sure? Ahmed has seen pictures of Misrata; the city destroyed, its buildings blackened like rotten teeth, its roads littered with shrapnel and the casings of bullets. He knows that many have died there, not just the fighters, but children, old people, brothers, sisters, aunts and cousins. What if the war moves to Tripoli? What then?

He stares gloomily out of the window. Grey and pink clouds like ribbons trail across a golden sky but it is a chilly evening and he shivers. How different the summers are here compared to the hot, dark nights of Tripoli. But Tripoli no longer appears real: it has become a film set, something he can only look at from a distance.

'Are you sure?' his father says sharply. 'Just a moment.' He snaps his fingers. 'Please go to your room, Ahmed.'

Ahmed fidgets on the chair.

'I need to speak privately with your aunt. Now go. I will explain later.'

Reluctantly Ahmed leaves, closing the door behind him. He lies on his bed and watches the shadows lengthen and the light fade, leaching all colour from the walls. A dog barks on the estate and a man shouts, 'Mattie! Come here, boy!' while from the living room comes the faint murmuring of his father and the silences in between.

The door opens. 'It is dark in here,' his father says. 'Don't you want the light on?'

'No,' Ahmed replies sullenly.

His father sits on the edge of the bed and ruffles his hair. 'I have news, Ahmed but it is not good news.'

Ahmed sits up, his heart suddenly beating too fast. 'Is she dead? Have they killed her?' He searches his father's face for an answer.

'No, Safia is not dead. Whatever made you think that?' His father places his fingers on his forehead as if he had a headache. 'She has disappeared. Your aunt has been making enquiries but she has no news. It is difficult now to get news.'

Ahmed's belly twists and turns. 'Where would she have gone, Father?'

'I do not know.'

'Are you angry with her?'

His father taps his fingers on his thigh. 'I am not angry. There is no reason for me to be angry. However, I am troubled and I cannot lie about this. Your mother did not like the regime. None of us liked it but we had to put up with it because we had no choice. But the day arrived when your mother could stand it no more. She spoke out against something she felt was unfair and for that she paid a very high price. I do not want your sister to pay that price.' He closes his eyes and covers his head with his hands. 'I cannot bear to lose her too.'

Ahmed feels suddenly afraid. His father's reassurances make no sense. What if they have Safia?

Surely they will imprison her? Or kill her. And if she does come back she will never be the same. He was only young when his mother returned from the prison but he saw how she had changed, how could he not? She had lost weight and her lovely dark hair was streaked with white. At first she seemed all right and he accepted the changes but when she began to laugh at the shadows on the walls, to mutter and curse, a strange look in her eyes as if she were peering into the depths of a well, he avoided her. Just as he avoided the beggar man he and his father used to pass on the way to the *souk*.

One day, when his father was at work and Safia out on an errand, his mother asked him to fetch her coat. When Ahmed hesitated, saying it was too warm for a coat his mother glared at him and said, 'Son, do you not hear how the wind howls?' She had smeared red lipstick on her mouth, lined her eyes with black and covered her face in pale powder. She looked like a ghoul, a ghost. But he did her bidding and fetched the coat and she took his hand and led him down the stairs. He was surprised to find her hand no longer soft: the skin there had turned dry and cracked like the desert.

They walked to the jewellers shop and along the way he tried not to cry when he noticed people staring and a man passing called his mother a terrible name. Things did not improve at the jeweller's. His mother tried on so many bracelets, necklaces and earrings that the assistants almost turned the shop upside down. Ahmed was so ashamed he could not look at anyone and instead spent the time studying his shoes.

After much sighing and bother, his mother bought a pair of expensive earrings. She asked him if he liked them and he nodded. The earrings were beautiful and sparkly but even Ahmed understood that they could not really be afforded. He thinks his father returned them the next day.

Yet there were days when his mother would get out of bed and walk in the garden and tell him stories and once, though only once, she chased him through the rooms of the house, that pink silk scarf billowing out like a cloud behind her.

'Safia is clever,' Ahmed says. 'She's probably hiding somewhere.' He is not sure he believes his own words.

His father smiles, a thin smile. 'I expect you are right.'

'How is Aunt Nafissa?'

'Life is not easy in Tripoli at the moment. Of course she is worried but she will survive, *insha'allah.*' His father glances at his watch. 'It is too dark to see the time,' he says with a small laugh, 'but I know it must be late.' He reaches over and switches on the light, and they both blink. 'Shall we have a story to take our minds off our own concerns? How about the King of Zamzar? That is a good story, is it not?'

Ahmed has heard the tale a dozen times before but he is happy to hear it again. The King of Zamzar, out hunting with his nobles, chased a golden gazelle through the desert. At sunset the gazelle turned into a beautiful, young woman and the King married her. However, it was not long before the new wife became jealous of the King's other wives. She complained to her husband and, one by one, each of the wives was imprisoned, though none had done anything wrong. Naturally the King's subjects grew suspicious but not even the most powerful families dared accuse their King without proof, and there was none.

Ahmed understands that his father is telling him this story because of the Colonel, for his father falls silent when it is finished and sits on the bed without moving.

'Well, that's that,' his father says after a while.

Ahmed reaches over and gives his father a hug. He smells of cologne. His mother used to buy his father's cologne although surely that particular bottle must have run dry by now. He expects his father has bought a replacement. 'I wish Safia was here,' Ahmed murmurs.

His father extricates himself from the embrace. 'I wish that too. But we must be patient and trust in Allah.'

The sulphurous light from the street lamp filters into the living room, turning the blooms on the carpet into living things, and Mohamed thinks of all the flowers he bought Nour over the years of his marriage and how, after she fell sick, she no longer wanted flowers but shut herself in her room with the blinds drawn. He does not blame his wife for speaking out even though many of his friends and colleagues turned away after she was imprisoned. It was hard to bear but he understood their fear: people were afraid because of the association. That must have hurt Nour too. But why, oh why, did he and Nour not speak of it?

How silenced he has been. Even here in the relative safety of this country, he has felt that silence pressing down on him. Few understand this: how the silences and the secrets become part of you, until you are no longer able to speak, how the gag becomes simply something you wear each and every day.

Sighing, he checks his watch. It is past ten. He switches on the news, the volume low. A massacre has taken place on an island in Norway. Dozens of young people have been shot dead. He wonders how one individual could do such a terrible thing but then he thinks of Gaddafi ordering the killing of more than a thousand inmates at Abu Salim prison, the young student activists hung in public and he realises he is not surprised.

Five minutes later Mohamed picks up the phone and dials Hashim.

When Ahmed wakes, his father is still at home. 'Are you ill, Father? It's not your day off, is it?'

'I have called work to say I am sick because there are things I need to arrange, important things. It pains me to do this but it is necessary, may Allah forgive me.'

'What things?' Ahmed heard his father talking on the phone again last night but he could not catch the words.

'I am going to return to Tripoli to look for Safia.' His father smears marmalade on his toast – he is partial to English marmalade. 'You will go to stay with your uncle Hashim in London.' His voice is quite calm.

'Tripoli? Now?' Ahmed turns cold inside.

'It is important that you understand how serious this situation is. I cannot ask Nafissa to take all the responsibility. This is not right.'

'I don't want to go to London. Why can't I come with you?'

His father sits back in the chair. Sunlight filters through the cheap Venetian blind, creating dark shadows on his father's face like the bars of a prison. 'It is not safe for you to come, Ahmed. The journey will be very difficult. I am afraid there is no choice.'

Ahmed pushes his own plate away. He is no longer hungry.

Chapter Thirteen

Savannah is crying in the downstairs lavatory, a soft and broken sound. Betty clacks down the hall, stopping briefly at the black and white picture of George, taken when he was young and handsome. No matter how many times a day she passes that picture it still cuts her to the heart. He was a good man: she was right to marry him, even if perhaps things were not always so easy between them. She looks into George's eyes and they stare back as if registering her presence. He is sitting on the edge of their boat, legs dangling, trousers rolled up and he is smiling that wonderful smile she will never forget.

Next to George's photograph is a photograph of Eva. How beautiful Eva looks. Everyone has a year when they are just perfect and that was Eva's time. She was twenty and, as Betty learned too late, in love.

She sighs and catches sight of herself in the hall mirror. How old she looks, her skin tired and lined, her once lustrous hair limp and grey. She rests on her stick, lifts up her chin and pulls up her shoulders. Walk tall, Betty. Don't slump so. Annette is always saying that Betty doesn't look her age but she certainly feels it today. She scrutinises her face. Perhaps she needs a new haircut. With her free hand she gathers her hair up, scraping it away from her face. Now that's better, not perfect but a definite improvement.

'Betty!' Savannah's voice echoes plaintively down the hall.

'I won't be a minute,' Betty calls back, turning away from the mirror. When she reaches the open door, she can see Savannah on the toilet seat, her pink dress scrunched up, her legs dangling like George's on the boat, her face stained with tears. 'What is it?'

'There's no toilet paper,' Savannah says, beginning to cry. So much for Betty's belief that things would seem better in the morning.

'I'll go and get some. Don't worry.'

'It's Ahmed's fault.'

'What is?' Betty leans against the doorframe. She feels unaccountably dizzy.

'He stole the paper to make streamers. I said you wouldn't mind.'

'Just a minute and I'll fetch you a roll.' Betty takes three deep breaths and leans against the wall until the dizziness passes.

When she returns with the paper, Savannah is still crying. 'Mummy should have waited for me! I want to be a bridesmaid and wear a pretty dress and satin shoes. It's not fair!'

Savannah isn't crying over the dress or the shoes, Betty understands that. But life is full of disappointments and small treacheries, and Savannah will have to learn to cope with those. 'We'll talk again when you've finished,' she says.

Betty is sitting on the sofa, examining the woven palm-leaf basket she bought on her final trip to Ghadames, when Savannah walks in.

'That's nice,' Savannah says. Her eyelids are swollen and red but she looks more cheerful.

'Yes, it is, isn't it?' Betty brings the basket to her nose. The musty smell carries with it a thousand memories of Omar. What is she doing? She puts the basket down. Sentimentality is a trap. She must never fall into that.

Savannah goes over to the window and picks up a small inlaid wooden box Betty bought in Zagora, Morocco. 'Is there anything inside?'

'I can't honestly remember.'

Savannah opens the lid and lifts out a small red drawstring bag Betty had quite forgotten about. 'What about this? Can you remember?'

'Yes, a snake, just a small one, mind.'

Savannah's hand flies to her mouth and she almost drops the bag. 'You're teasing me, aren't you?' She looks sad again.

'I didn't mean anything by it, Savannah. I was only trying to cheer you up.'

'I'm all right, Betty. I'm just...disappointed.'

Betty smiles. What a strange and grown-up thing to say. But that's Savannah, an odd mixture of child and sophisticate. Savannah smiles back, before dipping her hand into the bag and bringing out a tiny striped feather. Betty must have collected the feather in the woodland, years ago. 'That's a jay's feather,' Betty says. 'You can keep it, and the box. After all, I gave Ahmed the globe. It doesn't seem fair that you shouldn't have anything.'

'Thanks,' Savannah says. 'At school we had to write a poem about a magic box. My friend Crystal wrote that she found a big diamond and I wrote about a magic bird that can sing in all the languages of the world.'

'What a lovely idea.'

'My teacher liked it too. She put my story up on the wall.' Savannah snaps the box closed.

'Why don't we walk over to the shop on the estate and buy some Parma Violets? That'll cheer us up.' She and Savannah are both partial to Parma Violets.

'Are you sad too?' Savannah asks.

'I was just thinking about Ahmed's family. It must be difficult for them.'

⚜ ⚜ ⚜

When they return from the estate Ahmed is waiting by the front door, neat in loose trousers and a clean white shirt. But his face has a mournful look. It reminds Betty of the icon of the Virgin Mary that hangs upstairs in her bedroom.

'Are you all right, Ahmed? You look a little depressed.'

'I'm fine, thank you.'

Betty doesn't ask more. Ahmed will talk in his own time. That's what Annette doesn't realise. She's always pushing for answers but people must be given room, whatever age they are. 'I'll make lunch. You'd like lunch, wouldn't you? Will you be fasting for Ramadan?' Ahmed nods, though whether in reply to the question about lunch or Ramadan, Betty is not certain.

'I can help. I help at home with my father.'

'I appreciate your offer, Ahmed, but there's no need. Another time perhaps? Now where has Savannah gone?' Betty slips off her coat and hangs it on the peg.

'She ran upstairs,' Ahmed says. He is still standing awkwardly in the hall.

'You can go up too, if you like.'

Ahmed shrugs his shoulders, it's a habit he has, then he turns and she hears the slow thud of his feet on the treads. Betty steps into the kitchen as the clock in the hall strikes one. She switches on the radio and starts to slice the bread. She has just finished filling the sandwiches when the newsreader says, 'It looks as if the war is moving to Tripoli,' but Betty doesn't hear the details because Savannah comes flying into the kitchen, her face pink and angry.

'What is it?' Betty puts the cutlery down on the table with a bang; she can feel her patience ebbing away.

'Ahmed bowed down to the ground and I asked him what he was doing and he said he was praying. He said I could pray too if I liked but if I wasn't going to pray I had to leave. That wasn't very nice of him.' She folds her arms across her chest. 'I mean, it's not his house.'

'He's Muslim. Prayer is very important to him.'

'He said something else. If he does anything bad, his God will strike him down. How awful is that? Will God strike me down if I'm bad?'

Betty turns the radio off. 'I don't think God will worry, unless it's something really terrible.'

Savannah sits on the low chair, her chin resting on the edge of the table. 'Maybe God struck Ahmed's mother down.' She shivers and closes her eyes.

'People get ill, Savannah. It happens.'

'What if my Mummy gets ill and dies.'

'She won't. She's perfectly healthy. Now, I expect Ahmed has finished his prayers. Go and call him for me, will you? Lunch is ready.'

⚜ ⚜ ⚜

The ice-cream van on the estate is playing *Greensleeves*. A motorbike revs in the distance and overhead a seagull wheels, mewing like a cat. But the woodland is quiet.

'Let's go to the rope swing,' Savannah says. She and Betty found the rope by mistake when Betty took a wrong turn. Today, however, the swing proves difficult to locate.

'Was this it?' Betty asks, when they reach a fallen beech tree. 'Perhaps it came down in that wind we had.'

'I don't think so,' Savannah answers.

The fallen tree reminds Betty of the Roman columns at Leptis Magna, the Roman town not far from modern Tripoli. She first visited Leptis with George. They were bowled over by the scale of the place, the amphitheatre and triumphal arches, the stone head of Medusa staring out at them with her fearful snaky curls. The second time she went to Leptis, it was Omar who accompanied her, not George. They sat on the steps of the amphitheatre and he kissed her and for a few moments she entertained the thought that she would divorce George and move with Omar to Libya. Later, the broken columns of Leptis appeared like a metaphor for their relationship.

'This definitely isn't it,' Savannah says emphatically. But when Ahmed climbs up onto the massive trunk and begins to walk along its length, Savannah shouts, 'Wait for me!' and clambers up after him.

Betty stands a while longer, examining the beech. Its smooth trunk is marked in places like a tiger's pelt and where the branches grow out there are heavy folds in the bark which resemble loose flesh. She walks carefully across the rough ground to the base of the tree where some of the roots still cling to the earth, as if the tree could not quite let go.

'This is awesome.' Savannah waves her arm in the air and her legs wobble. She's showing off, Betty thinks.

The sun edges behind a cloud and Ahmed drops to the ground.

'I'm a bird, I can fly!' Savannah is swinging from one of the larger branches. If she falls she'll get no more than a few scratches and a bruise or two. All the same, Betty smiles, it's a good thing her mother isn't here to see.

Damn her mother. How selfish.

Ahmed is peering at a clump of moss at the base of the tree. His mouth is turned down, his head lowered, like a child ashamed. Something is bothering him, she is certain of it.

'What is Ahmed doing?' Savannah shouts. 'Why isn't he climbing?'

'He's looking at moss.' Betty leans on her stick and turns to Ahmed. 'Are you sure everything is all right?'

He slumps against the trunk of the tree. 'My father is worried because my sister Safia has disappeared and now he is going to Tripoli to look for her.'

'Your father's going to Tripoli?' She means to keep her voice calm but she can hear the anxiety in it, the name of the city flying up at the end.

'He says that there is always a path to the top of the highest mountain.' Ahmed tries to smile but the smile becomes caught in a great gulp, as if he were taking in water, as if he were drowning.

'I'm sure he is right.' Some paths are perilous, she thinks though she does not say this to Ahmed. 'Is he taking you with him?'

Ahmed scrabbles at the moss and throws a clump of it into the carpet of leaves. 'No. He says it's too dangerous. I've got to go to London and stay with my uncle.'

Dangerous? Yes. And foolish perhaps. But she would have done anything for Eva, if she could. 'You don't sound very keen on London.'

'I want to stay here. But I must go.'

A possibility forms in Betty's mind. 'Perhaps you could come and stay with me. Savannah is here for another few weeks and if you had to stay on longer it wouldn't be a problem. You could always go to your uncle later. Of course your father will have to agree. Will you ask him for me?'

Ahmed turns his sad and crumpled face towards her and a small light, like a candle in the darkness, appears in his eyes.

'Or would you prefer me to ask?' Betty says.

'No, no.' He sounds panicked. 'I will do it.'

'Your father is right not to take you, Ahmed. The situation is difficult in Tripoli right now. But you mustn't worry. I'm sure your father knows what he is doing.'

A cloud crosses the sun, fading the shadows. 'We don't have so many clouds in Libya,' he says, his voice turned small again.

How difficult it must be for Ahmed: his mother dead, his sister missing, his father going to a war-zone. Heavens, what has she agreed to now? She looks up at the sky. This is no time to lose courage. 'Well, we certainly get a lot of clouds in this country. Do you know the painter, Constable? He was a great painter of clouds.'

'I don't know him,' Ahmed says with a shake of the head.

'I have a book of his paintings at home.'

Savannah jumps off the tree onto the ground. 'Are you still looking at the moss?'

'No. We're looking at the clouds and talking about Constable, the painter.'

'Oh,' Savannah says.

They walk a little further into the woodland but the rope swing eludes them and finally they turn for home. On the way back, Betty suggests a game of cloud-spotting. She and Eva used to do that. Today they see sharks, stingrays, cats, crocodiles, dragons, doves and, just before they reach the house, Savannah shouts, 'Look at that! It's a dog eating the world.'

Betty examines the cloud and shivers. Savannah is right. The fact that clouds are merely water vapour gives Betty no comfort. She doesn't want Mohamed to go to Tripoli. She is afraid for him, afraid for them all.

Betty twists and turns in bed, listening to the clock tick out the minutes. When sleep finally arrives she dreams of falling columns and dark, fearful skies. In the early hours of the morning, awake again, she turns on the sidelight and picks up the novel she has been reading, but she soon drops it again.

To pass the time she takes out her wedding album.

Theirs wasn't a smart wedding. People didn't have posh weddings in those days, unless they were royalty. No one got married in Las Vegas or the Maldives. She and George married in the local church, the reception was held at his parent's house and Betty helped make the sandwiches. She turns the pages of the album: how young and innocent she looks in her homemade satin frock. How dashing George looks in his borrowed suit. But all that happened half a century ago. It was another age and she was almost another person.

She puts the album back on the shelf and opens the bottom drawer of her chest. It is here that she hides her photographs of Ghadames – not that she has any need to hide them now George is gone but the habit has remained with her. The small yellow pocket folder is tucked behind her underwear, a place George would never have looked. She hasn't looked at the photos in years: like the wedding album, they make her sad and nostalgic.

Or is it guilt?

In the sixties Omar's family still lived in the old town of Ghadames in one of the traditional adobe houses, its whitewashed interior decorated with traditional murals painted by women. When she first saw the murals she was entranced. She'd never seen anything like them. Later she learned that the patterns had meanings – the red cross-hatching symbolised the gardens of the city, the plants, moon, sun and the stars picked out in greens and yellows.

As the women explained and Omar translated, she began to understand that she could never really understand Omar's culture, that she would always remain an outsider. She picks up another photo, this one of the mosque. Its bold simple lines remind her of an abstract painting called *White on White.* Oh, but what is the name of the artist? She has quite forgotten. Next are the pictures she took of the town's roof terraces – reserved for women – and the dark covered walkways – only for the men. She was lucky for, as a Western woman, she had access to both worlds. She sighs. Both worlds and no worlds, that is a fact, Betty. The remainder of the photos – there are not many – include the town's large cistern, a grove of palm trees and three picture of sand-dunes. Perhaps she will show the pictures to Savannah and Ahmed.

However, there is one picture she will not show to anyone. This is the only close-up she has of Omar. He is smiling, his eyes squinting a little under the bright sun. But the colours on the print have faded, as though she had left it out in the Saharan sun. Betty gazes at Omar's face, as if by looking she could make him leap out of the paper and embrace her. There have been times when she has been sure she has heard his voice in the night. *Habibti* he murmurs, *habibiti,* my dearest. She will reach out for him but he is never there and so instead she clutches at the pillow while the chill air creeps in under the ill-fitting window.

No one lies in her bed now.

Chapter Fourteen

'I overslept.' Betty glances at the clock in the kitchen. It is almost half past nine. Savannah is already downstairs, spreading honey on a slice of bread shaped like a worn sarcophagus.

'I don't mind.' Savannah smiles; she looks happier. 'Mummy always gets up late when she's not working and I have to get my own breakfast. Did she call?'

Betty suddenly remembers that Delia was supposed to phone. 'Not yet.' She peers at the yellow stickers on the fridge. When is that eye appointment, and doesn't she have to go to the dentist soon? Nothing is written. Perhaps she has no appointments. She opens the cupboard to search for a jar of marmalade. 'We'll need to go to the shops later. But this morning I must do some work.'

'Are you making your bird house?'

'It's a head, Savannah. Yes, I think so. I'll find you a new pad of paper, if you like. You can do some drawing. Or cutting.' The sculpture is almost finished. It still looks like Baba Yaga's chicken hut but Betty no longer cares.

Savannah makes a smacking sound with her lips, and Napoleon ambles in and rubs himself against her legs.

'Have you seen Stealth lately?' Betty asks. She can't remember whether she last saw him a week ago or only the day before.

'He's in the bamboo patch.' Savannah takes a bite of her bread and honey. 'Do cats like honey?'

'I'm not sure. Goodness, that is a large slice of bread – not that I mind.'

'I was hungry. It's my second piece.' The girl always looks as if a gust of wind would blow her clean away but Betty isn't fooled by her appearance.

'When are we going to the beach?'

'Tomorrow, with Ahmed. The weather forecast is good.' Betty reaches down to twist one of her bracelets before she realises that she has not yet put them on. 'Ahmed might be coming to stay with us for a few days, perhaps longer. His father has to go away.'

'He's going to look for Ahmed's sister.'

'How do you know that?'

'Ahmed said. Ahmed can have the yellow room, can't he?'

'It's not quite arranged, Savannah. We'll have to wait and see. His father would prefer him to go to London.'

'Oh,' Savannah says, disappointed.

'But the beach is a definite, unless there's a hail-storm or a blizzard.'

'Don't be crazy, Betty. It's summertime!'

⚜ ⚜ ⚜

The morning passes slowly. There is no word from either Ahmed or his father. In the afternoon Betty takes Savannah to the supermarket for supplies and later they walk in the woodland searching for the fallen tree. And all day the phone remains resolutely silent.

Betty waits until Savannah is settled in bed before picking up the receiver, tapping the numbers in quickly to stop herself from changing her mind. Mohamed answers at the first ring. 'I'm sorry to call so late. It's about Ahmed. I was wondering.' She grips the arm of the chair. 'Wondering if you would allow Ahmed to stay with me while you are in Tripoli.' She gabbles, like Delia. On and on. A hundred reasons.

'I do not know about this,' Mohamed says when she has finished.

'It might be better for Ahmed than going to London.' He is silent: she's blown it. How stupid and tactless. She opens her mouth in an attempt to explain but the words tangle and twist like balls of wool and she too falls silent.

Then he says, 'I think it is possible.'

'Possible?' Did he really say that? Before he has time to change his mind, she says, 'Why don't you come by tomorrow and discuss it? There's no obligation, of course. I will quite understand if you prefer Ahmed to go to his uncle's house. But he will be near what he knows here, won't he?'

'How can I repay you?' Mohamed says unexpectedly. 'Ahmed will be most happy.'

This nervousness is quite ridiculous. Should she wear the Tuareg necklace again or not? The navy blue dress? No, that's too formal. In the end Betty chooses a plain white blouse and linen skirt but this time she hangs a simple silver chain around her neck, one that she chose with George. Today the Tuareg necklace feels somehow too awkward.

When the knock comes on the door, she is pacing the sitting room.

'*As-salam alaykum*,' Mohamed says, reaching out to shake her hand. Instead of his Western suit he is dressed in the traditional long white shirt and loose trousers. Just like the clothes Omar used to wear.

Betty's heart jumps. '*Wa alaykum e-salam*,' she says before turning to Ahmed to hide her confusion. 'Savannah's in the garden, Ahmed.'

Ahmed hesitates and his father bends down and says something to him in Arabic that Betty cannot quite catch. Her Arabic was never very good and now it is rusty through lack of use. When his father has spoken, Ahmed nods and walks off, out through the door, and onto the path.

Betty ushers Mohamed to the sofa by the window and offers tea. When she returns from the kitchen, Mohamed is sitting just as she left him, his arms rigid at his sides. She pours the tea, wondering how she can make him feel more at ease, but he is the one who initiates the conversation.

'I know you visit to my country,' he says, 'but I must be certain that Ahmed follows his religion while he is here.' His English may falter at times but there is nothing faltering in his statement.

'Of course.' She listens and reassures, and rules and practicalities are discussed – prayer times, the possibility that Ahmed may fast this Ramadan, what programmes he may and may not watch on the television, the time he should be in bed at night. Only when they have exhausted these does Betty allow herself to ask if there is any news of his daughter.

Mohamed lowers his head like a sheep ready for the Eid slaughter. No,' he says, his voice heavy and slow. 'There is no news and I am afraid for her because she is like her mother.' He pauses. 'The children are still in the garden, no?'

Betty looks over her shoulder. Savannah and Ahmed are down by the chicken coop, half-hidden by the trees. 'They're quite a way from the house.'

A cool breeze blows in through the open window, bringing with it the sound of the children's voices and the cluck of the hens. Mohamed is silent for a minute. He places the cup and saucer on the small table she has set at his side, before returning to his former, almost military pose. But his hands are not still. He clasps one in the other, then begins to pull at his fingers.

'My wife.' He stops and his hands fall to his lap. 'My wife is a teacher. She hates the regime. We all hate this. But we know what happens if we speak against. My wife, she changes after her cousin disappears. He is in prison we think, Abu Salim, you know this place? The cousin is disappeared because he writes against Gaddafi. We never see him again. We think he dies when the Gaddafi soldiers kills the prisoners in Abu Salim but we never know this certain. My wife is angry and she says something to a teacher in the school. I do not know what she says, or the teacher she speaks to. After this, they take her away. It is for re-education, this is what they say and she is there one year. But this is a prison and we see her only once in this time.' His voice rises and he digs his nails into the palm of his left hand. 'My children see her once!' He closes his eyes. 'When she is returned to us she is thin like grass.'

Betty is tempted to reach for his arm but he would be shocked by such intimacy. 'It must be very painful for you to think of it,' she says.

He opens his eyes, taps at his temple. 'My wife is not well when she returns. You understand? Here she is not well.' He taps again. 'I do not know what it is they do. She is never like this before.' Tears well up in the corners of his eyes but he does not attempt to wipe them away. 'I try to help. We all try to help but she does not get better. It is Ahmed who finds her. We do not know how she dies. I think the heart. A weakness.' He places his hands on his chest.

'I'm so sorry.'

'I work as a doctor but soon after my wife dies I have no job, I have nothing. It is not safe for us any more. I say we leave Libya, leave everything but my daughter says no, I am not coming. I say she must come but she says she cannot and so I leave her with the sister of my wife.' He speaks quickly in spite of the fact that he is not fluent in the language. 'Now, maybe the same happens to my daughter. Maybe she goes to the prison like my wife. Because I think she is with the young people who fights against the regime. They are flying the new flag and burning pictures of the tyrant and this is dangerous. If they are catched...' He raises his hands in despair.

'I understand,' Betty says. 'She is like my daughter.'

'You have a daughter too?'

'Yes.' She picks at a sequin which has worked its way loose from a sofa cushion. 'She went to Gaza at the end of the Intifada in 1993. She was twenty-one.'

'She is in Gaza?' His voice rises in surprise.

'She was there, yes, but it's a long time ago now. She believed in the Palestinian cause. I suppose that's what matters in the end, that the cause is just.'

An expression crosses his face that she cannot quite fathom. 'The cause, yes. Safia always believes in this.' He points to his chest. 'We older people, we become afraid. But the young people, maybe they do not see what we see. The hell. The black pit. If people fall into this pit there is no way out.'

She understands what he means: that black pit of despair and guilt. 'I am sure Gaddafi's days are numbered. The regime is weakened.'

He shakes his head. 'He still has peoples in Green Square chanting for him. I do not believe he has many but maybe it is enough.'

'He cannot win.'

A flash of anger crosses Mohamed's face. 'We are dogs, this is what Gaddafi says. Can you believe he calls us, his own people, like this? Dogs and rats, he says. He wants to kill all the peoples of Libya and he pays bad people from Chad to fight us.'

'Ahmed will be safe here. I can promise you that, at least.'

'You are most kind, Mrs Betty.' He takes an envelope out of his pocket and hands it to her. 'I speak to Hashim, Ahmed's uncle. He will take Ahmed if I do not return. Everything is here, all informations. I will ask Hashim to make you a telephone call.'

Betty does not open the envelope but turns it over in her hands, feeling the weight of it. What if Mohamed never returns? But it is too late for doubts.

'This is your daughter?'

She jumps. He is staring at the photograph of Eva.

'Yes, it is.'

'A beautiful young woman.'

He smiles. But now she is anxious. If he were to learn the truth about Eva, he would never allow Ahmed to stay. 'How do you plan to get to Tripoli? It can't be easy.'

'I take the aeroplane to Djerba in Tunisia. You know this place? It is not so far from the border. Then I arrange taxi. It is possible.'

'Yes, I know Djerba.' Betty can hear the children's footsteps. That's a relief. She is safe now from more questions.

'The children come,' Mohamed says, turning his gaze to the window. 'This garden is beautiful. Almost like paradise.' He laughs, just the once. 'I hope to be back soon and see it again.'

'Please come and have supper with us before you leave. Perhaps you could come tomorrow after we return from the beach, if you are not too busy.' She pushes herself up from the chair and holds out her hand. 'It has been a pleasure to meet you.'

His grip is firm, the feel of his hand in hers almost unexpected. 'My pleasure also,' he says. 'I will take your offer, thank you. But I cannot tomorrow. I think Thursday. This is the night before I go.'

After Mohamed and Ahmed have left, Betty stands at the front door, resting her hand against the wooden jamb, remembering all the goodbyes in her life: Omar, Eva, George. She turns and retreats into the sitting room, and picks up a book of poems by Mahmoud Darwish, opening it at random. *In exodus I love you more, soon you will lock up the city. I have no heart in your hands, no road carries me, and in exodus I love you more.* She closes the book and Savannah runs in, a bunch of wild flowers tight in her hand.

Chapter Fifteen

It has been years since Betty visited this beach, though it is barely twenty minutes drive from the house. She has quite got out of the habit. When Eva was small she was here every week, summer and winter. They loved the place – for its stark beauty, its limpid rock pools and grey, marled stones, the never ending dance of light on the water.

After Eva was gone, Betty came every day for weeks. She sat on the same rock, a flat boulder pitted with marks like drops of rain, listening to the sigh of the wind and the ceaseless rocking of the waves. Each time she would try and empty her mind but she often raged and cried, and once she waded into the sea in all her clothes, as if she might never come back.

That was then, a long time ago.

Betty places the picnic basket on the shingle and the children wander down to the shoreline. It is wonderful to have the children, even if Savannah can be hard work at times. Betty's memories of Eva at this age have faded like the bleached driftwood washed up on the beach. Memory is such a strange and fickle thing. Some events stand out in stark relief while others are as insubstantial as a mirage.

'Look at this, Betty, isn't it beautiful?' Savannah runs up, an oyster shell in the flat of her palm. 'Ahmed and I are going to make a shell house.'

'What a good idea,' Betty says, blinking against the shimmering light.

'Ahmed says there are more stars in the sky than grains of sand on the beach. Is that true?'

'I expect so,' she answers and Savannah runs off again until she is just a black shadow in the distance. Betty watches the children bobbing up and down like the oyster catchers on the shoreline, before settling back onto the picnic blanket and closing her eyes.

She has promised not to think of the past but Mohamed and his son have stirred up memories. Now a series of images flash into her mind from the Libya of 1969. Early March, George on an American lecture tour – he was beginning to make quite a name for himself. Betty working in the south-western desert of Libya – that unworldly landscape of dunes and twisted spires of rock. The research required that she measure and record the rock carvings and paintings, a slow and sometimes tedious task.

In the evening, before sunset, she would climb the escarpment and look down into the valley below at the spindly tufts of grass and thorny acacias threaded along the wadi, the rocks and sand turning golden, the shadows blue in the fading light. Up there, the wind whistled and moaned so that even she, always sceptical, understood why people might believe in the existence of djinns. Their Tuareg cook, who spoke only French – which she understood but could not speak well – said, 'There are places no one will visit.' His face was solemn. 'In these places you will hear and see many strange and terrible things.'

'What things?' she asked, while he placed the flat-bread in the hot coals to bake.

'They say a soldier lost his mind at Khaf Anjoun, the mountain of the ghosts. You must take great care in the desert. You people may not believe in the spirits but we know they live amongst us – the evil and the good. Be watchful and you will come to no harm.'

But Betty never did see a ghost or anything resembling one.

At the end of that expedition she returned home to England, but in late August she was back in Libya again to help organise the next survey. While awaiting the numerous permissions and papers required, she made a decision to visit the town of Ghadames. She and George had intended to see the place together but events always conspired against them.

How life can turn on a single road taken.

Omar was at her side the moment she stepped out of the ancient Land Rover. He was the tourist operator – not that Ghadames received many tourists in 1969 – and was wearing a long blue robe and black turban. He stood tall, surprisingly tall, quite unlike George. She felt his eyes on her and that made her uncomfortable, but when he invited her to meet his family, she agreed. No harm could come of that. In any case, she was a married woman and she made sure he knew it.

It was an experience to eat with his family and she felt honoured. But as the evening progressed, Omar kept meeting her eyes and she found it difficult to look away. She was drawn to him, that she could not deny. She attempted to shrug off her feelings, persuading herself that it was nothing more than a little harmless flirtation. However, later, in the darkness of the unfamiliar room she had rented, she could hardly sleep for thinking of him.

Rest came late and she woke with a start to the sound of the early morning muezzin.

That day Omar insisted on showing her every nook and cranny of the town. He teased her for wearing trousers and when he learned that she drank wine he said that wine was *haram* and he pretended to be deeply offended although she knew he was not.

Each hour that passed she felt herself falling for him – the way he spoke, the soft movement of his hands, the long strides he made along the paths – everything drew her closer and closer until her body tingled every time he looked at her. And yet when, at a grove of palm trees on the edge of town, he attempted to kiss her on the mouth she rebuffed him, reminding him of her married state, telling him he was taking advantage. He apologised and she said she'd slap his face if he tried again but they both knew she was playing.

She stayed almost a week in Ghadames, spending most of her waking hours with Omar, even though she sensed the beginnings of a whispering campaign against her. She understood the disapproval. After all, she was a Western woman, a foreigner with strange clothes and customs, but she could not tear herself away from him. They kept each other's gaze for longer and Betty felt sure he would see her heart pulsing in her chest, so fast did it beat. But he did not try and kiss her again and she began to regret her rebuff.

The minutes, hours and days ticked by. Even in that dusty, desert town where time appeared to slow to a trickle. All too soon it was time to leave for Tripoli to complete the expedition preparations. And after Tripoli, England.

Their parting was rather formal. Though Betty had expected this, she was disappointed, bitterly so. His family was there and he would not even meet her eyes. She felt abandoned, forgotten. How stupid she had been to imagine that anything should come of their flirtation. But perhaps it was a relief too.

She broke her journey in Gharyan, in the Nafusa mountains. She had only been in the town an hour when Omar drew up in a dusty, half-broken truck. He must have been following her. Was she surprised or not? She cannot be certain of that now. But she is certain of the rest – how he clasped her hand and swore he loved her and how she knew at that moment her resistance was over. So, when evening fell and the stars appeared in the desert sky she followed him to a secluded grain store, hidden from prying eyes – and here she gave herself to him, all and all.

Even after what came later she cannot say she has regrets.

Omar accompanied her to Tripoli, claiming he had business in the city. She had the rental of a room there and he stayed. The days were taken up with work – the expeditions required a great deal of planning – their nights were something that will stay with Betty to her dying day. She had never encountered such passion and desire.

With George there was companionship and perhaps, at the beginning, something akin to passion, but it was always muted and soon fell away. Yet now that she thinks about it, what she felt for Omar was precisely because she knew it would be temporary. All that week the thought of their imminent parting was a boulder in Betty's chest and she also dreaded facing George. He would never be unfaithful and she had broken his trust. What would she say? Or would she say nothing? But surely he would see that she was changed.

There was also change in Libya. A colonel in the army, a young man named Mu'ammar al-Gaddafi had set himself up as chairman of a new Revolutionary Command Council while the King was in Turkey. Yet few seemed bothered by the news, if anything people were glad. Gaddafi represented a break with the past, Omar said. A new wave of Arab nationalism was spreading. Betty too was pleased to be part of that. And in an odd way it was Gaddafi who saved Betty. Because when she got back to England, this was what she spoke of to George. The coup became her cover.

A fly lands on her arm and she opens her eyes. Ahmed and Savannah are running along the sand. She waves and they wave back. Forget the past, Betty. It is done and gone.

To her right is a large pile of granite rocks, ferried in for sea defences. How ugly the pile is, ugly and ultimately in vain. She moves and the rocks disappear from her vision. Now the view is perfect, nothing but the sea muzzling the sky and the white-tipped waves chasing each other to shore.

Life can be perfect. Sometimes.

'Savannah!' she calls. 'Ahmed!' They are too far away to hear.

Ahmed follows Savannah along the shoreline to where a clutch of dark pools lie, sheltered from the waves. The pools smell of salt and seaweed, their depths scattered with silver-blue shells and small, barnacled stones. Tiny transparent shrimps dart between the stones, and blood red anemones curl their tentacles like the aliens he sees on the *Doctor Who* programme he likes; that his father allows him to watch.

Savannah pokes her finger at an anemone. 'Ow!' she says, withdrawing her hand fast, 'That hurt.'

'It's only an anemone.' Ahmed is proud he knows this English word. To think that he knew so little English when he arrived. Now he knows many words: moss, minnow, tide, ripple, crab, anemone, limpet, barnacle. 'It looks like a plant but it's not. It's an animal, with stinging parts to catch prey.' He brushes his fingers against the flowing tentacles. 'They're too small to hurt us.'

Tentatively, Savannah replaces her hand in the water. 'Do you have an-enemies in your country?'

'Enemies?' He grins at her. 'Quite a few, I suppose but you mean *an-em-on-e.* We have those in Libya, yes. It's very hot there in summer. Not like here. In Tripoli the sand burns your feet.' The sea is a different colour here too, a minty green, with patches of grey and brown. It isn't the dazzling blue of Tripoli. But the city beaches used to get very crowded and it is good here where he can see no one, and not a single building.

The waves slosh softly on the stones and Ahmed murmurs the words of the song his father hummed when he had forgotten he was sad.

'What's that?'

'Something my father likes.'

Savannah frowns. 'It's nice but what does it say?'

'I don't know. It's not Arabic but the language of the desert.' He must ask his father. He will know. But when Ahmed thinks of his father he is afraid.

'Sing it again, Ahmed. Sing louder.'

He is not sure he can sing it again because the song is wide and open like the sea, and the sea reminds him of Tripoli and his mother.

'Don't you want to?' Savannah is looking at him, her face puzzled, her head to one side, her golden hair blowing in the breeze.

He breathes in and out like the waves and this time, when the song comes out, it is stronger. When he has finished Savannah claps her hands and says he sings like an angel and he feels himself blush and he is not sure if he is pleased or ashamed.

They walk back up the shingle. Betty is lying on the striped rug, her face hidden under the hat.

'She must be asleep,' Savannah says. 'Old people sleep a lot.'

'What if she's dead?' Ahmed thinks of his mother on the bed. Still and cold. Like a statue.

'Don't be stupid.'

'She might be.' He should stop now. But he can't. He wants to hurt Savannah, make her cry. He doesn't care that her mother is in America because she hasn't gone away forever, not like his mother.

Savannah kneels on the edge of the picnic blanket and places her ear close to Betty's chest. 'She's fine, Ahmed' Her eyes stare up at him, hard as the stones under his feet. 'Why did you say that? It's not very nice. You scared me.'

'I saw my mother dead.' Now he wants to shake Betty and wake her. What is she doing there, hidden under the hat as if she were really were gone?

'I don't believe you.' Savannah's face is white and scared.

Ahmed takes a step forward, his shadow falling dark across the shingle. 'I did see her. I touched her face and it was cold like ice.'

'Stop it, Ahmed, stop!'

'What's going on?' As Betty sits up her hat tumbles onto the stones and a breeze eddies up the beach, suddenly chill.

⚜ ⚜ ⚜

Ahmed is crouched on the shingle like a dog. Betty is at a loss. 'Let's have that picnic,' she says. Was he lying? Something in his expression makes her doubt it.

Ahmed scrambles to his feet and turns towards the sea. There is sand on the back of his faded red shorts.

Savannah taps Betty's bare arm. 'Do you think he did see his mother dead?'

Betty puts her hand into the basket and pulls out two sandwich boxes. 'I don't know,' she says quietly. 'Let's leave it for now, shall we?' She flips open the lids.

'OK.' Savannah sniffs and peers into the sandwich boxes. 'Would you like egg or tuna, Ahmed?'

'Tuna, please.'

'He wants tuna. That's good because I prefer egg.'

'Yes,' Betty says, handing out the sandwiches. 'It's even better that I like both.' A seagull flies overhead, cawking. She is tempted to make a joke about the seagull stealing their food but she bites her tongue. A joke probably isn't appropriate right now.

'I told Ahmed about Mummy getting married in America,' Savannah says, peeling the crust off the bread and throwing it onto the stones. 'Will your father get married again?'

Ahmed chews on his sandwich and stares at his feet.

'That's a rather personal question, Savannah, and in the circumstances I don't think it's appropriate.'

'He could marry you,' Savannah continues.

Betty feels her face grow warm. 'I'm too old to marry again.'

The seagull swoops down for the crusts and Savannah waves her arms to scare it away. 'Ahmed's father is old. He has grey hair like yours. When I get old my hair will be silver.'

'I know what we'll do when we've finished our lunch,' Betty says rather desperately.

'What will we?' Savannah asks.

'Beach-combing.'

'That sounds fun. You'll help, won't you, Ahmed?'

Betty breathes a sigh of relief. Well, that at least is sorted.

The earlier matter retreats like the tide and the beach-combing expedition is quite a success: one pink plastic child's sandal, an empty bottle of suntan oil, a broken lobster pot, an old tyre, a rusted pole and enough driftwood to start a fire.

'Are we going to take all this back with us?' Savannah is now holding a length of old fishing rope.

'I'll probably take the sandal and some of the smaller planks of wood for my sculptures,' Betty answers. 'Perhaps even that rope.' Ahmed says nothing.

'Betty is a proper artist,' Savannah says, folding her arms and trying to look important. 'She might even be Picasso.'

'I'd like to be an artist,' Ahmed says, his voice tiny as a barnacle, 'but science is more important, my father says.'

'You can be a scientist and an artist. Think of Leonardo da Vinci.' Betty bends down to pick up a mussel shell. Gaddafi is not fond of artists. Dictators prefer gold and weapons. Artists are too slippery. Like these rocks. But she won't say that. Not to Ahmed. Not now.

'Can you?' Ahmed says, a note of hope in his voice.

'It's perfectly possible.'

The waves shush and slosh. Seagulls squabble over a fish. The water is silver. Blue. Black. The tide edges out to reveal a long strip of sand. Beyond that, out in the Channel, a boat chugs by, its engine echoing along the low cliffs. And Ahmed finds a piece of wood riddled with tiny holes.

'Those are gribble holes,' Betty says. 'Gribbles nibble with their hundreds of tiny teeth.'

Ahmed turns the wood over in his hand and examines it suspiciously. 'Gribble? What's a gribble?'

'A tiny sea creature, almost transparent like glass, though they can be rather a nuisance. They like to eat through timbers.'

Ahmed brings the plank of driftwood close to his eye and peers through one of the holes. 'There are wormholes in space too.'

'Only stars live in space,' Savannah rolls her eyes. 'Oh, and planets.'

Ahmed reaches into his rucksack, pulls out a notebook and a stubby pencil and draws a wiggle in the middle of a blank page. 'This is a worm in two dimensions. Here it is moving on top of the page.' He jabs a hole in the paper. 'Now this is the hole the worm makes to move from one side to the other. But this is not a real worm. It is...an idea of a worm.'

He's clever this boy, Betty thinks. He'll go far.

'Yes,' Savannah says, although she doesn't sound very sure.

Ahmed rips the page out of the book, folds it up into a concertina and makes a hole through the folds with the pencil. 'Imagine...' He holds up the pencil. 'Imagine the top of the pencil is the worm, moving in space and time.' He smooths the paper flat and points to the holes the pencil has made. 'I've made only one hole but now the hole is in five places. It's like time travel.'

'Where does the worm go?' Savannah seems to have forgotten that a minute ago she didn't believe in the worms at all.

'Wherever it wants. From one part of space to a new part of space.'

'Let me try,' Savannah says.

Betty closes her eyes. She feels tired again. This is what happens when you reach your seventies. Instead of being excited by deep space, you fall asleep like a baby.

When Betty wakes again a warm wind is blowing and the sky has turned white. For a moment she cannot remember where she is. She sits up and looks around her. The beach, of course. The waves are slopping against the shoreline and the children are chattering nearby. Well, that's all right. No one has fallen in the water or got stung by a jellyfish. No one has really argued. Not badly anyway. Though that talk about Ahmed's mother has unsettled her. 'It's time to go,' she calls.

'Can't we stay longer?' Savannah calls back. 'Ahmed and I are making a dam.'

The dam is on a patch of sandy shoreline, but the tide has turned and the sand is fast disappearing. 'We'll come back another day,' Betty says, picking up her stick and walking towards them. 'The tide is coming in now. And the gribble might get you.'

'*Pfft!*' Savannah says, but already she is running onto the shingle. 'Gribbles are tiny. You already said.'

'So I did,' Betty answers. 'But they have strong teeth. They can even eat stars, you know.

Chapter Sixteen

'How was the beach?' His father is packing clothes for his trip into a small suitcase. Ahmed is sitting on the floor of the bedroom, watching.

'It was nice.'

'Is that all you can say? What did you do? What did you see?'

'I don't know.' Ahmed picks up one of his father's long white embroidered shirts. The fabric is soft from years of washing, the collar and cuffs frayed. His mother must have bought this shirt. The thought of that turns him sad again.

His father sits down on the edge of the bed. 'I understand how difficult it is for you, Ahmed. But I must go and look for Safia. You do understand?'

'If Safia had come with us, you wouldn't have to go,' Ahmed says angrily.

'*Leave each day behind, like flowing water, free of sadness. Yesterday is gone and its tale told. Today, new seeds are growing.*' His father reaches out and tousles his hair.

'What if something happens to you?'

'If the sun starts to move west, I will find a shady tree.'

Ahmed cannot stop the tear escaping. It rolls down his cheek and splashes onto his T-shirt leaving a damp patch there, like a drop of rain.

'Come and sit with me,' his father says.

Ahmed sits on the bed. He rarely comes in here. The room is like a cell, the walls blank and white, except for one framed picture: a quote from the Qu'ran in beautiful Arabic script. It is almost as if his father did not live here.

'Be strong for me. Promise me that.'

'I promise,' Ahmed says but his words feel faint and insignificant.

'Mrs Betty is a good woman. She will look after you well.'

'Yes,' Ahmed says, wiping away his tears, which are now spilling unchecked.

His father places a hand on his shoulder. 'Do not cry. I will ring you as soon as I can but quite when that will be, I cannot know. Nothing is working in Tripoli any more, if it ever worked. I shall be careful. There is no need to worry.'

'Can't you take a mobile phone? I can show you how it works.'

'I will manage, Ahmed. I will get a message to you one way or another. And the mobile is not always safe. Safia does not like me to use hers.'

'Where is Safia?'

His father sighs and tries to smile. 'She is strong, your sister. You have said so yourself. She is strong enough to face the lion and tell him that his breath stinks.'

'Do you mean Gaddafi, Father?'

'His time is coming to an end,' his father says, getting to his feet. 'Now, I must finish my packing. Then, if you like, we'll have another story.'

There is a stone in Ahmed's throat. He swallows hard but it won't go away. 'Mother used to tell us stories. You remember, don't you?'

'Of course I remember.'

The story his father chooses – about the famous Amazon women and Queen Myrina – is one Ahmed has heard many times before. It was one of his mother's favourites – until she stopped telling stories altogether and began to talk to the walls instead. During that mixed-up time, Safia read to Ahmed from *A Thousand and One Nights.* Now, in England, his father has become the teller of stories.

'Once upon a time Queen Myrina of the Amazons gathered together a large army in order to defeat their enemy, the Atlantians. To protect themselves, the Amazon women wore the skins of huge snakes. You know that we have huge snakes in Libya, do you not?'

'Do we?'

His father grins, showing his white teeth. 'I tease, Ahmed. Most Saharan snakes are small. But a great variety of animals lived in the desert, all those years ago. This was a time when the Sahara was green. Rivers ran through the canyons where now there is only sand and the place teemed with life.'

Ahmed has only thoughts for the snakes. 'Are the snakes in the desert dangerous?'

'The horned viper is poisonous, but most snakes in the desert are harmless. However scorpions can give a nasty bite. The ancient Garamantes, who lived in southern Libya thousands of years ago, are said to have had the sign of the goddess Tanit tattooed on their ankles, to protect them from bites. That was before Mohammed arrived, blessed be His name, to bring us our faith. Now, shall I continue with the story?'

His father describes the terrible battle fought, how thousands of the city's inhabitants were killed. Ahmed shudders and he thinks of Misrata again with its broken and burnt buildings, the streets littered with the debris of war and a photo he saw of three soldiers lying in the street, their uniforms stained with blood.

'When the fate of that city became known, the terrified Atlantians surrendered their remaining towns.'

'The people of Misrata didn't surrender.'

His father's face turns grave. 'No. The Misratans are brave people. They have driven the enemy from the city. But I do not think that what happened in Misrata will be repeated in Tripoli. In fact I am sure of it. Now let us return to the story. The Atlantians surrendered and Queen Myrina founded a new city to bear her name in place of the city she had destroyed. The Atlantian people, relieved that the Queen had shown mercy, presented her with magnificent gifts and in return she promised she would show kindness to their nation.' His father pauses. 'Always remember this, Ahmed. The victors must show mercy to those they have defeated.'

'I thought the Queen killed all the men in the city?'

'I do not think all were killed but, however you look at it, war is a terrible thing.' He waves his finger. 'We must not forget how the story ends. The Atlantians asked Myrina if she would invade the land of the Gorgons as the Gorgons had murdered many of their people. The Queen obliged, a mighty battle took place and many Gorgons were killed. So, you see, the Queen paid recompense to the Atlantians. This is very important.' Ahmed knows that the story does not quite end at this point. A few short years after this victory Queen Myrina died in another great battle. Ahmed also knows that his father cannot be certain about Tripoli. If the city does fall, what will happen to Safia and Nafissa, and to his father? But all Ahmed says is, 'Do you think it's true that there were Amazon women?'

His father's brow wrinkles. 'Perhaps. People believe our women are weak but this is far from the truth.'

Ahmed thinks of his mother. She started out strong and brave but when she came back to them she was as weak as a new-born kitten.

⚜ ⚜ ⚜

Savannah is helping Betty make salad. 'What day is Mummy coming home?' she asks, chopping a tomato.

'The end of August.'

Savannah walks over to the calendar on the kitchen wall and counts off the days. 'And when is Ahmed coming?'

'He'll be here again tomorrow so that his father can make arrangements without Ahmed getting in the way. But in the evening Mohamed will drop by and eat with us.'

'Is that his name, Mohamed?'

'Yes. Will you have cucumber as well?'

Savannah nods. She slices the remaining tomato and curls up in the chair like the cat. 'If Mummy is married, Scott will come and live with us, won't he?' She draws a pattern on the table with her damp fingers. 'Scott isn't my proper daddy.'

Betty peels the cucumber and cuts it into thin slices. 'Scott is a good man. Do you remember your father? You were quite small when he left, weren't you?'

'He's gone to a communication in Scotland. It's where lots of people live together.'

'I think you mean a commune.'

'Is it good to live in a commune?'

'That depends,' Betty says carefully, thinking of Gaddafi's communal experiments of the early 1970s. It all sounded fine, idealistic perhaps, but something any country might want to aspire to. However, by the time Betty returned to Libya with Eva in 1977 – when Eva was five – student protesters had been hung in public in the cities of Tripoli and Benghazi. Gaddafi had declared a 'people's revolution' and changed Libya's name to the Great Socialist People's Libyan Arab Jamahiriya. He'd also published the first volume of his infamous *Green Book*, a book packed with ridiculous statements which made him a laughing stock in the world. But life in Libya was no laugh. The country was quickly sliding towards disaster.

Betty's visit was a personal disaster too and she returned to England without meeting Omar. He had married by then. He also had a daughter, she heard. The news was perhaps only what she expected but it tore at her heart.

Savannah picks up a slice of tomato and pops it in her mouth. 'I wonder when I'll see Daddy again. He's got a girlfriend in that commune place. Mummy told me.' She chews the tomato slowly. When she has finished she says, 'I can't remember what he looks like any more.'

'I'm sure you'll see him again one day. When you're older you'll be able to visit, won't you?'

Savannah sighs. 'I don't know.'

'Scott will take you swimming. He's an excellent swimmer. He's won a few medals. After all, if you're going to be a diver, you'll need to swim well.'

'I can swim,' Savannah says. 'I'm quite good at it.'

'There's always room for improvement.'

'You sound just like my teacher.' With that, Savannah dives off the chair, almost knocking it over.

⚜ ⚜ ⚜

It is after nine. Ahmed is reading in bed, or perhaps he is playing that game on his computer. Mohamed does not know how to use a computer. Ahmed says he should learn but there has not been the time.

Mohamed paces from one side of the room to the other. He cannot settle. Safia is always in his thoughts but the truth is, he's also concerned for himself. What will it be like to return to Libya after an absence of three years? Will he be welcome or will he be an exile in his own country? It is not always easy to return to a place one has had to leave. People ask questions, sometimes disapprove. But coming to Britain was a matter of necessity, not choice. He likes England – there are many good things about it – but his heart has remained in Libya and that will never change.

He sits on the sofa and tries to concentrate on the television. Ahmed says he should watch to improve his English though he is not sure if that is now necessary. The programme is about a beach in the west of the country. He has never been there. Besides this place and London he has not travelled in this island. The beach looks beautiful and yet the people are complaining. He cannot understand. Surely they have everything they want? Isn't freedom enough? How would they like to live in Libya, when opening your mouth is forbidden, when a single sentence can result in imprisonment, torture and even death?

With a shake of his head, he gazes round the room. Even though this apartment has been their home for almost all of those three years, it looks like it belongs to a stranger. Apart from a few items, little is theirs. The crockery, the curtains and blinds, the choice of paper and carpet – all are someone else's. Is it not time to build a new and solid future? But how? And where? Whatever happens, he must go home. He wants to. He wants his family back, together again. The pain of separation is so deep it makes him gasp.

He cannot wait any longer. He picks up the phone and dials Nafissa's number and this time he is lucky; she answers at the first ring, as if she was waiting for him. 'It is all arranged,' he says. 'I should be with you by Sunday, *insha'Allah.*'

'This is good to hear,' she says, but her voice is strained and tired.

'Is that you, Nafissa?' He has been hasty and used her name.

'Of course it is. I am sorry...'

'What is it?'

'I am afraid I have bad news for you. The bird is in its cage.'

Her words send the room spinning like a top. He feels sick, struggles to breathe.

'Hello? Hello?' Her voice crackles down the line. 'Are you still there?'

'I am still here,' he gulps.

'This is only what I have heard. It is a rumour, not a fact. Do you understand?'

'Yes,' he says.

'Perhaps it is not even true.'

Nafissa is trying to reassure him but he is not reassured. The words have only one meaning, a code they agreed on long ago: Safia has been picked up by the regime.

When the call ends, Mohamed stays holding the phone, listening to the dead line, the words echoing in his mind: *the bird is in its cage.* He falls to his knees. Oh, Allah be merciful, I beg you. Please keep my daughter safe.

Chapter Seventeen

From the bench Betty can hear the papery sound of the bamboo, the cats rustling in the undergrowth and the chickens clucking, pecking at the seed she threw out earlier. The morning is perfect, cloudless, the leaves hanging limp and unmoving. How many more perfect mornings does she have left? This is something she has to consider at her age.

If she could be granted one wish it would be this: to pick out a morning at will. These are the ones she would choose. That morning in Gharyan, Omar at her side, the moon a pale crescent in the fragile blue sky. The early hours of her honeymoon with George, a view of St Giorgio Maggiore framed by the hotel window, the slightly rotten smell of the Grand Canal drifting into the room. An early sun shining on the Adriatic, a school of dolphins playing alongside the boat. Eva taking her first few faltering steps on this very lawn. The three of them – she, George and Eva, swimming off the south coast of Crete in crystal clear water.

Maybe there are others too, ones she has now forgotten.

The sun has reached the top of the wall and cars have begun speeding along the road – people out and about with their busy lives. She ought to have got up earlier. She always ought to have got up earlier.

She sips at her milky coffee and bites into the croissant. Savannah is not yet awake but she'll be up soon enough and the peace of the morning will be broken. But that's all right. She really doesn't mind. Since George's death, the house has been too silent. Sometimes she can hear nothing but the blood pumping in her ears and those damned clocks, ticking away.

An ant zigzags awkwardly across the brick path. It must be going somewhere; it looks as if it has a purpose. Betty thinks about that. Life seems to have passed by so quickly and unintentionally. A faint gloom settles. The ant, meanwhile, continues on its journey.

A call from deep in the house: 'Betty!' More like a bellow. A girl with strong lungs.

Savannah comes dashing into the walled garden in her pink night-dress, her bare feet pattering on the brick path. 'You have to come!'

'What is it?' Betty leans on her stick a moment.

Savannah screws up her eyes against the sun. 'There's a bird in the house.'

The bird – a swallow – is flying frantically from one end of the room to the other. Already it has left a white trail on the back of the sofa. Betty opens the door but the swallow continues its desperate beating.

'Why won't it fly out?' Savannah says, her eyes widening in panic.

Betty tries to coax the bird towards the door with her walking stick but it only flies about ever more crazily.

'What if it dies?'

The trapped bird makes Betty dizzy. 'Fetch me the phone, will you, Savannah?' She phones Fred to explain their predicament while Savannah perches on the edge of the chair, her fists pressed against her cheeks.

Fred arrives within five minutes, a net in his hand.

'Please don't hurt it,' Savannah pleads.

Fred holds up his hand. 'Don't fret, young lady. You stay still as a statue. Else she'll take fright and batter herself against the wall.'

They both sit, motionless. Fred raises the net into the air. The swallow dives, then shoots up to the ceiling. Savannah flinches and Betty reaches for her hand. Fred steps forward and slowly turns the net. The swallow dives again and Fred gives the net a sudden twist. 'There you are, my beauty.'

He releases the bird on the lawn. It rises into the sky and disappears from view. When it is gone, Savannah claps her hands and jumps up and down and claims she will be Fred's friend for ever and ever, but Betty feels the tug of the bird's flight deep in her heart.

'Well, that's done,' Fred says.

'What do I owe you?'

'You can't put a price on freedom.'

Betty tries to smile but the smile will not come. 'That's true. While you're here, perhaps you could put a price on my grass?'

'I'll be round tomorrow.'

After Fred has left, Savannah sings, 'Fred is awesome,' over and over until Betty can hardly bear it. 'I could have done that a year ago,' Betty says, more roughly than she intends. 'I'm a little slow on my legs now, that's all. I used to do all sorts of things. Things you could hardly imagine. I haven't always been old, you know.' She glares at the girl.

'You are old. You said so.'

'No, I am not!' Betty yells, sounding like a child herself.

Savannah's hands fly to her mouth and she flees from the room and Betty hears her feet thumping on the stairs. The door upstairs slams. Then silence.

Betty slumps down onto the sofa. What has she done? How stupid to get irritated over such a trifle and to upset Savannah like that. All this stuff about Libya is continuing to stir stuff up, things she ought to have kept locked away. She sits awhile, staring out of the window. The sky may appear perfect and unblemished but a storm has passed through Betty, leaving her quite exhausted.

Savannah is lying on the bed reading a book. This was once Eva's room but Betty had it re-decorated some years ago. The white walls Eva insisted on have been papered in a blue and cream stripe, the bamboo blind replaced with curtains. For many years Betty left the room as it was, not a thing moved. Eva's clothes remained draped on the chair, her comb on the dresser, a thumbprint on the mirror. As if she had only just left. But then the day arrived when Betty decided it was time to make changes. At first George was against the idea and that surprised her. In the end he came round.

Betty hands Savannah the breakfast tray she's prepared: her peace offering. It was something she used to do for Eva after they'd had some silly argument or other.

'Thank you,' Savannah says in that peculiar grown-up voice she uses sometimes. 'That looks nice.' Her hair is twisted into two thick strands.

'I shouldn't have got cranky.'

'It's all right,' Savannah says, dropping her book and reaching for the toast and honey. 'Mummy gets cranky too.'

'You remind me of Wing-Tip-the-Spick with your hair like that.'

'Who's Wing-Tip-the-Spick?'

'A girl in a book.'

'Do you have it? 'I'd like to see.' Savannah takes a bite of toast.

After she cleared the room, Betty got rid of most of Eva's stuff. Except for two shelves of books. She is surprised Savannah has not already looked at the books but then again, she doesn't read much. Not like Eva. This particular book was purchased for Eva's fourth birthday but the very next day Eva scribbled all over it with her crayons. How cross Betty was. She shouted and smacked Eva on the leg and Eva burst into tears. George, hearing the noise, rushed in to comfort Eva and by the time Betty came to her senses, it was too late, the damage was done.

'Was this yours?' Savannah bends over and sniffs the pages. 'It smells funny. Like old things.'

'It was my daughter's. Eva.'

'You never said about your daughter.' Savannah blinks. 'Where is she? Does she live a long way away like my daddy?'

'Yes. She is far away.' Betty feels the familiar contraction in her stomach but she soon composes herself; she has learned to do that over the long years.

'Do you really think she looks like me?' Savannah asks. She sounds dubious.

Betty peers at the illustration of Wing-Tip-the-Spick. 'She has two freckles on her chin like yours. And, if I remember correctly, her eyes are blue like cornflowers.'

'Do I have freckles?' Savannah clambers over to the mirror. 'I don't think they were there before, were they? How funny. Maybe just this darker one.'

'The sun brings them out. The darker one is a mole.'

'Shall we go outside to read the story?' Savannah picks up the empty tray and climbs off the bed. 'It's sunny today. We don't want to be inside and maybe I'll catch a few more freckles.'

'Why not?' Betty is glad to have been forgiven so easily. Eva was different. She bore grudges though perhaps she had her reasons.

They sit on a patch of grass under one of the apple trees. 'Do you want me to read it to you?' Betty asks. 'Or would you prefer to read it yourself?'

'You read.' Savannah pulls at her hair. 'Mummy never reads to me. We watch television instead. She likes that programme where famous people go to the jungle and eat horrible food like ants and bugs and snakes.'

'Hmm.' Betty never watches those programmes. Maybe she is a snob. Not that she cares what people think. She picks up the book. 'Wing-Tip-the-Spick lived in a village so light it had to be anchored to the ground on a long rope so that it wouldn't blow away in the wind.'

'I wish I lived in a village that floats in the sky like a kite. It would be awesome to live up with the birds.' Savannah peers through the apple leaves. 'I wonder where the swallow is?'

Betty tilts her head. 'I see her. She's catching insects for her young.'

Savannah jumps up. 'Where?'

'High above the chimney, far beyond the clouds.'

'There aren't any clouds.'

'I was being metaphorical.'

'That's not a metaphor, Betty. You need to say the swallow is an arrow in the sky or a blob of ink. It's when something is something else.'

Betty smiles. Savannah can be so like Eva. Determined. Stubborn. 'That's true, but do you know that in autumn the swallows leave England and fly south to Africa? I spotted a pair one February swooping for insects in the desert.' Betty's heart tumbles in her chest. If she could only visit one last time.

They hear someone calling.

'That's Ahmed,' Savannah says. They had quite forgotten he was coming.

Ahmed walks up through the gap in the hedge. He always goes that way. It is quicker than taking the path to the front of the house.

'Guess what happened?' Savannah says, running to meet him. 'There was a swallow in the house. Fred had to come with his net and rescue it.'

Ahmed is glad he was not there to see it. He still remembers the day his father came home with that pet bird for his mother. His mother smiled when she saw it, one of her rare smiles during that long illness. Safia complained to their father. She said they shouldn't have a bird as a pet, that it wasn't fair. The bird worried Ahmed too. He could not understand why his mother would want to put a living creature in a prison just like the one she had come from. It seemed cruel. However the bird stayed and their mother used to talk and coo to it through the bars of its cage.

'Is your father ready for his trip?' Betty asks.

'Yes, he is ready.' The words falter on his tongue like a missed step.

'Your father will be careful. He won't take any unnecessary risks.'

'Is he taking a gun?'

'Of course not,' Betty says, turning to Savannah. 'You aren't allowed to take guns when you travel abroad.'

'Won't he need a gun? You said it was a war.'

'Savannah,' Betty warns.

'He has a gun in Tripoli. He keeps it in the back of the wardrobe. It's very old. It belonged to my grandfather.'

'Is he going to shoot with it?' Savannah hops from one foot to the other. 'Is he?'

'That's enough.' Betty sounds irritated. 'Guns are dangerous, Savannah. It's not like in the films.'

⚜ ⚜ ⚜

An hour later and Savannah is lying on the grass by the pond, a pigeon pecking in the grass nearby. Ahmed crawled into the bamboo patch but Savannah refused to join him, saying she was scared. Now Ahmed has borrowed Betty's special garden scissors and cut a stick of bamboo. Betty didn't ask what he wanted them for. She just gave him the scissors and said he must put them back in the shed on the hook.

Holding the stick carefully in his right hand, Ahmed creeps up behind Savannah and aims it at the back of her head. '*Wheew!*' he shouts, trying to mimic the sound of a rifle.

The pigeon takes off, its wings slow and strong. 'What are you doing? If you wanted to scare me, well you haven't. I wasn't scared in the least little bit.' Savannah's cheeks have turned bright pink.

'I'm a sniper.'

'What's that?'

'A lone gunman who hunts people.'

'Are there snipers in Libya?'

He nods. In Misrata the snipers took over the big insurance building in the centre of the city and shot people on the street. Dead. Killed. What if there are snipers in Tripoli, creeping into buildings, waiting for their moment? If only he were old enough to fight. He'd have gone with his father to protect their family. But he isn't. He isn't anything.

'Betty says we've got to collect eggs,' Savannah says.

Ahmed points the stick at her head again. 'You're dead. You can't move.'

'I'm not dead.' She wiggles her fingers. 'See!'

'If this stick was real you'd be dead.' Now Ahmed mimics the sound of a machinegun. '*Tttttttt!*'

Savannah sticks out her tongue. 'That's stupid. Guns are stupid. Stupid, stupid!'

Ahmed throws the stick on the grass. He doesn't want to play any more.

Savannah shakes her finger. Like his teacher. 'It's a horrible game and I don't want you to play it again. If you do, I'll tell on you.' She glares at him.

'Stay there and don't move. I'm going in the house to fetch an egg box.'

He lies in the grass and gazes up at the sky. He and Safia used to argue. Because she's ten years older she used to win. Most times. He ought not to tease Savannah but sometimes he can't seem to help it. He wonders if that makes him a bad person and if Allah will punish him.

His mother wasn't bad and she got punished. But it wasn't Allah who punished her. The thought confuses him.

A butterfly lands on his hand, tickling the skin. He moves his head to get a better look at it but the insect flies off and disappears into the long grass. Tonight his father will come to supper and tomorrow he will disappear like the butterfly. If his father doesn't return, Ahmed will go to live at his uncle's house in London. It is all arranged. He thinks about that for a while, turning the possibility over in his mind like a heavy stone. Then he walks up the brick path to meet Savannah.

PART 2

Chapter One

Rising out of the sand, the Ras Jdir border post consists of a scattering of dusty palm trees and a low, white building, its window frames painted turquoise. A group of soldiers, dressed in green, guns slung nonchalantly over their shoulders, rest in the shade. The Libyan taxi driver, who Mohamed found outside the hotel in Djerba, turns off his engine, opens the windows and smokes a cigarette. 'Are you sure you don't want one?'

Mohamed shakes his head. He has paid for those cigarettes: he has had to pay the driver more than he cares to think and he hopes the amount will be worth the sacrifice. At least his story has held: an ailing mother, a spell in Egypt working as an engineer. It pains Mohamed to lie, more so in this holy month of Ramadan, but if he is to get back into Libya, he has no choice. For all he knows, the driver kisses the ground Gaddafi walks on.

The cars are few yet the queue moves at the weary pace of a snail. An hour passes. Mohamed checks his watch. It is eleven in the morning. His thirst increases and it becomes difficult to think of anything else, although perhaps that is a blessing because the discomfort overrides his anxiety.

The driver, whose name is also Mohamed, taps his fingers on the dashboard and chain-smokes cigarettes and, from time to time, the two Mohameds exchange idle comments. The engine ticks and the branches of the palm trees hang listless in the burning sun. A fly buzzes into the car and Mohamed the driver tries to swat it with his hand. Later, a man from the car in front, suitcases piled high on the roof of the car, gets into an argument with an official, breaking the monotony.

At last it is their turn. A border guard instructs them to leave the vehicle and takes their bags into the office. He proceeds to inspect the car, lifting up the blanket lying across the back seat and checking the glove compartment. Inside the building the waiting begins again. Mohamed's bag and passport are examined, questions are asked. His mouth is now so dry his tongue keeps sticking to his palate and his lips have turned cracked and salty. Anything could go wrong now. He could be slapped in jail or turned back to Tunisia. But this official, in his crumpled and sweat-stained shirt, appears bored, as if he couldn't care who was slipping over the border or for what purpose.

Time hangs heavy like the midday heat. Mohamed waits, seated on a metal chair. It is difficult to imagine that over the border people are dying in a war that has continued for months now. Drops of sweat trickle down his back. The chair is uncomfortable but he continues to sit without moving, staring steadily at the concrete floor. He does not wish to attract unwanted attention, to appear impatient or fearful. An ant zigzags past. Mohamed focuses his mind on the verses of the ant in the Qur'an, where Solomon and the language of the birds also appear, the story Ahmed loves so dearly.

His name is called, his passport stamped, the formalities are over. He steps out of the building into the harsh desert sun. Now only a few metres lie between him and the country of his birth. He wipes away the beads of sweat that have gathered on his forehead with the back of his hand and walks over to the car. The other Mohamed is already sitting in the driver's seat, the engine running, the air conditioning turned up.

'OK?' he says.

Mohamed nods. The car moves forward. It passes under a line of green flags and a signpost to Tripoli. 248 kilometres.

'We had good luck today,' the driver says, accelerating.

'Yes,' Mohamed replies. The stress of crossing the border has left him exhausted. His eyes dart to the window. Coils of wire glint in the sun and an empty drinks can dazzles his eyes. 'How long will it take?'

'It is hard to say. There are fifteen check-points to get through before we get to Tripoli.' The driver touches the *hamsa*, the palm-shaped blue amulet hanging off his mirror. 'That's if we don't get shot at, or blown up by a rocket.' He winks. 'Don't worry. We'll be all right, *insha'Allah.* I have done this journey many times before. More times than I care to remember.'

⚜ ⚜ ⚜

Dusk is falling as they enter the city's outskirts. Mohamed leans forward and looks out of the dusty windscreen. High up the sky is the colour of lapis but below, in the dust and smog of the city, the horizon has turned a smoky red. How strange it is to be home again, how strange and yet how wonderful. But Tripoli is not quite as he remembers. The ring road is almost empty of traffic, there are few people about and many of the shops are shuttered. New buildings have mushroomed too, ugly high-rises and new hotels.

The driver turns into a side street, passing the mosque with its green and white minaret, a landmark Mohamed knows so well he could draw it in his sleep. They turn into a second street, and another. There are butterflies in Mohamed's stomach now, excitement and fear.

'This is it,' the driver Mohamed says, pulling up in front of a dreary concrete building. 'Home sweet home,' he adds, in English. This is not Nafissa's place, she lives a ten minute walk from here. Mohamed cannot risk the driver knowing where he lives.

'Thank you,' Mohamed says and he hands the driver a tip, even though he has already paid the extortionate fare. The driver nods, takes the notes, rolls them into a bundle and places the cash behind the mirror. 'I hope your mother gets well soon,' he says.

'*Insha'Allah*,' Mohamed says, shaking the other Mohamed's hand. How he hates these lies. How he hates Gaddafi for forcing him into deceit.

'Peace be with you and your family.'

'And with yours.'

A pigeon flutters its wings in a nearby tamarisk and they both look up. The sky has darkened and a crescent moon has risen above the rooftops. But the moon is not alone; tonight it has a sister. This moon, slenderer than the one that hangs in the evening sky, is stamped on a striped flag, the flag of the revolution. The two Mohameds look at each other for a moment. Neither says a word and yet an understanding passes between them.

The driver hands Mohamed his business card. 'If ever you need me,' he says with a wink. With that he gets back into his car and drives away. Mohamed waits for the taxi to round the corner and disappear. Then he hoists the heavy bag over his shoulder and walks down the street. When he raises his eyes again, the flag has gone.

Nothing seems to have changed in the neighbourhood. The dusty streets and broken-down pavements, the green shutters and tatty concrete apartment blocks are just as he remembers. Two boys cycle by. The smaller boy sits on the saddle while the older one pedals from a standing position. He and

Hashim used to ride like that years ago. Sometimes he wishes for those days, when life was simple.

Wearily, he steps up to the apartment block and presses the buzzer.

Nafissa is waiting for him at the top of the stairs. 'Mohamed! How happy I am to see you! Come in, come in!' She is smiling but her eyes dart nervously into the dark hollow of the staircase.

He drags his feet up the remaining stairs and steps inside. 'I can't tell you how happy I am to see you too,' he says, embracing her.

She closes the door behind him. She has lost weight and her face is pale, her eyes ringed with fatigue. 'You can have your old room. Since you left I took over Ahmed's room and Safia has the room she and I shared. Here, let me help you with your bag. Then we must break our fast. You must be hungry after your long journey. Was it hard? I've been so worried. I thought you might not make it. You hear such terrible things.'

'It was long but there were no problems.'

'Allah must be smiling on you. I don't know what I would have done if you had not turned up.'

'You always find a way.' He smiles. She returns his smile but hers is fleeting and guarded.

He takes his bag into the bedroom. Once Nafissa and her husband shared this room, but Nafissa's husband died of cancer the year before Nour was imprisoned. There were no children and Nafissa never re-married.

Sitting down on the edge of the bed, Mohamed drinks greedily from his water bottle. A few moments later, on his way to the bathroom, he passes the room that is now Safia's. The door is ajar and he pushes it open. Safia's study books are stacked neatly on the shelf and a copy of the Qur'an is open on the bedside table. At the head of the bed is Safia's toy elephant, missing one ear. Nour bought Safia that elephant when Safia was three, almost two decades ago. Mohamed takes another step into the room. It smells faintly of the rose perfume Safia wears that was also a favourite of his wife's.

He steps back out into the hallway and, wiping away his tears, quietly closes the door.

Nafissa serves supper with an apology. 'I'm afraid it is not quite as you are used to. The shops are half-empty, Mohamed.'

'It looks delicious. In England there is no one to cook for me. ' In response, Nafissa laughs. It is good to see her laugh. 'No wonder you have no meat on you,' he adds.

In spite of Nafissa's protestations, there is plenty. The *iftar* meal is delicious and Mohamed is hungry. At first they talk only of family, of small things. But later Nafissa says angrily, 'That man has lost his mind. He wants to kill us all. That speech he made, vowing to hunt down protesters inch by inch, house by house, home by home, alleyway by alleyway, *zenga, zenga...* Those are the words of a madman.

'Shush,' Mohamed admonishes, placing his finger over his lips. 'Do they not say the walls have ears?'

'We are not afraid, not any more.' Nafissa lowers her voice all the same. 'But you want to hear about Safia.'

He nods.

'Safia has been helping the revolution. After the demonstrators were killed in February, she said she could no longer sit back and watch.'

He chews on a piece of chicken. Perhaps he did guess – she is her mother's daughter after all – but he has avoided thinking of it. Now his reaction is anger. 'Didn't you try and stop her?' He grips the fork so tight his fingers hurt.

'No, I did not.' A silence descends. Nafissa sighs and puts down her own fork. 'Forgive me, Mohamed. There is much I have not told you.'

Mohamed toys with the last few grains of rice on the plate.

'You are fearful. I can understand this,' Nafissa continues. 'It was hard to keep silent but if I had spoken to you I might have put us in greater danger. You know how it works here. The phones are tapped. People spy on each other. No one can be trusted.'

He sits back in the chair. 'When I phoned you from England recently I thought someone was impersonating you on the phone.'

'No, that was me,' she says, wearily.

'So, what do you know?' He is exhausted after the journey but his mind is a whirling sandstorm.

'Safia started running errands back in February. For the opposition.' Nafissa shudders and runs her hands through her greying hair.

A drop of sweat works its way down Mohamed's forehead. He wipes it away with the napkin. 'She is just like her mother,' he says tonelessly.

'No, Mohamed. Safia is not Nour.'

He feels himself bristle but he refrains from answering and they sit in silence again. Someone turns on a radio in a nearby apartment and the tinny music drifts in through the open window. Down in the street a car rumbles slowly by. Mohamed peers out of the window but all he can see are its red tail-lights disappearing into the darkness.

'Safia is young, Mohamed. This is a different generation.'

'The young are not always strong.' The lights in the apartment flicker and dim before turning bright again.

Nafissa snorts. 'Did the old people demonstrate? What did we do these past forty years?'

He forks up the last of the rice. What can he say? They tried, some tried, but it was not enough. He thinks of the public hangings, the disappearances, the dark rumours of torture and killings, the day Nour's cousin vanished. No one knew where he had gone. No one even dared speak of it. And when Nour spoke up, the regime set out to destroy her.

Oh, it is all very well talking about courage but where does it lead? To prison and the gallows, that's where. He looks up from his plate. On the wall next to the television there is a framed photograph of the *Umm-al Maa* lake at Ubari, blue as an eye against the yellow sand dunes, the palm trees at its edge mirrored perfectly in the still water. He has never seen the picture before. He wonders who took the photograph. Perhaps Safia and Nafissa visited the lakes and did not tell him. All the same, the picture calms him.

'Do you want me to go on?' Nafissa asks. She does not wait for his answer. 'The day Safia vanished I had such a bad feeling, I cannot explain it. When she hadn't returned by dark I thought of calling you but I was afraid and I did not wish to worry you. I sat at the table here and waited all night.'

She opens her mouth but instead of words a faint sob falls out. Mohamed reaches across the table and places his hand on hers. 'I should have been here for you,' he says, his anger vanishing.

She withdraws her hand and places it on her chest. 'Please Mohamed. You cannot change what has gone. I looked for Safia the next day. I walked around the neighbourhood and I walked to Green Square and on through the old town. I walked all day. How my feet ached. But who could I ask? Who is there to trust? Our family is scattered like blown seeds.' She shakes her head sadly. 'I did not come back until nightfall but before entering the apartment I called into the shop on the corner. Ali's father died last year – you remember him don't you? Ali and his brother run the place now. They are good people.' She leans in towards him and whispers. 'They are striped.'

'I do not understand.'

She rolls her eyes and for a brief moment becomes the Nafissa he remembers. 'You are either plain like the old flag or striped like the new one.'

This is the first time he has heard the phrase. There is much to learn.

'I wanted to buy rice but there was none to be had. "Try tomorrow, Nafissa," Ali said. "I will put some by for you." As no one was in the shop I told him about Safia but he said he knew nothing. He promised he would do whatever he could but what can anyone do in this city? Gaddafi will not give up Tripoli without a fight. It is not Misrata or Benghazi. People are afraid.' She pauses. 'Have you heard? The people in the east call us women! What an insult. As if we women don't work for the revolution! The men from Benghazi have even threatened to send women's underwear to the city. Do they not understand how hard it is for us here?'

Mohamed laughs. 'Is this what it has come to?'

'It is no laughing matter, brother-in-law,' Nafissa continues. 'So, I was about to leave when a young man walked into the shop, nobody I recognised. He looked straight at me. "Are you Nafissa?" he asked. I was scared hearing those words but Ali nodded and said, "I know this man, you can trust him." The young man claimed that Safia had been picked up in the street and bundled into a waiting car. He said he had witnessed it himself. He promised he would try and obtain more information and we arranged to meet at the shop the following day. But he did not turn up that day or the next. For five days I waited but still he did not appear.'

'Where do they hold people?'

Nafissa throws her hands in the air. 'If I knew, I would go there now.' She sips at the glass of water in front of her. 'I have been to the women's prison but she is not held there. I have not dared to visit Abu Salim but I don't think they would have taken her to that place. Even this regime has its limits.' Her hands fall to her lap.

'Limits? Do you think a regime that can murder its own people has limits?'

Her face pales. 'Perhaps not. They keep people in all sorts of places. I have heard of people locked in containers without food or water, and in the heat of summer too.'

A shudder passes through Mohamed's body. If Safia should be held in such a place, what hope is there? The lights flicker again and this time they are thrown into darkness. Nafissa gets up from the table. He hears her opening a drawer and striking a match. She places a candle on a mat in the middle of the table. 'This is quite usual. The electricity will come on later, *insha'Allah*.'

In the glow of the candle, Nafissa's face looks softer and he is reminded of Nour. A pain passes through his heart. 'How will it end?'

'That is for Allah, and only Allah to know.' She bows her head.

He feels ashamed. Nafissa has done so much for him over the years without complaint or admonishment. What has he done for her? But this is no time for regret. The rat-tat-tat of machinegun fire stuttering through the night, not too far away, reminds him of that.

'This too,' Nafissa says, 'Each and every day now.'

The next morning Mohamed picks up the walking stick that once belonged to Nour's father. The head is polished through years of use and it feels comfortable in his hands. He has no need for a stick but if he walks like an old man perhaps no one will bother him.

'Be careful,' Nafissa says, before he leaves. 'Age will not always save you.'

He walks down the stairs and out onto the street. Keeping his head bowed, the stick tip-tapping on the broken pavements, he walks slowly, avoiding eye-contact with the people he passes. He does not want anyone to recognise him: his position here is not safe.

The heat makes him sweat and every now and again he stops to wipe the moisture off his forehead. Yet in the daylight, the city appears almost unchanged. Here is the jewellery shop where he bought Nour's ring and the café at the Galleria del Bono where he and Nour would drink coffee from time to time. The café is empty but that is not unusual for Ramadan. By evening it will be buzzing with people.

He sits down on a bench in the middle of the square, close to the famous Italian fountain and its magnificent stone seahorses. When he thinks of the Italian occupation he feels sad again. So much blood has already been spilt. Must there be more? All the same, the fountain has a special place in his heart. He and Nour used to come here when they were courting. And it was here that he, Safia and Ahmed came that day, bringing Nour's pet bird. They set the cage down on the edge of the fountain under a palm tree. It had rained earlier but by the time they reached the square the sun had begun to shine and Mohamed could feel the warmth of spring in the air – though winter was in his heart.

Safia opened the cage door but the bird sat on its perch, its head cocked to one side, peering at them with its black eye. 'Why won't it fly away?' Safia asked in a quiet voice.

'I expect it is a little nervous. Clap your hands. Perhaps that will help it on its way.'

Safia brought her hands together. The bird ruffled its feathers and hopped off its perch.

'Fly away!' Ahmed shouted and he too clapped his hands.

The bird spread its tiny wings and fluttered up into the palm tree. And there it stayed.

Safia's face reddened and she stamped her foot like a child. 'Tell it to go, Father. The cats will eat it.'

A passer by stared at them and an old man muttered under his breath.

'The bird will be fine,' Mohamed said, though he knew it would not and when they arrived back at the apartment, Safia rushed into the room she shared with Nafissa and he heard her weeping and did not know how to comfort her.

The leaves of the palm rustle in the hot breeze blowing off the sea. Mohamed raises his head and tries to imagine the bird perched there still, waiting for them. But of course there is no sign of it. He leans forward to catch the cooling drops of spray from the fountain and watches the people walk by, the cars on the road. Nafissa says the city is suffering petrol shortages, that there are long queues at every garage. She has heard of people burning the green flag and destroying posters of Gaddafi. But Gaddafi's face still stares out from the wall of the fort opposite where the green flags of the regime flutter, and all seems as it was.

Mohamed takes out the photograph of Safia he always carries in his wallet. After prayer this evening, when the cafés and markets are busy, he will ask if anyone has seen her. Or will he? Is that wise? If only he knew what to do. He has lost touch with his old colleagues and friends, Hashim is in London and he has no one to turn to, only Nafissa. Plus it has been three years since he saw his daughter. Maybe she is changed.

Safia inherited Nour's wide mouth and thick, dark eyebrows but her eyes are more like her grandmother's, his own mother. His mother was part desert Tuareg and she spoke their language, but when she married Mohamed's father she moved to Tripoli, away from her roots.

He wonders what she would have thought of the war. They never discussed Gaddafi but he knew she hated him. Gaddafi liked to play games with the tribes, pitting each against the other, giving favours to some and not to others and he banned the Amazigh language. All the same, he doubts his mother would have supported the idea of an armed conflict. But she is no longer there to ask.

He turns the photograph over in his hands. Perhaps, as he sits here on the bench, Safia is being interrogated and beaten. They beat Nour. He saw the scars on her back, though she tried to hide them. But the scars were deeper than skin deep; that was the real problem. And he did not see that. Not then. Only when it was too late. He is deep in these thoughts when a man sits down next to him and in his nervous, fearful state Mohamed accidentally drops the photo to the ground.

'Is this your daughter?' The man is young, around Safia's age. 'Here,' he says, picking up the photo and handing it to Mohamed.

'Yes, it is.'

'She is very pretty.'

Mohamed studies his companion. The young man is smiling in an open, trustworthy way, but

Mohamed knows that anyone can be corrupted in this system. 'Are you a student?' he asks gruffly.

'I am.' The young man holds out his hand. 'My name is Abdul.'

'Mohamed.'

'Peace be with you, Mohamed. You're from Tripoli, I presume?'

He nods and smiles back at Abdul. Keep things polite. Reveal nothing. 'So, what are you studying?'

Abdul shrugs. 'I'm not studying at present. I was a student of engineering but there are no classes. Everything has stopped.' He peers over his shoulder and drops his voice. 'Do you understand?'

'I'm not sure I understand anything.'

'Who does?' Abdul replies.

Mohamed scrutinises the young man again. He is dressed in blue jeans and a red T-shirt. Might the red shirt be a clue to his allegiance? It is not possible to tell. He decides to take a risk. What can he lose? 'I'm looking for her – my daughter. She has disappeared. Perhaps you recognise her. She was studying at the university.'

Abdul looks to his right and then to his left. There is no one nearby. 'Many people have disappeared,' he says in a low voice. 'Let me see her face again.'

Mohamed hands over the photograph.

'I don't know her. But I will remember the face. Who could not remember such beauty? What is her name?'

'Safia.'

'You chose well. It is a lovely name.'

'She hasn't been seen for weeks.' He hopes the desperation does not show in his voice.

'I understand. There is no need to say more. I promise I will do what I can but if I hear anything, how will I contact you?'

Even a friendly engineering student with a broad smile can be your enemy. He meets Abdul's eyes and Abdul's own stare back unblinking. 'I am living with my sister-in-law.' Mohamed recites the address and telephone number. Abdul listens and nods. He writes nothing down.

'You may count on me.' Abdul is no longer smiling, his expression is grave. 'I give your my word, may Allah be my witness. Now I must go. We have been talking long enough. There are eyes and ears everywhere, even if we cannot see them.' He leans in close to Mohamed and puts his arm on Mohamed's shoulder. 'Things are changing,' he whispers. 'It will not be long now. But for some of us, the price of freedom will be our blood.' He stands up, bows his head and says loudly, 'Good day, Uncle,' before walking away across the square and vanishing.

Chapter Two

Betty wakes in the middle of the night, troubled. She walks over to the open window. Outside, the dark shapes of trees stand like sentinels against the orange-tinted sky and a moth beats its pale wings against the glass. As she stands in the cool night air, a fox barks, its cry sharp and unsettling and she wonders what Mohamed is doing, whether he is sleeping or wakeful. He shouldn't have to be looking for his daughter in a warzone but what choice does he have? If Betty had needed to travel to Gaza she would have done so without considering her own safety. However, there was no need.

She stretches, flexes her bad leg and places a hand on her aching hip. The pain is not so bad, perhaps she has been using it as an excuse. Seventy-three, it is not such a great age. She moves away from the window, sits on the edge of the bed and turns on the sidelight. Even in its soft glow, the knotted blue veins on her legs and the brown age spots mottling her hands are visible. Goodness, the year she met Omar she was hardly past thirty and yet she thought she was already over the hill. How ridiculous is the vanity of youth.

Over the years she has managed to forget Omar. The feelings she once had for him faded and life moved on. When George died, she grieved more than she thought was possible. The grief was shattering and she thought she would never get over it, but she has. She also believed she would avoid the past and live in the present. It was a promise she made herself. But now Omar is back, almost as if he never went away.

She reaches into the drawer next to her bed and takes out her old leather-bound notebook. A flick through its yellowing pages reveals her pen and ink drawings of Ghadames – the white mosque and traditional adobe houses – and her sketches of the rock art she researched in the Fezzan: giraffe, lion and elephants, red and white figures of humans, dogs hunting animals and vignettes of domestic life.

These sketches were done for her pleasure, not for scientific journals. She is still pleased with the results. They are really quite good. The book also contains other notes and reminders: place names, plant species, a few words of Arabic. But near the end of the notebook a sentence has been scribbled out and pages are missing. She tore those pages out after Omar left, the day he told her he was getting married, the day she sat in that shabby hotel room in Tripoli with the blinds closed, staring at the walls, the day she thought she would never believe in the world again.

That day. That day of a thousand tears, her heart ripped apart.

But when she returned to England, George was waiting for her, good old dependable George. And she had her work, that too a comfort. Nine months later Eva was born. A miracle, George said.

Eva. Born with sand between her toes.

She flicks back through the pages. Here is a pressed camomile flower she picked in a dry wadi with Omar. Here an aromatic herb which still emits a faint scent. She sighs and clasps the notebook to her chest. Those times in the desert were perhaps the happiest of her life. Bang! The notebook closes. Motes of dust rise into the air. Did she not promise to close the door on the past?

Footsteps pad along the landing to the bathroom, Ahmed's footsteps. Betty turns off the light. The house ticks and creaks and the moth flies in through the window and settles on the curtains. She yawns, pulls up the cover and closes her eyes. Damnation! Now there is a scratching sound at the door. It is Napoleon. But she cannot be angry with him. He always knows when he is needed.

Up she gets.

The door closes.

The car curls up on the bed.

The house sleeps.

Tic-tac the clock. Tic-tac, tic-tac, a strange mechanical creature. A shadow crosses the pillow and Ahmed is afraid and thinks of the djinns who inhabit the desert and sow evil in the world. Safia, where are you? Can you hear me? He shivers and pulls the duvet right up over his head, but then he remembers that he is safe here in Betty's house, that the deserts of Libya are far away.

A bee buzzes on the lawn. A rose petal drops onto the path with a faint whisper. And now the soft sound of a child's bare feet.

'Good morning,' Betty says, 'Have you seen Ahmed?'

Savannah shakes her head from side to side like a marionette. 'I think he's still asleep.' She bends down to pick a daisy from the path, holds the flower close to her nose. 'Why doesn't it smell?'

'Not all flowers have a scent. I prefer flowers that smell strong and sweet, like my old roses.'

'Roses are nice,' Savannah says, placing the daisy head in the pocket of her pink pyjamas, 'but they have sharp thorns.'

'Everything beautiful has thorns.'

'You say some funny things, Betty.'

'Do I? That comes from getting old, I suppose. Well, it must be time for breakfast. Let's go down to the coop and see if there are any eggs.'

'I can't remember their names. No, wait.' Savannah bites her lip. 'I know! *Urn, derr, troir...*'

'*Wahid, ithnan, thatlatha...*'

'That's not right.' Savannah sounds quite indignant.

'It's the hen's names in Arabic: one, two, three.'

'*Urn, derr, troir, waheed, eethnaan, thar...latha...* Now I can speak French *and* Arabic.' Savannah skips down the path, repeating the words over and over.

'So you can,' Betty says. 'Well, it's a start, isn't it?'

⚜ ⚜ ⚜

It is Annette's day for visiting. This afternoon she brings Betty a bunch of chrysanthemums. They smell like cat's wee.

'I can't believe you've got yet another child staying with you.'

'It's the least I could do,' Betty says sharply. 'His father had to go to Tripoli.'

'Isn't that rather foolish, going to Tripoli right now? In the middle of a war? He might get injured or even killed. Aren't we dropping bombs there?'

'He's gone to look for his daughter.'

'Who?' Annette holds her hand to her ear and adjusts her hearing aid.

'His daughter,' Betty repeats.

'Ah, now I understand,' Annette says with a knowing smile. She taps her long red nails on the edge of Betty's small sofa and turns to gaze out at the window. 'The children seem to get along. They're playing outside nicely.'

'Sometimes they argue.'

'You were in Libya.' Annette turns back to Betty. The expression on her face is hard to decipher. 'You met that man there, didn't you? Omar.'

It has been years since they discussed Omar. 'That's right,' Betty says carefully.

'You never did tell George, did you? Surely he must have had some idea?'

'No, I did not. But you know that.'

Annette holds up her hands. 'I didn't mean to upset you. I only brought it up because of the connection with Libya. Well, that and the daughter. Don't you think it's odd that this boy and his father have suddenly come into your life? Fate takes us on strange paths.' She takes a bite of the cake Betty has put out.

'I don't know. I haven't thought about it.'

Annette rolls her eyes and raises a pencilled eyebrow. 'Oh, never mind. I can see the topic is upsetting you.'

'It's not.'

'If you say so.' Annette takes another bite of cake and pushes at the crumbs that have fallen onto her plate. 'What I was going to say is... Well, maybe you could go back to Libya for a holiday when everything is settled. You always loved it there and you used to be such an adventurer. It seems a pity to throw all that away. Goodness, what have I done with my life, Betty? It doesn't amount to much. Just think of what you used to do.'

No one should regret the choices they have made, Betty thinks. 'You have your children and grandchildren. That's something, isn't it?'

'They have their own lives now.'

'At least you have children.'

Annette dabs at her linen trousers with a paper napkin. 'I'm sorry, Betty. I wasn't thinking. I am grateful for what I have, even if I don't always show it.'

'I'm the one who should apologise. I've never forgotten how you supported me during those dreadful few weeks. If it hadn't been for you I'd have gone under.'

There is a short silence, weighted with memory. George was wonderful, even though he too was suffering like Betty. But she could not tell him and that was perhaps the worst of it. Only Annette knew.

'I wish I could have done more.'

Betty reaches out and pats Annette on the hand. 'You did more than you could imagine.'

A long sigh falls from Annette's lips. 'So, what's happened to that man's daughter?'

'She's been missing for two weeks.' Betty eases herself up out of the chair. She doesn't want to discuss Libya any more, or Eva, or anything from the past. 'Let's take a walk around the garden. It's such a lovely day. It would be a pity to miss it.'

'I can't imagine how you still manage all this,' Annette says, as they step outside.

'Fred still comes once a week in the summer, though the garden has gone somewhat straggly, as you can see.'

'We've gone somewhat straggly ourselves, wouldn't you say?' Annette says, grinning at Betty.

'I'm the one who's straggly. You always manage to look chic and sophisticated.'

Annette plucks at Betty's cardigan. 'This is a little past it, I agree, but you were quite elegant in the old days, if you remember. That blue satin dress, what a dream you looked in that.'

Did she? Betty never thought it at the time. Oh, but wasn't that the dress she wore when she and George went out to eat at the new Italian restaurant in town and she told him she was pregnant? Yes, it was that dress. Wasn't it also that dress she wore the very last time she went to Tripoli? How a dress can tell a thousand stories. Of love and hate. Betrayal and trust. Each hand-print, stain and sweat mark a story.

But now the children call from down by the apple trees and a summer wind blows up, shaking the heads of the ox-eyed daisies and she realises she's doing it again, retreating to the past she must forget.

'I've got an idea,' Annette says. 'A shopping trip. The two of us. We haven't done that in such a long time. I'm sure we can find somewhere to park the children safely for an hour or two. It'll be fun.'

'I'm not sure.'

'Oh, for goodness sake, Betty, why can't you treat yourself for a change? Or is it against your principles these days?'

Betty feels her cheeks warm. 'I don't wear hair shirts, if that's what you mean.'

'So, that's a yes, I take it?'

'You're incorrigible, Annette,' Betty says, but she smiles all the same.

'Come on, live a little. You've been like a hermit these past few years. Neither of us has that much time left. We should make the best of it.'

⚜ ⚜ ⚜

It is just after half past eight when the phone rings, the sound of it echoing down the hall. Betty feels that familiar jolt to her stomach – a mix of hope, fear and anticipation. 'Hello,' she says carefully.

'Hello,' a voice replies.

Mohamed. The relief of hearing his voice is overwhelming.

'Are you OK?'

'Yes, yes. I am arrived in the city some days now. I am sorry I have not called before this time. I try but it is quite impossible.' He sounds tired.

'How is it there?' She must take care to ask the right questions. Nothing political. Nothing to put him at risk.

'I think it is OK. Sometimes there is noise at the night. You understand?'

'Yes,' she says although she is not quite sure what he means by that. 'Have you found what you are looking for?'

'No,' he responds, his voice suddenly quiet. 'I must continue with the searching but it is... I think you say in English like you look for a needle in the straw.'

'A needle in a haystack,' Betty corrects. He did not discuss this with her before he left – how he might go about looking for his daughter. Perhaps they ought to have talked about it. But the moment she thinks this she realises it would have been futile. What does she know of Libya now? A plate clatters in the background. That must be Nafissa, Ahmed's aunt. Oh, if only she could be with Mohamed, back in Libya. However, she has Ahmed and Savannah to consider. And an old woman like her would be a liability.

'How is Robert?' Mohamed asks.

This is the name they have agreed to use to protect Ahmed's identity. 'He is well.'

'And your roses?'

Betty wonders if this is part of the code. She cannot remember. 'My roses?'

'The roses in your garden.'

'Oh, yes. Thank you for asking. I'm afraid they are almost finished for this summer.'

'We wait for next summer.'

Mohamed's voice is strained, the tone flat and without modulation, like the stream in the woods when it has not rained in a long while. 'I'll fetch Robert for you.'

'Thank you. This will make me happy, to hear his voice.'

While Betty goes to find Ahmed, she wonders if she could have asked more, if perhaps she was over-cautious. Surely the regime doesn't have the capacity to listen in to every telephone conversation? Perhaps that is not the point. The regime has been successful in creating fear and suspicions. That's what matters. Even she feels it. How people have managed for over four decades in such circumstances is difficult to imagine.

She remembers that visit to Libya with George in the mid-80s. So much had changed: the shops were almost empty and the people they came into contact with were guarded and suspicious, even old friends were not the same.

George had wanted to take Betty back to the hotel in Tripoli where they had stayed during their first few visits to the city in the late 1960's. In those days the hotel was quite cosmopolitan. Betty remembers dances and laughter, a fancy-dress party, musical evenings. But they found the pool emptied, its tiles broken, the whole place turned shabby and depressing, and they chose another place to stay.

⚜ ⚜ ⚜

'Hello,' his father says in English. 'How are you?' He soon slips back into Arabic. 'Have you been to the beach again? Are you behaving?'

'I am fasting for Ramadan. I know you said I could wait until next year but I have decided.'

'That is good news,' his father says. 'I am proud of you.'

'How is Auntie?' Ahmed is happy his father has phoned but there are so many questions he wants to ask and he doesn't know how to begin.

'She is well.' His father coughs.

'Do you have a cold?'

'No, no, I am fine.' A pause. 'I am afraid I have no other news.' A silence descends, broken only by the hiss of the line, the sound like small waves washing along the shoreline. 'I will phone again as soon as I can, once I have news for you but you know how it is here.' His father's voice has turned distant, as if a black hole were swallowing it up. 'Your aunt is waiting to speak to you.'

Nafissa asks him how he is and if he has grown and he says that he is well and perhaps he'll soon be taller than his father. She laughs and then that awkward silence descends again. He wants to say, 'Where's my sister?' But he is afraid.

The call ends. Ahmed stands in the middle of Betty's sitting room, his heart thudding uneasily in his chest. While he stands there, waiting for his heart to settle, his eyes travel to a framed photograph of a young woman, the same woman whose photo hangs in the hall. He hesitates. Betty is in the kitchen; he can hear the tap running, the sound of the kettle being filled. Anyway, there is nothing wrong with picking up a photograph.

The young woman is about Safia's age. He examines her features. She has the same thick, black hair, the same dark eyes. They could almost be sisters. He wonders who she is.

Betty is sitting at the kitchen table.

'Savannah's eaten already. You know what she's like. She couldn't wait. Why don't you have a cup of tea while I fix your food?'

'Thank you, I will.' The phone call has left Ahmed thirsty, as if he had been speaking with cotton wool in his mouth.

Betty pours a spoonful of leaves into a small glass pot and the leaves float and then settle like the fish in the pond. 'Do you take sugar? I can't remember. My memory is like a colander sometimes.'

'One spoonful. Please.' He looks at her. Did his father tell her anything? But her expression is calm. 'What's a colander?'

Betty reaches for a large metal object hanging from a rack above the cooker, along with various other kitchen implements. 'This is a colander. It's like a sieve but with large holes.' She hands him the colander and he turns it in his hands.

'Ah, you wanted sugar, didn't you?' She fetches a teaspoon and the sugar bowl, then she sits down and runs her hands through her grey hair.

Ahmed has never seen her wear a hat or a scarf, except for that day on the beach. His sister always wears the *hijab*. His mother did not. But in those last few months, when his mother barely spoke, Safia's *hijab* was one of the few things that brought her to life. He remembers her shouting, 'What is it with you young girls? Do you want to turn the clock back?'

And Safia replying, 'It is not that, Mother. You don't understand. This is our identity now.'

Betty is talking to him. 'Don't worry too much, Ahmed. Your father will be fine, *insha'Allah.*'

How can she know that? And she shouldn't use that word, *insha'Allah.* She's not Muslim. He stirs the sugar into his tea, round and round. Now there is a vortex in the centre of the cup. Like a tornado. A black hole.

'You can have a biscuit while you're waiting. Just one mind, else you'll spoil your supper.'

He looks away from the tea. He should not get angry with Betty. She has done nothing wrong, not really. 'Thank you,' he says. He peers into the tin. Inside are chocolate digestives and malted milks, his favourites. He prefers these to the biscuits Mrs Preston used to bring round to their apartment. All the same, he wonders how she is now that he and his father are not there.

Betty and Annette have dropped the children at the library. Betty refused to go to the out-of-town shopping centre Annette recommended but she knew she had to agree to the local department store – not that she really wants to be here. She used to enjoy shopping but now it feels frivolous, a waste of time. Perhaps that too is something to do with getting older. She has no one to impress.

She browses through the racks of clothes but she has no idea what she wants. 'I can't wear this stuff,' she protests, picking up a flouncy dress. 'Can't we just go to the bookshop?'

'You're not getting off that easily!' Annette sniffs and waltzes off, swinging her faux leopard-skin handbag, leaving Betty to gape at the high-heeled shoes and the prices of everything.

Five minutes later Betty is wriggling into a pair of jeans in the changing room. She peers into the mirror and grimaces. 'These are too tight. I look like mutton dressed as lamb, and I never wear jeans, Annette, you know I don't.'

'OK.' Annette sighs. 'I thought you might like to modernise a little. There's no need to settle for grey and dowdy just because of your age, is there?'

'Well, I don't like the jeans or the T-shirts.' Betty flops down on the seat, hot and irritable.

Annette disappears again and returns with another armful of clothes. This time she comes up trumps and Betty chooses a pair of beige loose linen trousers and a long-sleeved sky-blue top, edged with white embroidery.

'Perfect,' Annette says, much to Betty's relief. 'Now – and don't complain – we'll go to the ground floor to buy you a new lipstick.'

Betty protests, but she is no match for Annette and the lipstick is purchased, along with a mascara wand and a blue eye shadow. Betty hasn't bought new make-up in years and though she is pleased with her purchases the shopping trip has left her uncomfortable. She thinks of Mohamed and his sister-in-law stuck in Tripoli with no way out, and a feeling of unease settles on her that she cannot shake off.

Savannah is sitting on a cushion in the corner of the library, reading a book with a pink bow on the cover. Ahmed is at a desk, a computer monitor in front him. The computer is, however, frustratingly slow and it takes a long time to find what he's looking for. Finally, here it is, a news report on Tripoli.

He scans the page. *Col Gaddafi's Information Minister put the trouble down to small, armed gangs. "Tripoli is safe, and completely under the control of the armed people committees and the honourable people of Tripoli." Col Gaddafi himself said, "The rats were attacked by the masses tonight and we eliminated them."*

Eliminated.

He shudders.

Another click on the computer. Now a photo of a man standing on a pile of rubble, waving the green Libyan flag, the caption below: *NATO murderers! This is the house of a family killed by NATO bombs.* Ahmed knows these bombs have come from America and Britain and he feels suddenly sick to his heart.

Click, click. A man sprawled in the back of a pick-up truck, his eyes closed, his jacket congealed with blood.

The tap makes him jump. 'What are you looking at?' It is Savannah.

Ahmed closes the window. He had not heard her coming. 'Nothing.'

'You were looking at a dead person.'

'I wasn't.'

The screen is now empty, apart from the library logo.

'You were. I saw.'

He looks at her and feels suddenly old, as if he had become grown-up in an instant. An odd feeling. 'All right,' he says. 'It was a dead person. In my country.'

Savannah's lip trembles. 'I'm sorry, Ahmed. I wish you didn't have a war there.'

'It's OK.'

'Why do people have wars?' She leans forward, touches him gently on the hand.

'I don't know. Maybe sometimes for people there's no choice. That day I came into Betty's garden, some boys were chasing me and I ran away. I thought if I ran I'd be safe. But then this boy ripped my shopping bag and he came back for me and I hit him. I didn't want to hit him but I did and now those boys leave me alone.'

'Girls fight too sometimes,' she says. 'But they don't often shoot.'

He smiles.

'Let's not talk about war any more. It's too sad. What shall we do? I'm bored and Betty has been ages and ages and ages.'

'We can look at Google Earth. They have it on the computer here.'

Savannah pulls up a chair and they are soon zooming over southern Libya as if they were flying a small plane. It is a relief to see Libya like this, to forget the destruction and blood.

'I thought you said it was desert,' Savannah says, peering at the screen. 'I can see rivers.' She points. 'See! There.'

'Those are dry rivers called wadis. Sometimes it rains and the rivers run again, although that doesn't happen very often. Thousands of years ago the desert was green and there were trees and animals.'

'Will it go green again?' Savannah's eyes are as round and blue as the marble he found in the grass.

'I don't know. Maybe one day. Not for a long time.'

He looks back to the screen. The dry rivers are like the veins in the rocks he examined on the beach the other day. He wonders what it was like when grass grew there and people hunted the animals, but it's hard to imagine the sand turned to green and trees growing where now there is only dry scrub and thorn and sometimes nothing at all. Just rock and sand and more sand.

'I wish I could go there,' Savannah says, pointing at a mass of sand dunes.

'You can't go now. Because of the war.' He thought he could forget the war. It seems he cannot.

'The war won't go on forever though, will it?'

'No, it won't.' But the words feel hollow and meaningless and he has to swallow to stop the tears rising.

⚜ ⚜ ⚜

Savannah is at the kitchen table drawing heads of queens in all colours of the rainbow. In three weeks she will be gone. How Betty will miss her. The children have eased the burden of loneliness that seems to have settled upon her in her old age, like a constant low-pressure system. 'What are you doing?' she asks, even though she can see perfectly well.

'Drawing queens,' Savannah says in a queenly voice, 'for stamps.'

'Who will you write to?'

'The Queen.' Savannah drops the pink marker. 'I'm going to ask if she needs a new doctor. Ahmed's father is a doctor but he hasn't got a doctor's job. When he comes back he'll need a job.'

'Indeed.' Betty sits down at the table. 'Would you like some lined paper to write on?'

'Yes, but only when I've finished the stamps.'

'Have you seen Ahmed?'

'He's in the garden with Stealth.' Savannah places a finger across her lips. 'He's in the bamboo patch again. I told him it's dangerous in there. But Ahmed will be all right.'

'I'm sure he will. I'm going upstairs for a while to have a lie down. The shopping has quite worn me out.'

⚜ ⚜ ⚜

It is peaceful by the pond. But Ahmed can't shake off the heavy feeling that has settled in his gut, as if he had swallowed a rock. Savannah and Betty are inside the house; only the thin grey cat is out in the garden, sneaking through the undergrowth on the lookout for a mouse, a vole or a bird. Why does the cat have to kill? Why does anything have to kill?

The cat emerges. When it sees him it stays completely still, as if it were a statue. And for a moment Ahmed hates it so much he feels like strangling it with his bare hands.

That won't do.

If only his father were here. To talk to, explain.

He lies on his stomach and stares into the still, green water. A fish swims by but it soon darts into the safety of the reeds, alerted by the movement of Ahmed's arm. He moves his arm across the water. It is reflected in the pond, a dark shadow and behind it, are the clouds, greeny-white. Now he punches at the water with his fist and everything shatters. As if he had broken a glass.

Savannah comes marching down the path in bare feet. 'Oh, here you are,' she says, settling down at his side. 'What are you doing?'

'Nothing,' he says.

'You must be doing something.' She peers at the pond, wrinkling her nose, frowning a little. 'Everything is upside down. The clouds are floating in the water.' She rolls onto her back. 'But the clouds are also close to heaven. Has your mother gone to heaven?'

'*What is with you must vanish, and what is with Allah will endure.*'

'Is that a prayer? Are you praying again?'

'It's a quotation from the Qur'an, our holy book.' Ahmed pushes himself up onto his elbows. 'I don't think my mother can go to heaven.'

Savannah's eyebrows knit together. 'You only get sent to hell if you're terribly wicked. Your mother can't have been that bad. Unless she killed somebody.'

'Of course she didn't.' But Savannah's words are an electric shock to his head. That half-remembered picture floats in his head like the watery clouds: the empty bottle of pills by her bed, the sickly smell in the room. His mother didn't kill anyone. She killed herself.

'I don't think she wanted to live any more. She just died,' he says. He looks at Savannah but her face is as calm as the pool with the ripples vanished.

'Your mother is in heaven, Ahmed. You mustn't worry about that. The angels will look after her. You know they will.'

Chapter Three

It is impossible to get a decent night's sleep. The apartment is hot and airless, the air-conditioner has broken down – Mohamed has no idea how to fix it – and the night is punctuated by gunfire and explosions.

He turns over in bed. The day, like the day before and the one before that, passed like a car caught in a long traffic jam. There is little to do. When the electricity works he and Nafissa watch state television but that is like eating a diet of deep fried food: it gives Mohamed indigestion. State television seems to consist only of the awful female newsreader with caked make-up and harsh voice who whines on and on about the 'rats', and a new talk-show, *Hope of the Nation,* also heavy on propaganda. Real news is difficult to come by without access to the satellite channels or the internet, and they have neither.

Earlier in the day Mohamed showed Safia's photo to the man who owns the nearby bakery. The man barely even glanced. 'I wouldn't let my daughter wander about the streets,' he said, as if somehow Mohamed was to blame. 'There are dangerous people about nowadays.' Mohamed did not say that he suspected Safia had been picked up by the secret police – that would be asking for trouble. But the man could have shown some sympathy.

Afterwards his eyes fell on a poster of Gaddafi tacked to a wall opposite and a fury swept over him like a tsunami. If only he'd had the courage to rip the poster down and tear out Gaddafi's eyes. But that would have been madness. Instead he reached into his pocket, pulled out a dinar note and, checking no one was looking, ripped it into pieces. From the gutter Gaddafi's torn and grinning face gazed up at him. It was a futile and stupid gesture but how futile and hopeless everything feels right now.

He wakes with a start; Nafissa is shaking him. 'Mohamed!'

'What is it?' His heart is hammering in his chest. He was dreaming of a falling building and a torn flag printed with the image of a skull.

'There's a fire at the end of the street.'

'I will get dressed and see what is going on. It is best that you stay here.'

In the bathroom, as Mohamed splashes cold water on his face, the tattered remnants of the dream gather in his mind like a flock of dark and menacing birds.

Outside, a knot of people has gathered, silently watching a building at the end of the street. Choking smoke pours from the blackened windows but there is no sign of flames.

'What happened?' Mohamed asks no one in particular. 'Has anyone been hurt?'

'I don't think so,' a man nearby replies. 'The building is empty.'

'It's the work of rats and traitors,' another man says.

'Is that so?' Mohamed answers in a sarcastic tone, turning towards the voice. The man's face is deep in shadow but the outline of a hawkish nose is just visible in the gloom. Now the man steps forward into the light of the building and stares right at Mohamed, his eyes flinty and unyielding. He looks like a man who has not eaten in weeks: his cheeks are sunken, his jaw sharp as a carving knife. But his jacket is smart, the shirt underneath white and pressed.

'The traitors are on our doorsteps and in our homes,' the man says. A murmur passes through the small crowd, although whether it is a murmur of assent or a form of self-protection, Mohamed cannot tell. He turns to his nearest neighbour, but in the darkness he cannot read the man's face and when he turns back to the speaker, he finds he has vanished.

The man closest to Mohamed offers him a cigarette. 'Thank you for your offer,' Mohamed says, 'But I gave up years ago.' He taps his chest. 'Doctor's orders.'

The man lights his cigarette. 'I had given up too, until all this started.' He gestures at the smouldering building. 'You're Nafissa's brother-in-law, am I right?'

There is little point in denying the fact. 'Yes, I am.'

The man looks over his shoulder, then beckons Mohamed to move closer. 'Be careful. That man you were just talking to – he's *mukhabarat*, secret police.'

⚜ ⚜ ⚜

'What was that all about?' Nafissa asks.

'No one seems to know. The fire has been put out but whoever started it must be long gone.' Mohamed sits down at the table. How tired he feels. 'Have you seen a man hanging around the block? With a thin face and a prominent, beak-like nose?'

'I see plenty of men like that. We'll all be like scarecrows soon if this food shortage continues. Why do you ask?'

'He's *mukhabarat*. He was outside just now.'

'I don't think he lives in this block. You better point him out if you see him again. Well, I must try and snatch some sleep, *mukhabarat* or not.' Nafissa yawns; she seems unconcerned. Another lesson to be relearnt.

'I'll sit here awhile. I don't think I will sleep.'

'I'm right out of coffee.'

'Don't worry. Coffee gives me indigestion at this time of night.' Mohamed rubs his stomach. It has never caused him any trouble but it feels suddenly painful and bloated. 'Bah, I already have indigestion.'

'Why don't you make yourself a mint tea?'

'I will, if you think it will help. Quite frankly I think the whole country is suffering indigestion, as well as insomnia, paranoia and tyrannophobia.'

"What in Allah's name is that last one?'

'Fear of tyrants.'

'Is there such a condition?' Nafissa giggles unexpectedly.

'There's a phobia for almost everything. You'd be surprised.'

Nafissa holds up her hands. 'Don't tell me, Mohammed. I don't wish to know. Now I really must go back to bed. My head is spinning.'

He boils the kettle, makes the tea. While he sips at it, he thinks about 'tyrannophobia'. He came across the term when he was at the hospital. The symptoms include anxiety, dread, irregular heartbeat, sweating, nausea and a dry mouth. '*Tyrannophobia, like other phobias, is illogical,*' he recalls reading. But it is not illogical to be scared in this country. To be without fear, now that really would be stupid.

⚜ ⚜ ⚜

The following morning Gaddafi broadcasts a message, though there is no sign of the man himself. '*Advance, challenge, pick up your weapons, and go to the fight to liberate Libya inch by inch from the traitors and*

NATO. Get ready to fight... The blood of martyrs is fuel for the battlefield.' On and on he rambles, his voice barely audible.

'He's finished,' Mohamed says rashly.

'Don't underestimate him,' Nafissa says. 'But let's forget him for a moment. He takes up enough of our thoughts. So, tell me about England. You haven't said much. I never understood why you moved away from your brother for one thing.'

'London didn't suit us.'

'But if you'd stayed there, could you not have found work as a doctor?'

Mohamed glances out of the window. There is no sign of the hawk-nosed man. There is no sign of anyone: the street is strangely empty. 'After I lost my job at the hospital I lost the will for that,' he says quietly. 'We have done all right, Ahmed and I. He is successful at school. His English is almost perfect.'

'And yours?' Nafissa says, with just the curl of a smile.

'It is not bad,' he says in English, before translating the phrase into Arabic. Nafissa would have liked to learn English but she has only a few words and phrases. She never had the chance of a good education – unlike her younger sister. Perhaps, when this is all over, he will take Nafissa to England for a holiday. She will like Betty, he is sure of it.

'It must be cold in the winter. Ahmed told me you had snow last winter.'

'It was cold and everyone complained. People there have no idea how lucky they are. Of course the country has its problems. Does not every country? Yet they have freedoms we can only dream of.'

Nafissa leans forward and taps him on the hand. 'We will have our freedom one day.' She sighs and throws her hands in the air. 'I would love to visit London. I've heard the shops are wonderful. We're a rich country but what do we have to show for it? That man has ruined everything. Do you remember when you and Nour were first married? She wanted to buy you a shirt and a pair of shoes but the only shoes available were sizes too large for your feet and the shirts only yellow.'

Mohamed laughs. 'I wore that yellow shirt for years even though I disliked the colour. I had no choice.' He looks at Nafissa. Her eyes are half-closed as if she were dreaming. 'I promise you a trip to London.'

She smiles, a slight smile. 'I would like that, yes.' She gets to her feet. 'Now I must attend to my chores.'

'I will help,' Mohamed says. He wants something to do. This waiting is driving him crazy.

'No. You sit. You should rest and recuperate. You need to get your strength up. Who knows when you might need it?'

The minutes tick by slowly. The hands on the watch Nour bought him move like an old donkey circling a well. Every now and again he taps the face to check that the watch is still working and later he stares out of the window at the street below but there is little to see.

By evening Mohamed's patience has vanished. 'I'm going out to see if I can find us some coffee. I need to stretch my legs, breathe some air. And perhaps the walking will help me think. I can't just sit here and hope Safia will come home. But where should I begin looking?'

Nafissa is at the table, sewing a button on one of his shirts. 'Do you really believe Gaddafi is finished?'

Mohamed picks a piece of fluff off the sleeve of his jacket. 'Yes,' he says, although now he regrets speaking words he is not sure he believes. But he must give Nafissa hope.

'What will we do?' Nafissa buries her head in her hands and begins to cry. 'Safia's laptop is missing, Mohamed,' she says, looking up at him with red-rimmed eyes. 'I thought she had left it here but I can't find it.'

He pulls out a chair and sits down. 'Was there anything important on it?'

Nafissa wipes her eyes with a tissue. 'She joined a dating site, although it wasn't a proper dating site. It was set up by the revolutionaries so that people could contact each other safely. I'm not sure exactly how it worked. Everyone used pseudonyms. Safia called herself Sweet Jasmine. They used words like that – jasmine, moon and stars – it meant you supported the revolution.'

'Do you think the regime knows this?'

She pulls and twists at her greying hair. 'It is possible. I'm sorry, Mohamed. It's my fault she disappeared. I ought to have taken better care of her.

But you know what she's like. Strong-willed. Hard to argue with. And she's nearly twenty-two. She's not the girl you left here three years ago. She's a woman now.'

He does not answer. He is not sure what he feels. A car passes in the street and a boy calls for his friend. Nafissa's eyes dart nervously towards the door. Then she picks up the needle and recommences sewing Mohamed's button.

'I must go out. Tomorrow we will plan a strategy for our search. While I'm out, keep an eye on the entrance door in case that man re-appears. And try not to worry.'

'What shall I do if I see him?'

'Can you whistle?'

She attempts a smile. 'Not well but well enough.'

'I will be back before midnight. Watch for me. If he is there when I return, whistle. Just the once. We do not want unwarranted attention.'

⚜ ⚜ ⚜

As Mohamed emerges from the side road into the main street that runs through the neighbourhood, a young boy leans out of the passenger window of a car and waves the green flag. Mohamed opens his mouth to say something though luckily the car speeds off before a single curse has dropped from his lips. But the episode leaves him bad-tempered.

The *souk* in the old town is a half hour walk. Once or twice, Mohamed hears a gunshot in the distance but other than that everything is quiet. He is relieved to be out of the apartment and when he reaches the *souk* he finds it full of goods and shoppers as if nothing outside were changed. There are mounds of spices, fruits, vegetables, dried beans, rice, and the same piles of cheap plastic goods he remembers. He even manages to locate a small jar of coffee. It is cheap coffee, not like the stuff he is used to in England but it will do.

But every time a young woman passes by his eyes fix on her face, in case by some miracle she might be Safia. Until one woman, accompanied by her brother or perhaps her boyfriend, sends him such a look of hatred and disgust he scurries out of the *souk* and then he hardly dares lift his gaze from the pavement.

There is a new café on the edge of Green Square, a modern, glassy building with small metal tables outside and orange chairs. He is surprised to see it. He goes inside and orders a cappuccino. 'How is everything?' he asks the man behind the counter.

'You're not local, I take it?' the man answers, skimming the froth from the heated milk onto the coffee.

'I've been away, working in Egypt,' Mohamed replies carefully.

The man's face breaks out in a huge grin, as if Mohamed had told him the funniest joke. 'This isn't Egypt! Everything here is *miyeh-miyeh*, one hundred per cent fine. You mustn't believe what you hear, brother.' He slaps his large chest. 'I used to be in the army. I fought in Chad. We are still strong. We will never be beaten by those NATO rats.' He raises a fist and shakes it in the air. 'We've had the Romans and the Italians and I say, that's enough. We refuse to be colonised again.'

There will be no invasion, Mohamed wants to say, but he understands the man's fears. A NATO bomb killed a number of civilians in the city in June. He knows this was a mistake but mistakes are costly: the man behind the counter is proof of that. And there are many others like him. He wonders just how many.

He takes his coffee and sits outside. The square is crowded. During Ramadan the cafés and shops always stay open late and this year is no different. Life in the city appears normal, as the man said, but Mohamed knows it is anything but. Everyone knows that, whatever they might say out loud.

A young couple stroll by with a baby in a push-chair. The man is dressed in a shirt and denim jeans. The young woman wears the *hijab* and a long buttoned coat, but under the coat she too is wearing jeans. Gaddafi banned jeans in 1986 after the American bombing of Tripoli. The American attack was retaliation for the regime's bombing of a Berlin night-club. The bombing killed a hundred people, including Gaddafi's adopted daughter, Hannah. Later, people whispered this was a lie in order to gain sympathy for the regime, although no one dared voice that in public. The regime has always relied on lies and rumours: it is a house of cards. But in many ways the bombing reinforced the regime. People were angry with the Americans. The law of unintended consequences is always there, waiting in the background.

Mohamed pushes such thoughts aside, sits back in the plastic chair and begins to relax. How warm and soft the air is here. He had almost forgotten how it felt. In England it is never possible to sit outside in the evening, not without a coat. An unexpected happiness courses through his veins. How good it is to be back. This is home: it will always be home. However his new mood lasts barely longer than five minutes. It is suddenly spoiled by blasts of loud, thumping music. He turns. Across the square, a group of young men are dancing and waving green flags: Gaddafi supporters. Do they really believe the regime can last or is this for show? He would like to ask but he won't.

He gulps the last of the coffee and leaves, his brief moment of content dissolved. He should get back anyway. Nafissa will be worrying about him.

⚜ ⚜ ⚜

He is fumbling for the key to the downstairs door when he feels a hand on his shoulder. 'Mohamed Masrata,' a voice says. It is the man from the other night, the *mukhabarat.*

'Yes,' Mohamed answers. He feels no anger or fear, only an intense weariness.

The man grabs Mohamed's arm, making escape impossible. 'We know where you've been.' His voice is thin and flat, like his body, and Mohamed has a sudden urge to laugh but he suppresses it.

'Only traitors leave.' The man turns and spits on the pavement, missing Mohamed's shoe by less than a coin's breadth.

Mohamed lifts his head in the vain hope of seeing Nafissa at the window but the blinds are drawn and the lights are out. Perhaps they have her too. Yet he feels strangely calm, as if he were watching the event from afar, as if it were happening to someone else altogether.

A car pulls up, white with darkened windows. He has no idea what sort of car it is. He has never been interested in cars, he cannot even drive. But for some reason he wants to know, as if the detail mattered. The passenger door swings open and a man eases himself out, a huge man, his belly large like a camel's. The headlights show the man to be impeccably attired in a pale linen suit, crisp white shirt and lavender tie. He does not address Mohamed but instead shouts at the man holding him who now shoves Mohamed roughly into the rear of the vehicle. The fat man re-seats himself in the back seat, slips a mask over Mohamed's head and handcuff his hands. The events happens quickly. Mohamed could not have resisted even if he had wanted to.

Ahmed can only remember a fragment of his nightmare – a gigantic bird with a beak like a sword and talons of steel. He takes a deep breath, rubs his eyes and goes to the window. There is a black and white bird on top of Betty's fir tree making a noise like a football rattle. He opens the window and claps his hands and the bird flutters its wings but does not fly away.

He turns to check the time. He cannot believe it: the clock on the bedside table reads eight. That means he has slept through the alarm, missing *suhoor,* the dawn meal and now it is too late to eat. He will have to wait until the evening. Oh, why didn't he wake up? He must be more disciplined. Then he remembers what he was thinking yesterday, about his mother. If only he could ask Safia. She would know. She would tell him.

Why would his mother leave them like that?

He goes to the bathroom, dresses, walks slowly down the stairs. Savannah is at the kitchen table, eating egg on toast. 'Hello, Ahmed,' she says. 'You've got toothpaste on your mouth.'

He wipes it away and Betty walks in, her grey hair damp and curling round her face. 'I don't think you got up earlier, did you?'

'I overslept.'

'It's a long time until evening. Do you really think you can manage?'

Ahmed nods. He will have to. He has made a promise not just to Allah but to his father. He cannot break that.

'Are you all right, Ahmed?' Betty is staring at him. But her face is kind. He knows she means well but he cannot say.

'I'm fine. Thank you, Betty. I'm only annoyed for sleeping through the alarm clock.'

'I have a lot of clocks in this house,' Betty answers. 'I can get you another one. That might help.' She smiles. 'Well, I have work to do. I'll let you two just get along, shall I?'

An hour later. Ahmed and Savannah are walking through the estate – past the grassy area littered with wrappers, the rose shrubs and spindly trees, and up to the apartment where he and his father live. Savannah wants to see but they can only look at it from the outside. Betty has a key but that is for emergencies only.

The block appears dull and ordinary after Betty's house but Ahmed dutifully points to his window. 'That's my room.'

Savannah bends her head back to get a better view. 'It's nice. Mummy and I live above a hairdresser's shop.'

'We lived in a big house in Tripoli, almost as big as Betty's house.' He is tempted to describe the house for Savannah – the view of the sea, the fountain in the courtyard but it feels like a dream. He never understood why they had to move but after his thought yesterday it dawns on him that the move was something to do with their mother. He feels another spark of anger. Why did she have to go and ruin their lives by speaking out? Why didn't she just keep quiet?

A cool wind blows across the grass, rattling an empty crisp packet. 'We should go back. We didn't tell Betty we were going.'

'She won't mind,' Savannah says with a snort. 'She never minds. She's probably not even noticed.'

A plane flies overhead. It appears to be hardly moving but it is travelling at hundreds of miles an hour. Ahmed wonders where it is going.

'I've never been on an aeroplane,' Savannah says. 'What's it like?'

He shrugs. 'I don't remember.' He does remember but he doesn't want to talk about that either because all he could think of on that journey was that he and his father were leaving everything. He did not care for the view out of the window, the boats below tiny as specks of dust, the islands like broken biscuits. Yet wasn't he just a little excited?

Perhaps.

'I wish I could go on a plane. I want to go everywhere.' Savannah waves her hand in the air.

'They can't see you.'

'I know,' she says.

'You can't go everywhere. You'd have to live for a thousand years.' Ahmed isn't sure he wants change or journeys. He looks up again but the aeroplane has vanished, leaving only a long vapour trail like the breath of something, but soon that too is gone.

Chapter Four

The car makes a left off the main highway. It turns right and left again down a bumpy road before taking several more turns. The car seems to be heading in a westerly direction but Mohamed is disorientated because of the blindfold and the many turns the car makes so he cannot be sure.

No one speaks, although someone lights up a cigarette and its acrid smoke drifts into the back of the car. Mohamed is not even certain how many people are in the vehicle, whether the thin man – the *mukhabarat* who originally held him – climbed into the front. Meanwhile, the large man, sat next to him in the back passenger seat, clicks his fingers continually, like a nervous tic.

Even on the bumpy surface the car moves fast. That, together with the smell of the new upholstery, the man's cheap cologne, the cigarette smoke and Mohamed's enforced blindness, make him slightly nauseous. In spite of the air conditioning he is also sweating. He has a handkerchief in his pocket but the handcuffs preclude him from using it.

After about twenty minutes the car slams to a halt and the man next to him jumps out of the car, surprisingly fast for such a large and weighty man. Footsteps. The car doors opening. An arm hooked under his armpit. Now he is pulled out and roughly manoeuvred across a flat surface, perhaps a car-park, then up three steps and into a building. Once he stumbles but the man heaves him up as if he were no more than a rag doll.

It is cool inside the building. They cross a large open hall, their footsteps echoing on a tiled floor. There are perhaps two more men following behind. The sound of the men's footsteps make Mohamed shiver. What will they do to him here? For a moment he remembers Ahmed but he pushes the thought of his son aside. To think of family here is dangerous.

Left down a long corridor. From an open door-way a man shouts while another pleads. Mohamed cannot make out the words.

'Move it,' his escort says sharply.

Mohamed tries to quicken his pace but it is difficult to walk with the man's arm pushed under his own. This man too stinks of cologne but Mohamed can detect another smell too and he thinks it might be whiskey.

A door opens. He is pushed into a room and shoved onto a hard metal chair. Before he has time to take in these new surroundings there is a scuffling sound behind him and a movement of air. The sudden jolt to his spine almost sends him flying off the chair and a man laughs in front of him, his laugh high-pitched like a girl's.

'Mohamed Masrata.'

Mohamed licks his lips but his mouth is so dry it makes little difference.

The man bellows his name.

'Yes,' Mohamed answers.

'What brings you to this place, Doctor Masrata?' The man laughs again, softer this time.

Mohamed would like to ask what place but he stays silent.

The man with the high laugh moves in his direction. His footsteps are not heavy like the other man's but appear to dance across the floor. Mohamed tenses the muscles in his body, waiting for the blow to arrive. It does not. Instead the man pushes his fist under Mohamed's chin, jerking it up. He removes the fabric mask with his other hand. Mohamed blinks. The room is bright but he cannot see the man's face, only a green uniform and polished black boots.

The man steps back, revealing himself. He is a slight man, neither tall nor short, and he has slicked-down greying hair peeking out from under a green beret. Even with the military uniform there is something effeminate about him. Mohamed can almost imagine him strutting down the catwalk, twirling a cane in his hand. But his eyes are two deep, empty holes.

'You are here, are you not, to look for your daughter?' He stares at Mohamed and taps his holster with his right hand. The gesture is not habit. It is designed to intimidate.

Mohamed nods and lowers his gaze. This floor is concrete. Close to one of the chair legs is a large, dark stain. Who else has been here? Is this where they torture people? Interrogate them? He wonders what terrible secrets the room holds.

The man takes hold of another chair, moves it next to Mohamed's own and sits down just inches from Mohamed's face. He has a woman's hands, the skin is smooth, the nails manicured. This is not a man who carries out the dirty work but a man who makes decisions. This one dies. This one lives. And now the man draws a piece of paper out of his pocket, smooths out the creases and begins to read.

'Fifteenth June of 2008, Dr. Masrata was removed from his post at the hospital for misconduct. Seventh July 2008, Dr. Masrata and his son, Ahmed, aged eight years, boarded a flight to London, Heathrow. Dr. Masrata's daughter, Safia, then aged eighteen, remained in Tripoli with her aunt.' He stops, refolds the paper and places it back in his pocket. 'Yet now, Doctor, you return. This is a odd time to return, would you not agree?'

'You know why I have come. You have said so yourself. And I am no longer a doctor.'

'Indeed. Do you expect to find your daughter here? Is that it?' The man's voice is calm and steady.

'I don't know where she is. In any case your men brought me here. I did not come of my own volition.'

The man smiles, a sickly smile that sends Mohamed's stomach churning. 'You are lucky, Doctor. I can be of assistance but this requires a certain amount of co-operation on your part. You are an intelligent man. Surely you must understand that this uprising, this stupidity, will only result in chaos. Is that what you want?'

'No,' Mohamed says, trying to suppress the bubble of fear that has risen into his gullet. This is how they always trick you. They sow confusion and doubt in your mind.

'We know that you are working for NATO, for the enemy.'

The blow comes so fast he has no means of protecting himself. And his hands are cuffed. The punch knocks the air from his lungs and sends him thudding onto the hard floor. As he lies there, doubled up with pain and gasping for breath, the big man standing behind kicks him in the back.

'Enough,' the man in charge commands, once the large man has aimed several more kicks. 'Get up!'

Mohamed does not move. The fear has gone. In its place is a strange admiration. So this is how the system works. It has worked for 42 years. Perhaps the man is right. No! He is falling for their trickery.

'Get up!'

Using one elbow, Mohamed rises painfully to his knees.

'Take off his cuffs.'

The large man unlocks the handcuffs and steps away. Mohamed takes hold of the chair and pulls himself up, and all the time the man in charge watches his every move. 'All right,' the man says. 'We will take you to see your daughter.' He smiles again, that devil's smile, before addressing the guard, or whoever he is. 'There's no need to handcuff him. Just use the blindfold.'

His daughter? Is this another of their tricks?

Mohamed is marched down another long corridor. His ribs ache from the kicks and each breath he takes hurts. They pass through a heavy metal door and across a square of open ground. The other man, the commander, moves in front, his footsteps crunching across the gritty earth. A warm breeze is blowing and Mohamed can smell the tang of the sea. There is no sound of traffic.

A door opens. Another building. It smells bad in here – urine, sweat and human excrement. Sounds reach his ears, pitiful groans, a low sobbing. Now he is truly afraid. Surely Safia cannot be in this filthy place, with all these men? The thought of that makes him afraid and he has not been afraid. This is what they want. To create fear, to maintain it. The threat of the noose, the barrel of a gun, the walls of a prison. All to keep people silent.

Another door, another corridor, this one silent but musty. That smell of cheap cologne. A room. What smell is this? He is becoming disorientated. Is it not his wife's perfume, or the sweet smell of Betty's roses?

'Here!' the commander barks.

Mohamed's blindfold is removed a second time. This room is gloomy, unlike the previous one. The only light comes from a dim bulb in the centre, hanging on a length of twisted wire. He blinks. The room is cavernous. Perhaps it was once used for storage. Now it is empty. Dark. He turns his head. Not completely empty. In the corner there is a metal cage, just like the lion's cage at Tripoli zoo, and inside the cage is a figure, sitting huddled, head bowed. He blinks again, focuses.

A bitter taste floods his mouth. 'Safia!' Is that really his daughter or is he hallucinating? 'Safia?'

'Father?'

He cannot trust his eyes or ears. He waits for his sight to adjust to the gloom; takes a step forward.

'Father?'

It is Safia, his beloved daughter. Any doubts he had have now vanished. But isn't that a bruise on her face, blood congealing at the corner of her mouth? And why is she so weak, her voice only a whisper?

If he had a gun now he would shoot them down with not a thought. That is how evil works in this world. One evil begets another and another. But he is weak. He has nothing. Only his mind.

'The daughter is like the mother,' the man in charge says. He turns to Mohamed, a putrid smile curling his lips. 'It is a pity that you are unable to control your women. She is a pretty little thing, is she not?'

A surge of anger courses through Mohamed. He is no longer handcuffed: he could easily lash out and hit the man. But he knows this is another of their tricks. He takes a deep breath and says, 'What is it you want?' He can hear the quavering in his voice. He sounds like an old man. They will wear him down. Safia is the bait. How will he resist?

'We want nothing.' The man smiles again. 'We are men of honour. We are not rats, but this is where we keep the rats, Doctor Masrata – or should I say Mr Masrata? We cannot have rats running around outside, infecting the population, can we?'

To argue will only result in greater pain – for both of them. Mohamed digs his nails hard into the palms of his hands and the words of the *hadith* come to his mind. *You who believe, care for yourselves; he who goes astray cannot harm you when you are rightly guided.*

'Mr Masrata, what is your answer?'

It takes a supreme act of will to say the words. 'She is no longer my daughter. She must remain here. This is the fate she deserves, the fate of all traitors. I would only ask you that, as she is a woman, you will show her some leniency. You are correct. She is her mother's daughter. I never wish to see her again.' He turns from the cage to face his captors and, in that small moment, he flutters his right hand behind his back like the wings of a bird. He hopes Safia understands his gesture, that she does not believe the awful words he has just uttered. It was his only choice.

The blindfold is replaced. The door closes with a bang, echoing down the corridor. Mohamed wants to weep and cry like the men he heard earlier, but he must keep his mind blank as a wordless page.

The same metal chair. The same room and its concrete floor, the same bloodstain, the same smell of cologne.

The blindfold is taken off. Now they will start. Mohamed is not afraid of dying but he does not want to die this way. An image of Ahmed floats into his mind but he pushes it away.

'You can go,' the man in charge says. He seems suddenly weary. Mohamed hesitates. Is this yet another trick? How many do they have? He looks at the man and the man returns his gaze coolly: he does not seem like a man who has doubts. 'Go! Before I change my mind.'

The big man steps up close and Mohamed flinches, expecting another blow. Instead the man replaces the blindfold, pulls Mohamed to his feet and drags him back out through the building and into a car, a different car. This one smells of stale sweat and when Mohamed is pushed onto the back, the seat sags and he can feel the springs underneath.

Perhaps twenty minutes later, brakes screeching, the car comes to a juddering halt. The passenger door opens and Mohamed is pushed out, still blindfolded. He loses his balance and falls, banging his head.

The car drives away fast, its tyres hissing on the road, the noisy engine disappearing into the night.

Slowly, he sits up, removes the blindfold and rubs at his scalp. There is a trickle of blood but the cut does not appear to be deep and he is not dizzy or in pain. Now, he can make out clumps of small, scruffy trees and the line of a path. Of course. It is the park at Suq al Juma. There, below is the dark sea, mottled with the reflected lights of the city and the ships at anchor in the harbour.

He stays where he is, gulping the fresh air. My child, my child, what will become of you? The agony of that is a knife to his chest. But a choice had to be made. He can only hope it was the right one, may Allah forgive him if it is not.

He glances at his watch but in the darkness he cannot see the hands.

Chapter Five

Betty opens the curtains. Nothing stirs in the garden. The ox-eyed daisies, the long grass, the bamboo stems, are still, as if waiting for something. The summer has begun to turn: the shadows stretch all the way across the lawn, the birds no longer sing loudly in the mornings and the roses are over-blown, the petals dropped.

She slips on her dressing gown and switches on the radio. The news reader announces that the rebel forces are within a few miles of Tripoli. The information sets her head aching. She sits on the edge of the bed and rubs at her temples but her head thumps even more and she has to go to the bathroom for a painkiller.

Ahmed is at the kitchen table, drawing. Each evening she lays out his breakfast and he eats it before dawn, before even she is awake. In ten days it will be the end of Ramadan. How wonderful if Mohamed were back in England by then, but that does not seem likely.

What should she say to Ahmed? He probably knows already. He is watching the television. 'This might be Tripoli's day,' she says carefully.

He looks up from his drawing. She recognises her garden but the trees are bent under an invisible wind and the pencil lines are dark and thick as if everything were suffering under a terrible storm.

'The rebels – the revolutionaries – have almost reached the city.' Ahmed looks at her wordlessly. 'Your father knows how to keep himself safe.' Her words sound as frothy and inconsequential as Savannah's pink ribbons. A sniper's bullet is indiscriminate. A bomb can fall anywhere, on the good and the bad, the young and old.

'What about my sister?' Ahmed picks up the pencil and chews at the stub. 'Will she be safe?'

Betty pulls up a chair. '*Do not try to run away from trials and tribulations, but endure them with patience. They cannot be avoided, and there is nothing for it but to endure them with patience.* Do you know this saying?'

Ahmed shakes his head.

'It is from Jilani, an Islamic preacher who lived almost a thousand years ago.' Betty draws a spiral on the table with her finger. 'Never stop learning, Ahmed. It's important to take an interest in the world. Ignorance creates fear and prejudice.'

'Yes,' Ahmed says, almost impatiently. He points to the drawing. 'Is this any good?'

'I think it's excellent. You have real feeling. Art is not just a technical skill, although that is important too.' She hesitates. 'I can't promise your sister will be all right, Ahmed. We just have to hope.'

'Yes,' he says again, jabbing the pencil at the paper.

At the same moment Savannah jumps through the open door like a Jack-in-the-Box. 'What's for breakfast? I could eat a scabby horse.'

Betty laughs, Ahmed too. It is good to hear him laugh.

'What's funny?' Savannah frowns at them both.

'The scabby horse, that's what's funny. Where on earth did you learn that?'

'She learnt if off the television,' Ahmed says.

⚜ ⚜ ⚜

The phone rings after lunch. It is only Delia. She must be feeling guilty. This is the second time she has rung in as many days.

'How is it going there?' she says.

'We're doing well,' Betty answers.

A short silence. 'Is Savannah about?'

Betty considers saying, Oh no, she's run away, but she bites her lip. 'I'll get her. She's out in the garden with Ahmed. We're about to drive to the seaside. It's a lovely day.'

'That sounds nice,' Delia says but she sounds distracted, as if she wasn't really listening.

'Is everything OK?' A bad feeling has settled in Betty's stomach. Delia is always so chatty. Something is up, she can feel it.

'Fine,' Delia says in precisely that kind of voice people use when things just aren't.

'I'll call Savannah.'

But as Betty closes the sitting room door, she hears Savannah say plaintively down the phone, 'You promised. You did promise.'

Betty stands at the back door, watching Ahmed on his hands and knees near the bamboo patch. She wonders what he is doing, but then Savannah's voice carries through the house, shrill and uncomprehending. 'A baby? You're having a baby?'

The sun is shining hot and bright as if all were well in the world. Betty has brought the children to the pier. A change from the house felt necessary, essential even. Savannah was very upset and angry about the baby. She still is. Betty ought to have guessed. The clues were there right from the start – Delia's guarded comments, the rushed marriage in Las Vegas, the strained telephone calls. But this isn't the 1950s. It is quite unlike in Betty's day when a young, unmarried mother was considered a scandal, when an affair had to be hushed up, hidden. All the same, she can't understand why Delia didn't wait to give Savannah the news. First Delia doesn't want to tell her daughter she's married, now she's rushing to tell Savannah about the baby. As if Betty didn't have enough to deal with. She leans on the metal railing. Perhaps she is being too harsh. Who is she to judge other people? Yet it seems so unfair.

Ahmed has been quiet all day. He said nothing when Betty explained Savannah's upset. Now

Savannah is kicking the metal railing and staring out to sea.

'Would you like an ice-cream?'

No reply.

She turns to Ahmed. It must take quite some discipline not to eat during the daylight hours. She is not sure she could do it.

'Maybe I will have one,' Ahmed says, jiggling his feet uneasily.

The wooden planks of the pier are sticky with chewing gum and melted ice-cream. A flock of seagulls circles hungrily overhead and in the shade below a dog edges its way along the shingle.

'I thought you weren't supposed to eat in the daytime,' Savannah says, scowling.

'My mother used to buy me ice-cream.' Ahmed's voice is thin and insubstantial, like the shadow of a passing seagull.

The sun glints on the gilded dome of the ballroom at the end of the pier and notes of music drift on the breeze. 'Well,' Betty says. She glances at Ahmed again. 'Only you can decide.'

⚜ ⚜ ⚜

The day is turning out all wrong. But he won't break his fast; he won't let his father down.

'I want a Magnum.' Savannah's eyes are like the ice Ahmed has seen on the television in those nature programmes, the ice that lies under the sea or in deep crevasses, cold and blue. Why does she have to be so upset about a baby? Then he wonders what it would have been like if his father had decided to marry again after his mother died. He wouldn't have liked that, not at all.

'A Magnum is a gun,' he says.

'No, it's not, it's an ice-cream. Are you having an ice-cream?'

'I can't eat or drink until sunset.'

'Why can't you? It's such a stupid idea.'

'Savannah,' Betty says in a warning voice.

'Well I do think it's silly even if it is Ahmed's religion.'

'Sometimes it's necessary to keep things to yourself.' Betty sounds angry. He has never heard her angry before. Savannah wrinkles up her nose but she doesn't answer back.

They sit at one of the tables set up outside. No one talks. Betty sips her tea and nibbles at an iced bun. Savannah slurps her ice-cream and stares furiously into the distance. The seagulls wheel overhead. The sun shines. The sky is blue. But Ahmed still feels bad inside. As if a chasm had opened up inside him, swallowing him up.

Betty sits down on the shingle bank. She opens her book and tries to read but she can't concentrate. After every few lines her mind wanders to Tripoli – not the Tripoli she remembers from the past but the Tripoli of the present. Why is there no news from Mohamed?

She closes the book, walks down the shingle, using her stick as a support and, taking off her shoes, digs her feet into the wet, muddy sand. The sand oozes up between her toes, cold and surprising. How many years has it been since she last went barefoot? Ten, twenty?

She turns to glance at the pier, delicate in the afternoon light, its rusted and barnacled struts perfectly reflected in the sand below. She turns back to the children. They are laughing together on the shoreline. This is what it means to be young; wars, families and upsets can be forgotten in an instant and, like the sparkling light, everything can be made anew.

Chapter Six

Mohamed's body aches all over. He is not bothered by his bruises, it is his heart that bothers him; it feels as heavy as the tanks he has seen rolling into cities all across the world – Sarajevo, Grozny, Beirut. Countless cities. Countless wars. Countless dead.

Will they spare Safia now? Or will they still seek to punish him?

He walks out of the park and down into the city streets. From time to time he hears gunshots and artillery fire, men shouting, and he is afraid. But he keeps to the back ways and alleys and only once does he meet trouble. He rounds a corner, sees a man running down the street, rifle in hand. As Mohamed steps into a doorway for safety, a second man dashes out of a building in pursuit. A volley of gunfire follows, then silence. He waits another few minutes, says a short prayer and continues on his way.

The whole street, the whole apartment block, is in darkness. He fumbles with the lock and pushes the door open.

⚜ ⚜ ⚜

When Mohamed emerges from his room, sunlight is streaming into the apartment and Nafissa is at the sink, washing dishes.

'Where were you last night?' she says. 'I was frightened half to death. I didn't hear you come back. It must have been late.'

'Just walking.'

She rinses the dishes and places them on the draining board. 'Walking? No one walks around at that hour, not now.' She peers at him, as if he were a bacterium on a microscope slide. 'Look at you. You're a mess.'

He sits down heavily, grimacing.

'Something has happened. I know it.'

She sits in the chair opposite, rocking back and forth. Now and again she asks questions. What time did they take him? Where did they take him? How did Safia seem? What did they do to him? Why did they let him go? He tells her everything. When he has finished, he expects her to be angry but all she says is, 'I am so sorry, Mohamed. I didn't see or hear a thing. The electricity went off and I must have fallen asleep.'

'I thought they'd taken you too.'

'Praise Allah, no.' Nafissa taps her fingers on the table. 'I wish you could work out where this place is. We have to find it.'

Mohamed rests his chin in his hand. He hasn't shaved and the stubble there is rough and prickly under his fingers. 'I have tried, Nafissa. I keep on going over the route in my mind but I cannot work it out. Now what shall we do?'

'It's essential we remain calm and logical. We mustn't allow our emotions to muddle our thinking. I will ask my contacts again and Safia will do whatever she can to protect herself. She's a strong young woman, she's not Nour.' Nafissa raises a palm. 'I know it is difficult to speak of this. You tried to shield me from the truth, Mohamed, but I knew.'

They have never discussed the circumstances and details of Nour's death. The grief and shame was too much.

'It's a terrible sin to take your own life,' Nafissa continues. 'Allah forbids it.' She begins to cry. 'I'm sorry. Here I am talking about keeping calm and now I bring this up. I should not have spoken of it.' Tears cascade down her face.

'*They* killed Nour,' Mohamed says. He is suddenly cold in spite of the heat in the apartment. 'When she came back from that place she was dead already. They might as well have murdered her in cold blood for all the difference it made. It wasn't my wife or your sister who returned from the prison, it was someone else.' He thumps the table. 'Don't preach to me about what is right!'

Nafissa reaches for a tissue and wipes her eyes. How silent it is suddenly, as if the world outside had turned to smoke.

'I have forgiven her,' Nafissa says after a while. 'Even so.'

He too has struggled to forgive Nour for taking her own life.

'She swallowed her sleeping pills.' Nafissa tears the tissue into shreds. 'The pills you prescribed for her. That's what happened, isn't it?'

'Yes,' he says. There is no point in denying it now.

'Why weren't you honest with me? Did you think I'd talk, was that it?' She picks up another tissue and proceeds to shred that too.

'I thought it would be safer to say nothing.'

'Safer?' Nafissa snorts. She shakes her head and the colour drains from her cheeks. 'Safia knows. We have talked about it at length. She's not a child, Mohamed. She needed to hear. But you should have been the one to tell her.'

Did he know that? Is that why Safia decided to stay with Nafissa in Tripoli? Perhaps he did. But he has nothing more to say.

He and Nafissa sit without speaking. The hot sun streams in through the windows and their unsaid words gather in the air. Until a single gunshot rings out and echoes down the street, sending Mohamed to his feet.

'What time is it?' he asks, tapping his watch.

'Almost noon.'

He taps the watch again but it is no longer working. The hands are stuck at thirty minutes past one. 'I'm going out.'

'Are you crazy? Didn't you hear that shot just now?'

'I cannot stay here all day. I have to do something. Look at me. What use am I? My daughter is in prison and I sit here, talking. It's unforgivable!' He is shouting again.

'Please calm down, Mohamed, and listen to me. What if they take you again? What use will you be?'

'They have Safia. They have no need of me.'

Nafissa slumps in the chair like a rag doll. 'I'm not sure I can take any more of this. Oh, when will it end?'

Mohamed places his hand on her shoulder. 'We must be patient. Unless you think I should be out on the streets fighting. That reminds me, I looked for my father's old rifle but it has gone missing. Do you know where it is?'

Nafissa looks up at him and a tear splashes down her cheek. 'One of Safia's friends took it.'

'You gave it away?'

She sits up, straight again, the moment of vulnerability gone. 'What would you have them fight with, their own hands?'

'Of course not,' he says. He gives her hand a squeeze. '*Weep like the waterwheel, that green herbs may spring up from the courtyard of your soul.*'

'You've always loved Rumi. Try not to stay out too long, Mohamed. At least promise me that.'

Mohamed picks up the stick from its place near the door. 'It's only been three years in England and I've forgotten what it is like to live here.'

'Yes, but perhaps it is good to forget.' She smiles. 'That stick quite suits you.'

'Indeed,' he says. With that he opens the door, walks down the stairs and out into the heat of the street.

A long queue has formed outside the bank. Mohamed brought dollars, the notes stuffed into his pockets, suitcase, even his shoes. But if things get worse, even dollars will be useless.

'There is no money,' the policeman on guard is shouting. 'No money.'

A woman bawls back, 'Shame on you!'

The small crowd jostles and jeers, and Mohamed walks by quickly but he does not go far. The crowd outside the bank has unsettled him. Then a car passing down the street slows down as it reaches him. He panics, thinking he is to be picked up again. The car, however, moves on. Perhaps it was nothing. Only his paranoia. He walks a little further, turns round. What can he do, pacing the streets? He may only be putting himself at risk.

Before returning to the apartment he decided to call in at the corner shop. Perhaps there is something he can take to Nafissa to make amends: a bar of soap, a packet of tea. But the shelves are almost empty.

'I'm sorry. We are still waiting for supplies,' the boy behind the counter says and he peers at Mohamed, his brown eyes unblinking. 'You're Nafissa's brother-in-law, aren't you? The one who lives in England.'

This must be Ali's youngest brother. He must be about twelve or thirteen, though he looks older, his face thin and tired, dark circles under his eyes.

'I'm striped,' Mohamed says, remembering the flag.

The boy grins. He looks younger when he smiles. 'Yes,' he says. 'I know.'

Mohamed reaches out and shakes the boy's hand. 'My name is Mohamed.' He uses the English.

'Pleased to meet you,' the boy replies, also in English. 'My name is Faheem.' He drops his voice to a whisper and adds, now in Arabic, 'Have you heard? The *thuwar* are in the city. My brother has seen with his own eyes. He has gone to fight with them. I wish I could fight too but I have to stay here and guard the shop.'

'Ah, but that is a good job. Someone has to do it.' Mohamed clears his throat. The heat and dust of the street has turned it scratchy. 'Are you sure the *thuwar* are here?'

The door opens and someone walks into the shop. Faheem taps his hand on the counter and says in a loud voice, 'I am sorry, Mister. We are right out of soaps today.'

Mohamed walks towards the exit but the man blocks his way and grabs at his sleeve. 'Mohamed. It is Mohamed, is it not?'

Memories of the interrogation flash through Mohamed's mind: the smell of the man's cologne, the kicks to his ribs, the spots of dried blood on the concrete floor, his daughter locked up in that cage. He steps back and his hands fly involuntarily to his chest.

'Mohamed,' the man repeats.

There is something familiar in his voice. Mohamed drops his arms and stares at the man's broad cheeks, the prominent nose, the slightly shabby and ill-fitting suit. Can it be? Yes. Yes. It's Khalid, his old doctor colleague. 'Khalid?'

'What are you doing here?' Khalid says. He lowers his voice. 'Can you speak?'

Mohamed nods in the direction of the boy. 'Do not worry. He is one of us.'

Khalid places a hand on his forehead as if he had a headache. 'I thought you were in England.'

'I was. I have come back to look for Safia.'

'Safia has gone missing? This is not good news.' Khalid steers Mohamed towards the rear of the shop. 'Let's talk here. If someone comes in I will pick up this bag of flour and go straight to the counter. Do not look at me. You understand?'

'I have not forgotten how it is here.' He examines his colleague. How far can he trust him? No one stood by when Mohamed lost his job at the hospital, not even Khalid.

'Do you have any idea where she might be?'

'If I knew, I would not still be looking.'

Khalid sighs and pulls on his greying beard. He didn't have a beard before, did he? Mohamed cannot quite remember. 'These are terrible times, Mohamed, my friend. Tarik, my youngest, was shot in February, during the demonstrations here.'

'Shot? I am sorry to hear this. Is he...?'

'He is OK. He was wounded in the thigh but he is making good progress.' Khalid bows his head. 'I am sorry too, sorry that I did not support you when you were thrown out of your job, may Allah forgive me. I was afraid. We all were. That is the truth. But we are afraid no longer. What is it they say? You can step on the flowers but you cannot delay the spring. Oh, how I have missed you, my dear friend.' He throws his arms around Mohamed and kisses him, one kiss for each cheek.

'It is good to be back,' Mohamed says, returning the embrace.

Khalid glances over his shoulder. The shop is still empty. 'The *thuwar* are about to enter the city. This is the beginning of free Tripoli.'

'So I have heard. Do you have any more information?'

'Hashim, my eldest, has been fighting in Zawiyah. He left there last night. They have air support, supplies. It won't be long now, everyone knows this, even the regime.' He tugs on his beard again. 'But I fear the price of freedom will be high.'

As if in response to Khalid's statement, a loud boom fills the air and they both instinctively dive behind a pile of boxes.

'Air support. NATO,' Mohamed says.

The explosion is followed by two more in quick succession. He and Khalid run out into the street, the boy following. A plume of dark smoke rises up above the buildings and a fighter jet flies overhead, the sound of its engines troubling the clear summer sky.

'I ought to get home,' Khalid says. 'Back to my family. They will be worrying. What about you, Mohamed, where are you staying?'

'With my sister-in-law.'

'That is good.' Khalid reaches out and clasps Mohamed's hand. 'What a dreadful tragedy, your wife.'

'Yes, it was.'

'When this is over, you must visit. We are still in the same place.' A faint blush stains Khalid's cheeks. Guilt or shame? But they all feel that. For all the disappeared and the dead, the ones no one could save.

'I will do,' Mohamed answers. He watches Khalid disappear down the street. He is limping slightly. He never used to limp.

The boy, Faheem, taps him on the shoulder. 'I can get you a car.'

'A car?' Mohamed shakes his head. 'What for?'

'So you can look for your daughter.' He grins. 'We know these things, Mr Mohamed. Nothing is hidden from us.'

⚜ ⚜ ⚜

The battered pick-up truck turns up ten minutes later, the rear weighted down with sacks of rice. The driver steps out and, with Faheem's help, carries three of the sacks inside. The driver looks to be about Mohamed's age but he is a bulky man with a fierce face and a large black beard. His head is covered with a red and white chequered *keffiyeh*. He introduces himself as Ahmed.

'That is also my son's name.'

'It is a good name.' A faint and brief smile plays across Ahmed's lips. 'So, where are we to go?'

Mohamed explains. Ahmed merely shrugs and says, 'If we are stopped we are making a delivery of rice. I have the papers.'

For three hours they drive around the city, though they avoid the area near Gaddafi's citadel where the smoke rises. Is that where the bombs hit? And there is no sign of the regime's troops, only the usual road-blocks. Mohamed asks Ahmed what he thinks but Ahmed merely shrugs and says he has no opinion. He speaks little as they drive and his silence makes Mohamed uncomfortable but he too keeps quiet, only directing Ahmed from time to time.

The roads and pavements are almost empty and most of the shops are closed, although once a flotilla of brand new vehicles, each with darkened glass, speeds along the road. This time Ahmed snaps his fingers and says, 'The regime fleeing the sinking ship.'

'Do you think so?'

'I am certain of it.'

At each road-block, Mohamed freezes, sure they will run into trouble. But Ahmed calmly shows his papers and they are waved through. It is almost as if nothing were happening, as if the war were only in Mohamed's head. But late in the afternoon, at the end of a dusty street in Janzour, close to a half-built development, they hear machinegun fire.

'We should go back,' Mohamed says. He has had enough of driving round in circles, as if they were lions in the city zoo. The task is hopeless. He will never be able to recognise the place they are holding Safia, even if by some miracle they should drive right by it.

'It's only a little buckshot,' Ahmed says, grinning for once. But he shoves the truck into reverse and they spin back down the road, spurting sand and pebbles.

'Impressive,' Mohamed says.

'I don't just deliver rice,' Ahmed says. He does not elaborate.

Back at Ali's shop Mohamed pays Ahmed the agreed fee – in dollars – and climbs out of the truck.

'I hope you find her,' Ahmed says, leaning out of the window. 'I lost my youngest son in May. He was only seventeen. He was killed at Dafniya, outside Misrata.' He shakes his fist in the air. 'I will make them pay. They will suffer like I have suffered.'

It is strange, Mohamed thinks, as he walks away, how suddenly and unexpectedly a man can break his silence.

There are more explosions in the night. These too sound as if they are coming from the area of Gaddafi's complex.

Mohamed taps his watch. The hands still refuse to budge. He guesses it must be well beyond midnight, which means it is Saturday the 20th August, in the Islamic year 1422. He remembers when Gaddafi required Libyans to change from the Western calendrical system to the Islamic one. At the same time Gaddafi decreed Libya was not to count the year from the Prophet's move to Medina, as other Islamic countries do – but that they were to count from the year of the Prophet's death. Later this was changed again – the count beginning with the date of the Prophet's birth, until everyone became so confused they had no idea what year they were living in. Gaddafi even renamed the months of July and August. July became Hannibal, and August became Nasser.

It might have been almost funny. But it was not.

Boom! Boom! This is what has become of the country. Death and bloodshed.

Where will it end? Nafissa's words.

Mohamed peers though the blind. Safia may be stronger than Nour, but no one is strong enough to resist a bullet to the head or a knife to the throat. At least a bullet at close range would be instant. She would not suffer. But if they have done to his daughter what they did to Nour, he will kill them with his bare hands.

Chapter Seven

The small red brick house is perched at the top of the grassy meadow. To the left is a rough track, rusted with leaves from a line of sycamores and chestnuts, which leads up to the ridge. Beyond the ridge is a valley and beyond that a line of hills, blue in the distance. Behind those hills lies the sea.

'I'm going to live in that house one day,' Savannah says, pulling at her pink sunhat and jumping over an ant-hill.

'That? But it's old and dirty.' Ahmed climbs up onto the wooden stile. Next to the stile is a finger post carved with a green acorn.

Betty can't remember seeing the post before. She may have forgotten. It has been a long while since she walked up here. A very long while. Perhaps before George died.

'It's not that old, Ahmed. It just needs painting on the windows.' Savannah looks thoughtful. 'Blue would be nice.'

Betty negotiates the stile with difficulty. Afterwards, she leans on her stick and inspects the house. It must have been pretty once but now it has an eerie, unkempt air. The paint on the eaves is flaking, the downstairs window frames are rotten, the net curtains torn and grubby and behind the choking tangle of brambles and willow-herb which make up the front garden, a line of dark firs scratches the sky like Baba Yaga's fingernails. She pushes open the creaky gate. 'Why don't we take a proper look?'

'What if there are people hiding inside?' Ahmed sounds fearful.

Last night Betty thought she heard him crying but when she listened at the door she could hear nothing.

'I'll knock, in case.' She walks down the cobbled, mossy path and lifts the brass knocker.

'If someone answers, what will you say?' Savannah says.

'I'll say we want to buy the house.' Betty lets the knocker go with a bang, startling a crow perched in one of the fir trees.

'There's no sale sign.' Savannah hops from one foot to the other. 'And we're not buying it, are we?'

They wait. Betty tries the door but it is locked. She peers in through the dusty windowpane. The room is empty except for a sagging sofa and a chair with only three legs, and the bare floorboards are spattered with white paint. 'No one lives here, I'm sure.'

'Can I look?' Savannah stands on her tiptoes and presses her nose to the glass. 'It's not very nice, is it, Betty? But we could make it pretty if we tried.'

Betty laughs. 'It's not our house.'

Savannah's face droops. 'I wish it was mine,' she says wistfully.

They walk back up the weedy path and out through the gate. Ahmed is still on the stile. He has his back to the house and is staring out towards the sea. Below him the grass is rippling in the breeze and the wood pigeons are making a soft, yawning sound. Betty considers the house. It is in a lovely position and it's not too large. But it needs so much work. All the same, it's a thought.

'One day that will be my house,' Savannah says to Ahmed. 'I'll paint the rooms white and I'll have lots of books, like Betty.'

Betty glances at Ahmed but she can't read his expression: his face is half hidden under his fringe. How quickly his hair has grown. She must get him to the barber's before his father returns.

'Someone took our house in Tripoli,' he suddenly blurts out. 'We had a big house with a courtyard but we had to leave and move into an apartment.'

'That's stealing.' Savannah's eyes are as wide and open as the sea. 'How can someone steal a house?'

They can rob everything, Betty thinks. Your house, your freedom and your life.

When they get back from the empty house the red light is blinking on Betty's phone.

'It's probably my friend, Annette,' Betty says, placing her walking stick in the big blue and white vase in the hall.

Let it be his father.

Please let it be good news.

Betty picks up the receiver and places it against her ear and her head nods like those toy dogs people have in the back of their cars and her bracelets go jingle-jangle, clink-clink and Ahmed can't breathe and time slows to almost nothing like it does at school when the teacher is boring and they have to sit still and listen.

But now she is smiling and saying, 'It's your father. Here, listen.'

However, the message is short and his father says nothing of Safia.

'He can't say much, you know that.' Betty takes the receiver and places it back in the cradle. This time she does not smile. 'It's good that he called. Perhaps he'll call again later.'

Betty is not lying but she is not telling the truth either. Ahmed has noticed this in people. He saw it in his father when his mother came back from the prison, and in the end they all became part of the lie. 'She'll get better,' they said. 'She will be fine.' It was easier to pretend. But it didn't help.

'Yes,' he says.

He hopes the disappointment does not show in his face.

⚜ ⚜ ⚜

'Was that your daddy on the phone?' Savannah is sitting cross-legged by the pond, that blonde-haired doll she sometimes plays with lying in her arms.

'Yes.'

'When is he coming back?'

A bat flies overhead, its dark shape zigzagging against the golden sky. 'I don't know. When he's found my sister, I suppose.'

'Will you go back to Libya with him?'

He shrugs. 'I don't know.'

'Mummy says we might be moving to America.' Savannah twists the arm on her doll and throws it into the long grass. In the shadowy darkness the doll's long pale legs stick up like bones.

'Don't you want to live in America?'

'No, I want to stay here.'

The hens cluck softly and a breeze sighs in the trees.

'It might not be forever,' Ahmed says. 'You'll soon make new friends. When I came to England I couldn't even speak English. At least they speak English in America.'

'I suppose.'

A sudden rustling in the bamboo makes Savannah sit bolt upright. 'What's that?'

Ahmed wants to say that it's Betty's cat but no cat makes such a crashing noise. He jumps to his feet and tightens his fists. He does not want to admit he is afraid. What if it is one of those boys?

Savannah clutches at his sleeve. 'Oh, what is it? Perhaps it's the monster.'

'There isn't a monster.' He wants to sound strong but his voice is less than the whispers in the trees.

Crash, crash, crash. Now it comes into view, ghostly in the gloom, not human. A large, lumbering creature. Ahmed claps a hand over his mouth and Savannah yelps.

'It's a badger,' Ahmed shouts. How happy he is to see it, and relieved. He's never seen a badger before. What a magnificent animal it is with its long snout and striped face. The badger sniffs and peers at them for a moment, before lumbering off in the direction of the hen coop.

Savannah giggles. 'Were you scared? I was.'

'A little,' Ahmed answers.

'I really thought it was the monster. Do you believe in monsters?'

He doesn't know how to answer Savannah's question. It's true that he no longer believes in fictitious monsters, but that doesn't mean monsters don't exist in the real world. He has begun to realise that it is humans who can be the monsters, humans who create chaos, who make wars and kill. The thought knots up his stomach.

A sudden 'boo' in his ear makes him jump.

'That scared you,' Savannah says, giggling again. And they both fall to the ground, pealing with laughter.

The sky turns a deeper blue and the evening star begins to sparkle, solitary and splendid. It is time to return to the house. The light fades. The Japanese wind flowers glow like eyes. And later it rains, the drops making small crackling sounds on the dry leaves.

Chapter Eight

A long and monotonous day. Explosions continue across the city and the rattle of machine-gun fire is almost constant. A long, tense day with nothing to do but wait and wait until the waiting is almost a torture. Then, in the late afternoon, a shouting in the street – '*Malashy, shafshoufa,* it's nothing, Gaddafi!' – sends Mohamed and Nafissa hurrying to the window. A group of local men is building a blockade at the end of the street out of piles of old mattresses, chairs and worn car tyres.

'Take that chair down for me, will you?' Nafissa says. She points to the rickety wooden chair that sits under the photograph of the Ubari lakes. 'I don't need it.'

Mohamed manoeuvres the chair down the concrete stairs and out onto the street. But when he starts to ask questions, the men are reluctant to answer.

'It's a precaution,' one man says. 'Nothing more.'

Mohamed retreats inside. Nafissa makes a few telephone calls. 'I'm looking for Jasmine,' he hears her say each and every time. But she has no luck. And so they continue to sit, saying little, fidgeting with their hands, listening to the steady sound of gunfire in the distance and the time passes slowly, slowly.

At last the sun dips behind the buildings, casting long shadows in the apartment. The smoke drifting across the rooftops turns momentarily red. Finally, the call for evening prayer echoes out from the minarets across the city.

'I should go and pray at the mosque,' Mohamed says. 'It is not right for me to continue to pray at home.'

'Please don't go tonight,' Nafissa says. 'Not with all that's going on.'

Reluctantly Mohamed agrees. He is doing this for Safia, not for himself, for as Nafissa keeps on reminding him, what good would it be if he were killed? All the same he feels like a coward. He rolls out the *sajjadah* and begins his prayers. Yet the call, instead of stopping, continues on and on: *la ilaha illa-Allah, la ilaha illa-Allah.* He can hardly concentrate for the sound of it.

When Nafissa hands him three dates, the traditional way of breaking the day's fast, she says excitedly, 'This is the signal.'

'What signal?'

'The fight for Tripoli. A call to arms.' She goes to the window. 'I can't see anything.'

'Before we eat, I will go outside and check.'

The street is eerily quiet. Mohamed has barely walked two steps when a shadowy figure looms out from the darkness. For a heart-stopping moment Mohamed thinks it is the man who took him that night, but it is not.

The man hisses, 'Stay inside, grandfather. It will be over soon.'

'Is there nothing I can do?'

'It is best you return to your house.'

The man dissolves into the darkness. Mohamed walks up the concrete stairs and back into the apartment. As he does he hears the sound of gunfire.

Mohamed turns over and over in the bed until the sheet is wrapped round him like a shroud. Boom, boom. Tat-tat-tat-tat-tat. Boom. A machinegun. Shots. Explosions. Anxiously, he untangles himself from the bedclothes and peers out under the blind. Tracer fire lights up the sky and exposes the rash of rooftop aerials and satellite dishes. But when the sulphurous blaze vanishes, Mohamed can see nothing but the city lights blinking in the darkness.

Nafissa crashes into something in the room next door and he calls out to ask if she is all right. A moment later she appears at his door, blanketed in an oversized dressing gown. 'I can't sleep.'

'No one can sleep.'

She wanders off and his eyes close. Another loud explosion shakes the apartment block, and he is wide-awake. Throwing off the bedclothes, he lifts the blind again. A plume of smoke is rising in the distance. Now a siren sounds, and another. He sits on the edge of the bed and bites at his nails. This is it. This will decide everything, it is out of his hands and there is some relief in that. Later, perhaps, he will have a role to play but for now he can do nothing, just as the man said.

Another blast, louder, rattling at the windows. Mohamed smiles. Allah has decided to test everyone in the city tonight: only the deaf and the dead could sleep through such noise.

'Wake up! It is time for *sahoor.*'

'What time is it?' Mohamed calls. He must have fallen asleep after all. He switches on the sidelight. At least the electricity is still working.

'A little after four.'

In the bathroom, he splashes his face and hands with cold water. His face stares out at him from the mirror, haggard and tired, the growth on his chin like frosted stubble in an English field. He picks up the comb and runs it through his hair. That at least has remained thick and dark, though it is threaded with silver in places.

'I have *bsisa* for you this morning,' Nafissa says, when Mohamed finds his way into the kitchen. 'I know you are fond of it.'

Nour always prepared *bsisa* for Ramadan.

'Here.' Nafissa lays the plate in front of him. 'Taste.'

He takes a spoonful of the *bsisa,* savouring the familiar mix of sweetness and bitter cumin. 'It is good, very good. Oh, how I have missed Libyan food.'

'You must have missed more than just the food.' Nafissa brings him a cup of black tea and sits opposite. The circles under her eyes are as dark as bruises.

'Did you sleep?'

She throws her hands in the air. 'Sleep? I thought we were going to be hit by a rocket. How could I sleep?' She takes a sip of the tea but leaves the plate untouched.

'Aren't you going to eat? Or have you poisoned the *bsisa*?'

'I'm not hungry.' She pushes at the *bsisa* with her spoon, does not smile at his joke. Not that he blames her.

'You must eat,' he says, shaking his finger at her. 'And you know how we men like to be obeyed.'

This time she smiles, though faintly. 'Things are changing, Mohamed. Even here in Libya. Women are not like they used to be. All the same, I will try the *bsisa*. You are right. I should eat.'

She eats but two spoonfuls. He understands. The *bsisa* is delicious but his appetite too is gone.

After the *sahoor* meal Mohamed recites verses from the Qur'an. But he would do so even if bullets were raining out of the sky.

⚜ ⚜ ⚜

When Mohammed wakes again, the bed-cover is striped with shadows from the slatted blind. He checks his watch – one-thirty – and taps the face anxiously. Surely it cannot be that late. Oh, but he has forgotten, the watch no longer works, it must have broken during his interrogation. But it must be late for the sun is already burning in the city sky.

He finds Nafissa lying on the sofa watching television with the sound turned down. 'What garbage are they spewing out today?' Mohamed asks, staring at the screen.

She shrugs. 'The usual. Gaddafi was broadcasting again but I couldn't catch all the words. He kept on mumbling about purifying the city of rats. The sound was so bad I thought perhaps he was broadcasting from the sewers himself.'

Mohamed laughs. 'The rat-hunter turned rat?'

Nafissa smiles, but her smile is like half of an equation, it goes nowhere. 'I wonder where he is. You don't think he's still in Tripoli after all this bombing, do you?'

'I don't know.' Mohamed sits in the armchair, his hands on his knees, peering intently at the television screen as if willing it to give him an answer.

'He'll never leave Libya. There are rumours that he's fled south, that's he's hiding out in the desert somewhere.' Nafissa sighs and cups her chin in her hands in a gesture that reminds him of Nour. 'No matter where he is, he can still rally support. We shouldn't underestimate him.'

Now the young woman presenter, a known Gaddafi supporter, brandishes a Kalashnikov on air.

'That's too much! Do they think we are idiots?' Nafissa's face burns with indignation and she jumps up and switches the television off. 'I wish I had bought a satellite dish so we didn't have to watch such rubbish. But satellite is expensive, Mohamed. I don't know how people afford it.'

'Doesn't anyone else have it in the block?'

She frowns. 'Yes, but who knows if they are informants, secret police. You have forgotten what it is like to live here. Who informed on you? Perhaps it was the man upstairs or the family living on the ground floor. None of us can be certain who is whispering. You of all people must remember that.' She bangs her fist on the coffee table. 'Four decades of fear! How can we have lived with it? Are we to blame for keeping silent?'

'You know what happened to those who talked.' Mohamed walks to the window. The street below is empty, but close to the city centre another large plume of grey smoke is billowing into the air.

'Public executions! Hangings! Disappearances!' Nafissa hits the table again but then she crumples and the tears spill down her cheeks.

'Nafissa,' Mohamed says. 'My dear Nafissa.'

That Sunday will remain in Mohamed's memory forever. Etched in his mind like his wife's death. Like Safia in that cage. All day the bombardment continues. All day the guns and rockets, the acrid smoke drifting across the city. All day he and Nafissa sit, hardly speaking, glued to the television. But without satellite or the internet they are starved of real news and when Mohamed ventures out to the corner shop to see if he can find Ali or his son, he finds the place shuttered and closed.

He and Nafissa do not speak of Safia, but her absence seems to fill the very air they breathe.

Perhaps it is already too late.

The afternoon is almost gone when a sudden change reaches their ears – a commotion, a cacophony of car horns, a steady volley of gunshots.

Nafissa almost drops the Qu'ran she is holding. 'That's not random shooting, Mohamed. Listen!' She puts her hand to her ear. 'That is celebratory gunfire!' Her tired, grey face turns light and hopeful.

'Maybe,' Mohamed answers cautiously.

Now the chanting of many voices streams in through the open window: *Allahu Akbar, Allahu Akbar. God is great. God is great.*

'I'll go down and take a look.'

'You're not going without me, not this time.' Nafissa picks up her headscarf. 'You can't be trusted.'

'OK, but if I say run, you must run as fast as you can.'

'Do you really think that running can save us from a sniper's bullet?'

A sound of breaking glass. Mohamed flinches.

Nafissa dashes to the window. 'People are coming out onto the street!' Her voice is as excitable as a young girl's. 'This is it, the freedom we have been waiting for.' She pulls at his arm. 'Come on!'

The main road in the neighbourhood is thronged with people and everyone, old and young, is cheering and shouting. '*Hurriya, hurriya*! Freedom, freedom!' The excitement is like something you could almost hold in your hands.

'Praise Allah!' Nafissa says. She clutches at the sleeve of his shirt. 'We have waited so long for this.'

Mohamed holds back. He cannot quite believe that victory can come this quickly. All the same, when, five minutes later, a convoy of rebel trucks rumbles down the pot-holed road flying the new flag, his doubts begin to ease.

'I wish Nour could have lived to witness this,' he says and hot, salty tears course down his cheeks, to his embarrassment.

Nafissa squeezes his hand. 'I wish it too.'

An old man totters out from the crowd and kisses one of the green, white and black flags that flutter from every vehicle. The crowd roars and the rebels fire their guns into the air and Mohamed is forced to put his hands to his ears.

'Who would think that a flag could inspire such emotion,' Nafissa says, when the commotion has died down a little. She is standing on tiptoe to get a better view. 'I'm so happy we are to rid ourselves of that plain green square. The sight of it makes me feel quite sick.'

Mohamed taps her arm. '*Our deeds are the colour of white, our battles are black, our meadows green and our swords red.* Those words were written by an Iraqi poet. I'm afraid I have forgotten his name.'

Nafissa throws back her head and laughs. 'However did Safia and I manage without our daily diet of quotations?'

'With great difficulty, no doubt,' Mohamed says cheerfully. But as soon as the words are out of his mouth, his spirits sink. How can he even think of celebrating while his daughter is in that unspeakable place? He blinks against the harsh sunlight and an image of a young woman sprawled out on a concrete floor replaces the cheering crowds. Her eyes are wide open; they stare not at this world but at the one beyond.

He shudders.

'What's wrong?' Nafissa asks. 'Surely you are not cold?'

'I am worried for Safia. People who have nothing to lose are dangerous.'

Nafissa sighs. 'Have faith, Mohamed. We will place copies of Safia's photograph all over the city. Someone will recognise her.'

He cannot share Nafissa's optimism. 'Time is running out,' he says.

'If something had happened to her I would know it.' Nafissa places a hand across her chest. 'I would feel it in my heart.'

'Yes,' he says, though he doubts her faith. How can she remain so relentlessly optimistic in the face of such odds? He closes his eyes again, trying to picture Safia as she was, smiling and full of life, but all he can see is that dark, stinking cage.

They push on. The entire population appears to be out on the street: women, children, babies, the old. A wizened woman leaning on a stick. A huge, bearded man carrying a guitar. A kid dribbling a football. A young man with a bandaged head. A small girl dressed head to toe in pink. And through everything drifts the smell of sweat, petrol fumes and cigarette smoke, and sometimes a heady scent of perfume. But above the throng, the sun burns merciless and indifferent.

At the edge of the neighbourhood they come across a checkpoint, manned by three armed fighters. Mohamed is about to order Nafissa to turn back when she shouts, 'Ali! What are you doing here? Shouldn't you be behind your counter?'

'My dear Nafissa.' Ali beams and, to Mohamed's astonishment, flings his arms around Nafissa. 'What a day! The city is liberated. We're making history. ' He turns and slaps Mohamed on the back. 'What a time to come home, eh?'

'The whole of the city is free?' Mohamed has no wish to squash anyone's enthusiasm but the news seems doubtful.

'There are pockets of resistance but I do not think they will last long.' Ali fingers his ammunition belt as if he had always carried it. 'You must have heard the call for prayer last night. That was our signal.'

Mohamed feels ashamed. What has he done to help the revolution? All he has done is sit in Nafissa's apartment while others have risked their lives.

'Is there any sign of the Gaddafi family?' Nafissa asks.

'There are rumours Saif has been captured, that Mohammed has surrendered but as for the man himself, nothing. Our people are already on their way to his palace.' Ali groans and moves his hands to his lower back. 'Standing all day like this makes my back ache. I am not so young as I was.'

'None of us are,' Nafissa says, smiling.

Ali's feet are shod only in a pair of cheap, plastic sandals. Is this all he has to fight in? As for storming Gaddafi's citadel, that hardly seems possible. The place is surrounded by a thick concrete wall and there are watchtowers, perhaps even secret tunnels. Yes, the rebels have NATO help but they have no boots on the ground, only men like Ali with his sandals.

Ali turns to the man next to him, a burly, bearded man dressed in green fatigues. At least this man is wearing good, strong boots. 'Meet my friend, Desert Lion. He's just arrived from Al Zawiyah.'

Mohamed extends his hand. 'Desert Lion is not my real name,' the man says, smiling broadly. 'But now everyone has a new name.'

'Do you have one, Ali?' Mohamed asks.

'I am Ali Baba, who else?'

'Where are your forty thieves?'

The joke is forced. But Ali grins and slaps Mohamed on the back again. 'I see you have not lost your sense of humour.' He points to the crowd. 'Here are my thieves.' His grin widens, then falls away. 'My son told me that you went out looking for Safia. We will do everything we can to find her.'

'Thank you,' Mohamed says. 'I know you will.'

Ali whistles through his teeth. The middle tooth, Mohamed notes, is missing, the remainder blackened. So much for Gaddafi's health reforms, he thinks, his promises to the masses.

'Many people are lost,' Ali continues. 'It will be a huge task to find everyone but do not despair.' He catches Mohamed's eye. 'Despair is not an option.' He turns back to Nafissa, softening his voice a little. 'We owe Safia and Nafissa a huge debt. Without their help, and others like them, we would not be here today.'

'It was nothing,' Nafissa says, her face as serene as the Ubari lakes.

⚜ ⚜ ⚜

It is late when Mohamed and Nafissa walk to the main square to join in the celebrations. Mohamed was reluctant to go but Nafissa insisted.

Halfway to the square they meet a group of young men flying the new flag. The men are standing on the corner, dressed in dirty jeans and T-shirts and carrying heavy weapons. They look exhausted, as if they had not slept in weeks. 'Be careful,' one of them warns, as they pass. 'The green slime is not quite disappeared. We are still taking some casualties.'

'Thank you for the warning.' Mohamed takes out the picture of Safia from his wallet. 'This is my daughter.'

The men listen patiently to his story. They peer at the photograph and shake their heads. 'Try posting her picture up,' the youngest says. 'There is a place in the square for that. I hope you find her. But many people are missing, father.'

Mohamed looks away. The word 'father' makes him want to weep.

'She's my niece,' Nafissa says. She has been silent up till then. 'You owe her, brothers. She smuggled ammunition for men like you.'

'We'll do all we can,' one says. 'Give me your address and number. If we find her, we'll bring her home, *insha'Allah*.'

'Why didn't you tell me before?' Mohamed blurts out, once they have moved on. 'Didn't you trust me?'

'It's not a question of trust, Mohamed. You were in England, or have you forgotten?' Nafissa's voice is hard-edged.

He shrinks into his jacket. How small and useless he feels. 'Ammunition? Surely that was dangerous?'

'Everything was dangerous, walking in the street, talking, thinking.' Nafissa flicks her fingers as if he were a fly. 'To stand back and watch people being slaughtered, to lose the possibility of freedom, now that would have killed us.'

'How did you do it?'

'Safia and I used to drop off bullets at the perfumery, the place you used to buy perfume for Nour. We named the bullets "stoppers" – after the stoppers in perfume bottles.'

'That place?' He is surprised. He had always considered them die-hard supporters of the regime.

'We hid everything there.'

'They must know something.'

'I have already asked.' Nafissa peers at him through narrowed eyes. 'What's the matter, Mohamed, don't you approve?'

'It is not that.' He hesitates. 'I don't blame you, Nafissa, but if Safia had kept out of this...'

She turns to face him, her arms folded across her chest and he is struck by how much she resembles her sister – his wife – in their early days together. That obstinate stare. The set of her lips. 'You weren't here, Mohamed. You made your choice. Safia and I made ours. Neither is better than the other. Blame, on the other hand, only plays into the regime's hands. Now, come on, let's get to the square before we miss everything.'

The square, like the street earlier, is packed. There are cheers, embraces, smiles and laughter. Tears too. In the old days fear permeated everything. It ran like a silent poison through people's hearts and minds. Whenever there was any sort of celebration, it felt staged and wooden. Tonight Mohamed can sense pure, spontaneous joy.

'Look,' Nafissa says, pointing to a group of young men burning green flags and tearing down posters of Gaddafi. 'Imagine doing that only a day ago.'

'It's over, frizz-head,' people chant. 'It's over!'

Maybe not just yet, Mohamed thinks, but he too raises a cheer.

CHAPTER NINE

Betty and Ahmed are watching the news. The rebels are inside Gaddafi's walled compound at Bab-Al-Aziziyah, flying the new Libyan flag and a young fighter is trying on Gaddafi's hat. The whole thing seems impossible. Astonishing. Ahmed is watching with such intent that Betty wonders if he might be looking for his father among the crowds of fighters. Not that there is any real possibility. But where is Mohamed? There has been no word from him in days.

'Why is it called Babel-Ziya?' Savannah asks.

Betty plumps up the cushion slipped behind her back. 'It's not Babel – although that's perhaps a better name – it's Bab-Al-Aziziyah. In Arabic it means Splendid Gate.'

The cameras are now showing bombed-out buildings in the compound; many are already covered in layers of graffiti.

'It's not splendid, it's horrible.' Savannah wrinkles her nose as if she were sniffing one of Betty's fish-paste sandwiches.

'I suppose the name sounded imposing, though it's quite a mess now. Mind you, I don't think it ever was very splendid.'

'Look!' Savannah jumps up and points to the screen. 'I wish I had a sofa like that.'

Betty snorts. 'That thing?' The news team has moved into the living quarters of the Gaddafi family and the camera is focussed on a gilded sofa, one end of which has been carved into the likeness of a mermaid. 'It belonged to the dictator's daughter. That's her face. Goodness, how vain.'

'Well, I think it's pretty.' Savannah sounds peevish. 'Who's going to have it now?'

'I expect it will get smashed up and burnt.'

Savannah scrapes back her hair and tucks it into her gold plastic Alice band. 'That's not right. They should give it to a poor person.'

Ahmed has been sitting silently, chewing on his fingernails, but now he grins at Betty and Betty gives him a sly wink. 'I don't think anyone will want something that reminds them of the bad old days. They'll want to make something new.'

'When I'm rich I'm going to have a sofa like that.'

'Just so long as you don't behave like the Gaddafi family.'

'I'll be peaceful. I won't have any wars and I'll allow people to make horrible pictures of me if they want. But they won't want to.'

'So, you're going to be a ruler, are you?'

Savannah sits down on the rug and crosses her bare legs. 'I'll be a *benivelont* ruler.'

'I think you mean benevolent. It means to do good.'

'Why was that man bad, Betty?' A picture of Gaddafi wearing his trademark mustard Bedouin style robe and *checheya* cap has flashed up on the screen.

Betty hesitates. What answer can she give the girl? 'I'm not sure he started out bad,' she says carefully. She glances at Ahmed but his eyes are glued to the set again.

'Apples aren't bad on the tree,' Savannah continues. 'They just turn horrible when they drop on the ground and worms get inside them.'

'Yes, it is something like that.'

Savannah steps in front of the television set, takes off her Alice band and waves it imperiously. 'Your honour,' she says, taking a bow. 'I command you to give me this mermaid sofa.'

'Please move,' Betty says. 'We want to watch.'

Savannah shuffles sideways. 'But you've been watching all day.'

'This is important, historic.'

'Well, I'm going out.' Savannah flings open the door and Betty watches her march down the garden path and out of view.

She turns back to the television. The sculpture Gaddafi commissioned after the American bombing of Libya in 1986 – a huge hand squeezing an American fighter plane, a real gesture of defiance –

is on screen. She wonders how the history of Libya could have played out differently and what might lie ahead. The path to a new and stable future will be a long one, of that she is in no doubt. But for the first time in decades she sees hope for the country that will always have a place in her heart.

The clock chimes in the hall. Napoleon wanders in and settles himself on a cushion. Betty glances out of the window but Savannah is out of sight. 'What's happening?' she asks. Ahmed still hasn't spoken a word.

'There are fighters in the palace and everything is smashed up. Why do they do that?'

'They're angry, Ahmed, and when people are angry they sometimes do bad things.'

Ahmed frowns and leans towards the television, his hands clasped, the nails almost digging into his skin. It must be hard for him watching this, waiting for his father to phone with news.

She switches off the set. 'I think that's enough for now. We can catch up again later.'

'OK.' His face is pale.

'Let's try telephoning your father, shall we?'

Betty does not say that she has tried already; that no one answered.

In the darkness of the bamboo patch, a breeze rustles the papery leaves. Once Ahmed hears the patter of a bird, but there is nothing else, not even Betty's thin grey cat. As he creeps deeper into the undergrowth he wonders what it would be like to stalk a man with a gun in your hand, to have the power of life and death. What if you were the prey instead? What then? That thought makes him fearful. Why aren't his father and Nafissa at home? Where have they gone?

'Can you see the badger?' Savannah calls from the nettle patch.

'No,' he shouts. 'Badgers are nocturnal.'

He crawls further into the thicket. How dark and silent it is, but there is something comforting about the place too. If you hid in this thicket, you would be safe from danger. But what if you couldn't get out? Then you'd die and your body would rot and nothing would be left but bones. Safia would never disappear of her own accord. If she was staying with a friend she'd have let them know. That's why his father has never said anything; Safia has been taken by the Colonel and his soldiers and they have hidden her somewhere dark and terrible.

Betty says the war isn't over even though the freedom fighters are in Tripoli. She says the fighters have released prisoners from Abu Salim, the famous prison but Ahmed knows there are other prisons across the city, like the one his mother was sent to.

Where is Safia?

Maybe they have killed her.

He crawls back into the light. He is trembling now and he feels nauseous. He gets to his feet. Something is crossing the sky, white and strange, and he blinks though he still cannot tell what it is. A seagull? A plastic bag? He blinks again but now all he can see are stars, millions and millions of them, tiny and faraway.

'Are you all right, Ahmed?'

He must lie down. It is only a slight dizziness.

He hears Savannah jump through the nettles and feels the smallness of her hand in his.

When he opens his eyes there is a blue and green mosaic above his head. The pattern reminds him of the tiles in the old town mosque he and his father used to visit sometimes. He rubs his eyes and the mosaic transforms into clusters of green leaves and patches of blue sky. He isn't in Tripoli. He is in Betty's garden. For this he feels relief, mixed with not a little sadness.

'You fainted.' Savannah is tapping him on the arm. 'But it was only for a minute or I would have fetched Betty.'

Ahmed sits up. The shadows of the trees are long and inky. Gnats whirl in a shaft of light over by the chicken coop.

'Are you OK now?'

'I think so.'

'Your face went very white. Like a ghost's. You looked very funny.' She giggles but then she turns serious. 'You're worried about your sister, aren't you, Ahmed? Do you think she will be all right?'

'I don't know,' he says. 'No one knows.' He turns away from Savannah and plucks at a stalk of long grass. He can feel the tears prickling his eyes and he doesn't want her to see his weakness. Whatever happens he must remain strong. Boys don't cry, do they?

Savannah sits down close by. 'Can I meet her when she comes back?' she says softly.

'When she comes back?' The words surprise him. 'Yes,' he says. 'Oh yes.'

'That's good.' With that, Savannah gets up and cartwheels across the lawn.

There is always a path to the highest mountain. He remembers that now.

Chapter Ten

Nafissa has gone out to help at the new missing person's bureau. She asked Mohamed if he wanted to accompany her, but he refused. He would only have got in the way. Now he is sitting in the overheated apartment with nothing to do except think.

He has just spread out the mat for noon prayers when the intercom buzzes. Perhaps Nafissa has forgotten her key. Reluctantly, he gets up to answer it. 'Is that you, Nafissa?'

A male voice answers. 'No, this is Abdul. Do I have the right address? I am looking for Mohamed.'

'Abdul?'

'We met on the bench by the fountain.'

'Yes, I remember.' Mohamed hesitates, then presses the buzzer to open the downstairs doorway.

'I might have some news,' Abdul says, springing up the stairs.

'What news?' Mohamed calls anxiously from the doorway.

'News of your daughter.' The young man is quite out of breath. Pools of sweat stain his T-shirt, his cheeks are flushed and his eyes are bloodshot, as if he hadn't slept in a while.

'Safia?' Mohamed puts his hand to the wall to steady himself.

Abdul bounds up the final step and embraces Mohamed.

'Please sit down,' Mohamed says, pulling away. He gestures to the sofa and Abdul falls onto it, still breathing heavily, beads of sweat running down his forehead.

'My brother says a young woman escaped from a building the rebels stormed last night. He thinks her name is Safia.'

Mohamed's head begins to spin. 'Where is she now?'

'He is not sure, 'Abdul stutters. 'Maybe a safe house.'

'Why isn't she here? Why hasn't she come home?' Mohamed is bewildered. There is nothing he can grasp at; he is like a man thirsting in the desert, seeing only mirages. He wipes his forehead with the back of his hand. Beads of sweat have formed there. The air conditioner is not working again and it is uncomfortably hot in the small apartment, even with the blinds half-closed.

'I will phone my brother.' Abdul reaches into his pocket and brings out a battered mobile phone. 'Do not worry. It will be all right.' Abdul tries once, twice, three times, but his brother does not answer.

'He is probably busy. He - Sami - he's with the rebels, fighting. I should be with him but I felt I had to come here and bring you this news.' Abdul runs his hands through his damp hair. 'Do you have family? I mean, besides your daughter.'

'A son,' Mohamed says. 'Ahmed.' He thinks of Ahmed so very far away. At least Ahmed is safe but when Mohamed thinks of his son, he feels split in two.

'How old is your son?'

'Eleven.'

Abdul gazes round the apartment. He is looking for evidence of a child, for books and toys. Mohamed does not want to explain that Ahmed is in England. For all he knows, this young man could be a spy, someone to throw him off course, confuse him. Perhaps he is even the one who alerted the *mukhabarat.* The thought of that makes him shiver, despite the heat. How tragic it is, not to be able to trust anyone.

The mobile buzzes. 'Sami!' Abdul moves the device from one ear to the other. 'What?' He looks puzzled; then his lip trembles. 'No. How? When? I understand. Yes. We will talk later.' He snaps the mobile shut and places it on Nafissa's table, adjusting it precisely so that it sits at a perfect ninety-degree angle. Then he cradles his head in his hands and begins to cry quietly.

'Is something wrong?' Perhaps there is more to the story, something Abdul is keeping from him. 'What is it?' Mohamed wants to shake the young man. *What about my daughter? Tell me, where is my daughter?* But the words choke in his throat and he does not utter them.

'My cousin is dead, killed by a Zombie sniper,' Abdul says brokenly.

'Zombie?' Mohamed does not understand.

'We call Gaddafi's supporters the Zombies. Because they do not think. They just follow orders and kill.' Abdul looks up. Tears are streaming down his cheeks. 'My brother saw Harid shot. They drove Harid to the hospital but he died on the way.'

A tear rolls down Mohamed's own cheek. He is still not sure if he can trust this young man but the idea of a man gunned down in his prime distresses him.

'Both of us weeping like women,' Abdul continues. He wipes his eyes on his T-shirt. 'See what the tyrant has done to us.'

'Here, take this.' Mohamed reaches for the box of tissues.

Abdul blows his nose. 'This is so hard for me. Harid and I are...were...the same age and close, like brothers.' He begins to cry again, though softer than before.

The mobile buzzes on the table. Abdul wipes his eyes again and picks it up. 'How is Auntie? Yes...I'm at his house... Yes. What shall we do?' Abdul places the mobile in the pocket of his jeans. 'My brother has more news. He knows where she is, your daughter. Come, come. We must go. My brother is on his way.'

'Now?' Mohamed shakes his head. 'I cannot go now.' He does not know what to do. If only Nafissa were here. She would know. Abdul's tears appear genuine but the whole episode could have been staged. Oh, how will they ever get back to something like normalcy here? This pains him more than he could ever say.

Abdul frowns. 'Is there a problem?'

'I don't know you, or your brother.' It had to be said.

'Of course. I am sorry.' Abdul sits back down. 'And I do understand but how can I convince you? I really want to help.' He puts his hand on his chest. 'My heart is good.' Then he taps his fingers on the edge of the sofa, looks around the room and sighs. 'Ah,' he says, suddenly, picking up the mobile. 'Here, take a look at this. My brother took the photo last night.'

Mohamed peers at the image: a man, clearly Abdul, is burning a green flag on a rooftop.

'I hate that slime.' Abdul presses the mobile into Mohamed's hand. 'Phone my mother if you do not believe me. She will vouch for me, I promise. Please. I will show you the number.'

'There's no need.'

'You are still not sure. I see it in your eyes.'

'I was picked up the other night, here in the street. You know how they work,' Mohamed says angrily.

'I promise that was not me.' Abdul falls to his knees. 'In the name of Allah, the most gracious, most merciful...'

'All right,' Mohamed says. 'I will go with you.'

A dirty white Toyota pick-up truck draws up outside barely ten minutes later. The side of the vehicle is covered in green and red graffiti and two rebel flag stickers have been placed at the top of the dusty windscreen. These people are clearly with the revolution. However, the sight of two young men sitting in the rear next to a heavy machinegun unnerves him. The young men may be with the revolution but the vehicle is a sitting duck. To get in that truck is to court death, whichever side you are on. But what choice does he have if he is to find Safia? He has to take this chance. And if that means his death, so be it. He has sat around long enough. It is time to act.

Abdul shouts a greeting to the two men, walks up to the driver's door and opens it. As Mohamed watches the two brothers embrace, he feels like an intruder.

'Come, come!' Abdul shouts.

'Welcome,' Sami says, proffering his hand. His eyes are shaded by dark glasses, his chin covered in several days of beard growth. Like the others he is dressed in civilian clothes – jeans, a yellow T-shirt, a leather bracelet on his right wrist. 'We will do what we can to help you.'

'I am sorry to hear of the death of your cousin,' Mohamed says, squeezing into the middle seat.

'Yes, it is a sad day for us. But victory is almost ours now.' Sami's voice is hard, as if he didn't care what had happened to his cousin. Mohamed knows this to be a lie. He understands, perhaps more than most, the way a wound cannot always be seen and he hopes that Sami's bravado will not later descend into something dark. But he has little time to think;

Sami shoves the truck into gear and they move off down the street, swerving several times to avoid the potholes.

'Is it far?'

'No,' Sami replies. 'Not far.'

The main highway is chaos. There are rebel trucks everywhere, horns blaring and once a volley of gunfire comes in their direction, although whether it's from Gaddafi supporters or mistaken fire from the rebels, Mohamed cannot tell. Sami curses and leans on his horn but they are not hit. Mohamed closes his eyes and tries to conjure up Betty's garden – the sweet smell of the roses, the lazy buzz of bees, the clouds white and slow – he cannot.

The truck skids to a halt outside Gaddafi's compound. Surely Safia is not here? Mohamed stares out of the window, his eyes straining against the glare. The area is littered with men of all ages, carrying weapons and firing from the back of their camouflaged pick-up trucks, everyone shouting *'Allahu akbar, allahu akbar'* and the air is thick with smoke and diesel fumes. He is about to ask what they are doing when, without a word of explanation, Sami dives out of the vehicle and accosts a giant of a man who is dressed in army fatigues.

'Why have we stopped?'

Abdul shrugs. 'I don't know.'

While they wait, Mohamed's eyes are drawn to the scrubby grass close to the compound wall. The scene here is something he never wishes to witness again. Not far away from where they are, the bodies of three young Gaddafi supporters lie, faces to the ground, hands tied with plastic tape behind their backs. The three men can only be in their twenties and all are black- skinned. None are in military uniform. They are clothed in T-shirts and ragged trousers, their feet shod in cheap rubber plimsolls.

This is the brutality of war. Young men on both sides dying in the most horrible circumstances. He looks away. A few metres from the dead men are several burnt-out tents, small piles of discarded clothes and three plastic chairs, deformed by heat.

'*Allahu akbar!*' the men shout. Their guns blaze and smoke rises into the sky like a great djinn, and a bitter taste rises into Mohamed's mouth.

Sami returns and they move off again. Mohamed is confused. 'Where's my daughter?'

'We are going there now.' Sami presses his foot hard on the accelerator. The truck veers left down a side street, and soon halts in front of a nondescript concrete building. 'This is it,' Sami says and Abdul goes running inside.

'Shall I go too?' Mohamed pushes forward on the seat. His back is slick with sweat.

'Wait,' Sami orders.

Abdul is back within seconds. 'No, this is not the place.'

'I'll make some calls,' Sami says.

Sweat prickles Mohamed's back. His mouth is dry, his hands clammy and there is a griping sensation in his stomach. The tension he feels is almost too much to bear and yet bear it he must.

'Yes, yes,' Sami says to whoever is on the end of the phone. He sounds impatient. He finishes the call and places the mobile on the dusty dashboard. 'We have to go elsewhere,' he says to Mohamed. 'It's not far.'

This time they park in a smart residential street. Trembling, Mohamed gets out and follows Abdul towards a spacious white edifice, surrounded by a garden of palm trees and oleander bushes. They walk up the low steps and into a large tiled hallway swarming with men and thick with cigarette smoke. The majority of the men are casually dressed although some – perhaps a quarter – wear military-style uniforms. The new flag is everywhere and the men appear relaxed, even exuberant. But Mohamed is in turmoil; the words he last spoke to his daughter run round his head like an incessant drum-roll. *She is no longer my daughter. No longer. No longer.*

He is distracted by the sight of Sami approaching a man in an elegant grey suit. Words are exchanged although Mohamed cannot hear through the hubbub of noise. The man clicks his fingers and Mohamed, along with Sami and Abdul, are led into a side room. A hush descends like a thick fog, cutting out all the noise from the lobby. The room is carpeted pale blue and a chandelier hangs from the centre of the ceiling like a wave of tears. Under the window, which looks out onto a green lawn, there is an Ottoman with gilded legs and a brocade cover. After the chaos of the streets it is as if he had walked into a dream, another world.

'The man Sami just spoke to thinks this woman might be your daughter,' Abdul whispers, pointing to a modern sofa which looks oddly out of place amongst the Italian style décor. 'I hope you won't be disappointed. Sami and I will wait outside.'

Three women are seated on the sofa. The two women each side sit silent and upright and both wear plain beige head scarves, which contrast with their dark *abayas.* In between sits a younger, slighter woman, her head bowed, her hands motionless in her lap.

It is her, is it not? Yes, yes.

He takes a step forward. 'Safia, Safia,' he calls. His legs have turned weak and the room blurs in and out of focus. Come on, come on, he says to himself. Don't let her down at the last minute. Come on.

The woman on the right glances his way. Her face is creased and lined. She meets his eyes for a moment, then pats the young woman lightly on her shoulder and whispers something.

'Safia,' Mohamed repeats, his words hanging in the stifling air.

Does she not see him?

It seems as if minutes pass yet in reality it can only be seconds. Mohamed's heart beats fast in his chest, sweat trickles down his back, his hands shake, he feels nauseous. Safia, turn. Safia, look at me. Finally, she lifts her head. Praise Allah! His baby, his beloved daughter. Oh, how long it is since he last set eyes on her. And he sees her as she was when she was a tiny baby, wrapped in a shawl, plump and smiling, a curl of dark hair falling onto her forehead, her chin dimpled by her smile. Then he sees a serious little girl, heading out for her first day at school, her backpack almost as large as she is, that she refuses to let anyone carry.

Now he sees his daughter as she is today, a grown woman, courageous like his wife. But she is trembling and there is a vivid purple bruise around her eye.

Another step, his hand outstretched.

Still she does not move. Nothing moves but the motes of dust in the air. Outside the shouts of the men suddenly float into the room, but here, all is silent.

'Safia!'

She is on her feet. In his arms. Nothing else matters, nothing at all.

Chapter Eleven

The walls of Nafissa's apartment are like hands pressing against him, squeezing the air from his chest. 'Why won't she talk?' Mohamed says. He can hear the anxiety in his own voice.

Safia is asleep on her bed, still in her clothes.

'She's exhausted. Give her time.'

'She hardly spoke on the way back.' On the return journey, they sat squashed up together in the front seat of the truck and Safia held on to the door handle and would not look at him, seemed almost to shrink from his presence. And yet in that room in front of strangers she had leant her head on his shoulder and let him wrap his arms around her.

'What did you expect? She's in shock.'

Gunshots ring down the street. Shouts. Footsteps.

'What was that?'

Nafissa shrugs. 'It's normal. It will be normal for some time to come. Though I hope for not too long. We have suffered enough.' She sighs and leans forward in the chair. 'We talked about Nour the other day but there is something else we need to discuss. If we don't talk of it now, we never will.' Nafissa's feet are bare. Yet she always wears slippers. Why isn't she wearing them now, he wants to ask. As if it mattered.

'Mohamed? Do you hear me?'

An icy cold has crept into his limbs.

'They raped Nour in that prison. Did you know that? Did you?'

He focuses on the photograph of the lake. The water is limpid and clear, the mirrored reflection of the palm trees perfect. Perhaps the photograph is a lie. It is possible, Ahmed told him. Computers manipulate. Things are not always as they seem.

'Mohamed! I'm talking about your wife.'

His wife. The bruises on her legs, the fear and shame in her eyes. Yes, he knew. He knew and he did nothing. Oh, but he is suffocating. There is no air. He gasps and jerks his head up, tries to speak. Cannot.

'I am not judging, Mohamed. I know you blame yourself for what happened but I also must take a share of that blame, may Allah forgive me.' Nafissa's voice has turned flat and emotionless.

He gulps at the stifling air. 'I didn't know how to save her. Can you understand? And then it was too late.'

'None of us did enough.' Nafissa rests her head in her hands.

'No. We did not.'

The gunshots are gone. It is quiet again outside.

'Did she ever speak to you?' His voice sounds strangled, unlike his own. He does not want to talk of this. Not now. Not ever. But it seems he must.

Nafissa sits up. 'I would have told you, Mohamed, if she had.' She pauses. 'Although there was one day – I thought she was a little better – when I asked if she had been harmed by any man in that prison. Those were my exact words. I remember them well. She looked into my eyes and for a moment I caught a flicker of her old self. She laughed and said, "Say what you mean, Nafissa. Don't speak in riddles." I repeated my question but this time I said, "I meant harmed you as a woman." She laughed again but her eyes had gone dead. Then she grabbed my arm, hurting me, and said, "We are never to speak of this again. I absolutely forbid it." Now I think I was wrong in not pursuing the matter. Now, I think we should have done more. Perhaps if we had, she might still be with us.'

Nafissa is right though he is the one who should have done more. He is the one whose pride got in the way. A man's pride. A husband's pride. But now he must think of Safia and Ahmed. They are what matters. It is time to shed the guilt and the sorrow; he has carried them far too long.

Mohamed gets up and rests his hand on Nafissa's shoulder. '*Silence is medication for sorrow.* What is done is done.' He feels calmer. As if some of the weight were already lifted from him. 'How much does Safia know?'

'We have talked of Nour but not of this.' She lifts his hand from her shoulder and clasps it. 'Oh, how I wish you didn't have to make the journey back to England.'

'I need to collect Ahmed. This is our country and we need to be a family again. It has been too long.'

'I understand. It is what I want too.' Nafissa releases his hand and he steps away. 'Mohamed?'

'Yes?'

'What if something should happen to you on the way?' She chews anxiously at a nail.

'I have to take the risk. I have no choice.'

'And if you do not return? What happens to Ahmed then?'

'Call Betty. She will come to Tripoli with Ahmed, if that is necessary. Hashim would come but the truth is, I would prefer Betty to accompany Ahmed.'

'She would do that?' Nafissa raises her eyebrows a fraction.

'Yes, I believe so.'

'She must be a good woman, this Betty.' Nafissa smiles mischievously.

'I trust her,' Mohamed says. 'That is what matters.' All the same, he feels the colour rise in his cheeks.

⚜ ⚜ ⚜

'Safia,' Mohamed whispers, sitting on the edge of the bed. She is curled up tight and her long dark hair – so reminiscent of Nour's in her youth – spills across the cover. She stirs and murmurs something but does not wake. He continues to sit, staring at her face and listening to her breathing, as he did when she was small. He does not know how long he sits. Perhaps half an hour. Perhaps it is more. Her eye is swollen, the bruise angry. Yet she sleeps without moving, as if nothing disturbed her.

He shifts on the edge of the bed. He should leave. There will be time. He need not be too hasty. But now her eyelids flicker and suddenly she is looking right into his eyes.

He reaches for her hand.

'Father,' she says weakly.

'How are you? I see they hurt you. Did they hurt you?'

She grimaces at him through cracked lips. 'It's only a black eye.'

Has she forgiven him? He can only hope. 'A black eye? Nothing more?' The fear of what might have happened to her is a black pit in his stomach.

'I'm all right, Father, really. Just a little tired.'

'I'll get you some water. You must drink.'

'It is Ramadan.'

'Even so. You are dehydrated.'

She sits up and gives his hand a squeeze. 'If you insist.' She shakes her head. 'It is true, they did not give me much to drink or eat in that place and the food I did receive was disgusting, worse than you'd feed a dog.'

'I am sorry,' he says.

He looks around the room. How cramped and shabby it is in here. Nafissa keeps the apartment spotlessly clean but she has little money for repairs or frivolous items. When they had to move, Mohamed offered Nafissa some of their surplus furniture, but she did not have room to accommodate more than one or two pieces. In their old house, Safia had a spacious room looking out over the courtyard with its fig tree and oleanders: none of them ever imagined how quickly that place would become just a memory.

'Sorry?' Safia repeats. 'Yes, there is a great deal to be sorry about.' Her eyes are two dark pebbles, her mouth now set in a tight line. He is not forgiven then. He ought to have explained. But the moment has passed.

⚜ ⚜ ⚜

'Ahmed!' The back door opens and Betty comes flying out of the house. He has never seen her move so fast. 'It's your father on the phone!'

He opens his mouth to speak but no words form and when he tries to put one foot in front of the other it is as if he were in a dream, as if his legs had taken root in the path, like the weeds Betty complains of.

'Ahmed. Your father. On the phone.'

The receiver is lying on the table in the hallway. A polished table of dark wood. There is a small drawer in the table, edged with paler wood. He has never noticed it before.

He reaches out. The receiver is warm and slightly sticky to the touch.

A deep breath. 'Father?'

'Ahmed,' his father says.

His real name. Perhaps this is a good sign.

'I am sorry I did not phone before.'

'It's OK.' Ahmed glances at his reflection in the polished surface of the wood. How strange it looks, all shadowy and dark. Like another being. Something that exists in another place. A ghost. Like his mother.

'Are you still there?'

'Yes.' He wants to ask about Safia but he is afraid.

'Wait. I have someone who wishes to speak to you.'

In that time of waiting, and it feels like a long time, Ahmed thinks of his mother's bird on the day the three of them set it free; how it perched on the branch, trembling, how he wondered if it was afraid or excited. But perhaps it was neither, only suspended between two worlds – neither flying or falling.

A voice on the line. A crackle. 'Little brother, how are you?'

Is this really his sister?

'Ahmed, why are you silent? Don't you want to speak to me?'

'Are you all right, Safia? Where were you? What happened? How did you get back?' The words tumble out and now he hears her say, 'Hasn't father explained?' and he replies that, no, he knows nothing.

'I was locked up by the *mukhabarat* but the rebels stormed the building and the regime soldiers ran away.'

'Did you have a gun? Did you shoot anyone?'

'No, Ahmed.'

Perhaps he should not have said that for now she sounds tired. He scuffs his feet on the black and white tiles of the hall, looks up and his eye falls on the framed photograph of the young woman who looks so like his sister. 'Did the *mukhabarat* hurt you? Like mother?'

'Like mother?' She is quiet. Only her breathing down the line. 'No,' she says. 'They didn't hurt me.' She pauses again and he wishes he could take the words back. 'My situation was different,' she continues, speaking quickly. 'I was given awful food to eat but no one hurt me, Ahmed, although they asked questions, day and night.'

'What questions?'

She laughs. At least she can laugh. 'Stupid questions. Let's not talk of those people. I don't want ever to think of them again. So, what of you, my dear brother? I hear you are fluent in English. Is that true?'

'I am,' he replies, in English. 'I know a thousand words, Safia. Minnow, mole, mackerel, monster...'

'What is this minnow?' Safia says, also using the English.

'A small fish.' Ahmed thinks of the fish in Betty's pond, how they circle and hide under the weed, how sometimes the light falls on their scales so that they look like ghosts.

'Ah, a fish.'

'Did they ask about Mother?'

He's done it again but this time her voice is soft. 'No, Ahmed. For them two and two equals five.'

'*All that is round is not a cake.* That's what you mean, isn't it?'

'You're getting like Father. Soon you'll be quoting Darwish and Dostoevsky at me.'

She is teasing but he doesn't mind. 'Will you come to England soon?'

'You are coming back here, that's what Father says. I would like to see London again. I often think about the time we went with mother.' She falls silent.

'Uncle Hashim took me to Trafalgar Square. I saw that big column and all the pigeons. Do you remember that, Safia? Do you?'

'Yes, I remember. You ask a lot of questions.' She laughs again. 'You would make an excellent interrogator.' He hears her sigh down the line, a small, soft sigh. 'I'm sorry but I must go now. I promise I will speak to you again soon. *Salaam.*'

'*Salaam.*'

The phone clicks and she is gone. So, he and his father will return to Tripoli, most probably forever. His time in England is coming to an end. He is not sure how he feels about that. Before leaving the hall, he glances at the photograph again and this time the young woman seems to be smiling at him. Soon, perhaps quite soon, he will see Safia's smile again and that thought is definitely a happy one.

Chapter Twelve

Betty is in the kitchen preparing a meal to celebrate the end of Ramadan. It should be a joyous occasion now they have the good news about Ahmed's sister but Betty's heart is like a stone in her chest because today marks another anniversary – one Betty has fought her way through for almost two decades, an anniversary she dreads, one she shares with no one. For now George is gone, only Annette knows.

She and George didn't receive word until the following day. A man called from the Foreign Office. At first Betty thought the call was a hoax; she had always imagined that if something ever happened to Eva she would know. Yet the night before she and George had gone out for a meal together with friends, they'd joked and laughed and all that time Eva had been lying dead in a morgue a thousand miles away and Betty had not felt the slightest shiver of premonition.

An accident, they said. What justice in that? If Eva hadn't been left in that truck in the stifling midday heat, she might never have died. Yet the verdict was clear – accidental death due to an underlying and undetected heart problem.

Betty never talked about Eva's death, except to answer questions from people in the immediate aftermath. Nor did she travel out to Gaza. Eva's body was repatriated, a funeral was held and that was it. Yes, there were cards, condolences and tears but she threw herself into work and tried to forget.

Forget? It is never possible to forget. She thought of little else. For hours and hours each day she would sit at her desk and write reports, study photographs and read articles, but she could not concentrate. She suffered from terrible insomnia and she lost her appetite, could barely eat. George tried to persuade her to see a doctor. She refused. She wanted to deal with the grief alone. Had to. Now she wonders if she was punishing herself.

Why did she not fight the verdict? She could have done that. It would have been a long fight but it would have been worth fighting for, would it not? George spoke of that in the weeks afterwards but she said, no, it would kill me.

Should she not have done things differently?

She picks up Eva's photograph and stares into her daughter's eyes. How she wants to summon up Eva's voice, the scent of her skin, but there is nothing, only the coldness of glass, the smooth edge of the frame. No life. No breath. Just emptiness.

'Can we pick some flowers for the table?'

Betty jumps. It is Savannah. She had not heard the girl's footsteps. 'Go ahead.'

'What are you doing?'

Betty realises she is cradling the photograph like a baby. 'It's Eva, my daughter.'

Savannah gives her a sideways look. 'I know. But why are you holding her picture like that?'

'Today is a special anniversary.'

'Is is her birthday?' Savannah's blue eyes stare up at Betty.

'No.' She wipes the glass with her sleeve and places the photograph back on the shelf. 'Eva died a long time ago. Today is the anniversary of her death.'

She has said it. She has said the words and there has been no thunderclap, no earthquake. She is not even crying.

'What did she die of?'

Betty almost laughs. She still sometimes forgets how direct children can be. 'She had a bad heart and it stopped.' A wave of grief washes over her. But there is guilt too and the guilt is perhaps the worst of it. Three months before Eva made the decision to go to Gaza, Betty told Eva the truth. 'George isn't your real father. Your father is Libyan, he lives in Libya.'

'Why has it taken you so long to tell me?' Eva screamed. 'I'm twenty-one years old, for fuck's sake. I've been able to vote for three years. I'm at university. I have a boyfriend. We even sleep together!'

She remembers the words she said, the excuses she made and she thinks of Delia. They are more alike than she wants to admit. Because Betty knows why she kept the truth from Eva. She was protecting herself, not her daughter. Oddly, Eva didn't ask if George knew. That was unexpected. When the shouting came to an end, Eva picked up her rucksack and stormed out of the house, and when George asked why she'd gone, Betty lied. Yes, she lied. She told George they'd had a row about Eva's boyfriend. George wanted to phone Eva but Betty persuaded George to give Eva time. He was so easy to persuade.

Eva wrote to George telling him of her plans in Gaza and George showed Betty the letter. It mentioned nothing of the boyfriend, and, to Betty's relief, nothing of their argument. Eva went to Gaza that very same month. If Eva hadn't gone to Gaza, she might have lived. The worst of it was that she and Eva did not even speak before Eva left and then it was too late.

'Are you all right, Betty?' Savannah's hand is touching her arm.

'I'm all right, a little sad, perhaps.' She smiles at Savannah. A little sad, yes, that's true. But the shattering grief and guilt is gone now.

'Why did her heart stop? She wasn't an old person.'

'Sometimes even young people's hearts stop working.'

Savannah's hands fly to her chest. 'Oh!' she says.

'Don't worry. Eva was born with a weak heart. Then she was put in a stressful situation and she wasn't able to get to the hospital in time. If there were a problem with your heart, it would have been picked up by now. These days doctors know a lot more. Let's get some scissors so you can cut those flowers. Be careful though, they're rather sharp.'

⚜ ⚜ ⚜

The arrangements for his return to England are giving Mohamed a headache. He will not be taking Safia with him – he cannot risk that. Better to travel alone. He taps the face of his watch. A habit. He still hasn't got used to the idea that it no longer works. When he is back to Tripoli he will take it to the watch mender in the *souk*. That man can mend anything.

Nafissa is out, gone to get supplies and Safia is asleep. He paces up and down the small room. He does not want to leave Safia again but he must go back for Ahmed. The intercom buzzes. Nafissa. He opens the door and walks down the stairs, takes the bags from her.

'There are still shortages,' she says. 'I couldn't get coffee or sugar. How is Safia?'

'She's sleeping.'

'Still? I will go and check on her.'

'I checked an hour ago.'

Nafissa returns, shaking her head. 'She's not in her room.'

'Not in her room? Where is she?' How could Safia have left without him knowing? She must have slipped out when he was in the bathroom. He bangs his fist on the table. 'What is the matter with her?' He is shouting now.

'Calm down. I expect she's gone out to see her friends.'

'Without saying anything? Creeping out like a thief? She knows we will be worried. It is not safe out there. Is this how she behaves?'

Nafissa collapses into a chair. 'No,' she says quietly. 'This is not like her, Mohamed.'

'She has a mobile phone. She must have that with her.'

There is no answer on the mobile and no sign of Safia. It is as if he doesn't know her any more, his own daughter.

'Now what will we do?' he cries. Just as everything was going to be all right, it is taken away from him again.

'We will wait. As we have waited before.'

Betty picks up the card Savannah has drawn and props it up against her wine glass. Here they all are like one happy family: Betty in a long blue dress, a row of coloured bracelets on her arm, Savannah in pink, a bow in her hair, holding hands with a rather spiky-haired Ahmed, his knees knobbly like two apples, Mohamed in a grey Western suit, Delia with her mobile phone and handbag, and Scott in blue jeans and black boots. Attached to Delia's handbag is a wiggly line and at the end, a baby – a boy Betty presumes as he's all in blue. Perhaps Savannah is coming round after all. Betty certainly hopes so.

She lights the candles and turns to look at Eva's face again. In the flickering light her daughter appears almost alive, although she would not look so young now if she were still living: she would be forty, perhaps married with children. Betty wonders how Mohamed coped, believing his daughter might be dead, how he managed the tragic death of his wife.

Darkness is falling. The nights are drawing in. Autumn is on its way. She walks over to the window. The edges of the curtains have faded in the sun. But that is how things are. Everything fades and disappears in time. As she reaches for the cord a shape catches her eye and she presses her nose to the glass. A fox is on the lawn, staring at her. She stands awhile, looking at it. Once, just the once, a desert fox crossed the road in front of the vehicle she was driving. Libya, somewhere south of Sabha. That was so very long ago.

The sky is threaded with streaks of red. Nafissa is in the kitchen chopping vegetables while Mohamed taps his foot on the rug and changes channels on the television. He's been doing the same for hours.

The door opens and Safia stands in the doorway.

'Where have you been?' He does not consider himself an angry man but at this moment he is tempted to slap her. Not that he will. But the feeling is there. And to think only yesterday his feelings were only tenderness and gratitude.

She is wearing a bright blue hijab, the bruise around her eye camouflaged with make-up. 'I had to go out,' she answers quietly.

'Out? You think this is freedom, doing what you please, leaving the house without a word?'

She pales. 'There was something I had to do.'

Nafissa is in the kitchen, hunched over the chopping board, a knife in her hand.

'Something you had to do?' he repeats. 'So secret was it, that you had to slip out of the door like a common thief?' When she does not answer, his anger turns cold. 'Or is this "thing" a person? Is that it? A boyfriend?'

'I don't have a boyfriend.' Her eyes blaze and he remembers Nour, how worked up she used to get. But that was before. 'All right!' She raises her hands and her voice softens. 'I should have told you I was going out. I'm sorry I didn't. But things have changed, Father. We've had a revolution, or haven't you noticed?'

He is weakening. He feels it. 'I should have stayed. I never should have gone to England.'

'Why did you go? Was it really so necessary? I stayed. Nafissa stayed.' She puts her hands on her hips and stares at him.

Nafissa walks out from the kitchen. 'Safia, that's really not fair.'

'Isn't it?' Safia turns to face her aunt. 'Why did he have to go?'

'You know why,' Nafissa replies, her voice curt.

Mohamed slumps into the chair. He feels old and lost. Why are they having this row? All he wants is their happiness, for Ahmed to return, for them to be a proper family again, together. He rubs his fore-head, as he might have a headache coming on. 'Can you imagine what it has been like for us here today, waiting? We tried your phone but it was switched off. I mean, I thought, we thought...'

'I don't have the mobile. It got lost somewhere in all that mess.'

'You could have left a note or called out to me. And if you must go out, make sure you tell us. It's dangerous out there, Safia. '

'As if I didn't know,' she says angrily. 'You have no idea what we've been doing to help the revolu-tion, Nafissa and I, the risks we've had to take.'

He holds up his hand now. 'I understand. But that doesn't give you the right to be disrespectful.'

She bows her head and a tear rolls down her cheek. He walks over to her and takes her in his arms. This time she does not shrink from him. How fragile she feels, as if she might break at any moment. But Nafissa is right – she is strong. He thinks of the first time he held her, the day of her birth, his sur-prise when she sucked forcefully at his finger. What a miracle she was. She is still a miracle.

'It's over,' he says. And he holds her until her sobs subside.

'I know you blame me for what happened to your mother,' he says, when he has let her go.

Safia perches on the edge of the chair. Her tears have run through the make-up and exposed the yellowing bruise.

'It is not so long ago, ' he continues. 'But, as you have just said, much has changed since then. We found it difficult to talk, even as man and wife. It's not like the West where these issues are discussed more openly. I felt ashamed. I felt responsible, as if I had allowed it to happen.' He looks to Nafissa for help. She nods and he continues. 'Your mother suffered a great deal in the prison. She never talked of it but I...but we... Nafissa and I believe your mother was violated there. But at the time I just didn't know how to talk to her. You know how she was, Safia. Please believe me. I felt like I was no longer a man because I hadn't been able to protect her. She was protecting me and it was supposed to be the other way round.'

Now Safia has her chin rested in her hand, her head to one side. The hijab has slipped, showing the edges of her dark hair, her mother's hair. 'I know you tried to get her out of the prison,' she says softly, 'and that nothing could be done. But when she came back home she was so sick. I wish I had understood why.'

'I was trying to protect you and Ahmed too,' Mohamed says.

She nods. 'I understand. But perhaps too much protection is not always a good thing.' She brushes away her tears and smiles, and he smiles back.

⚜ ⚜ ⚜

Sami has offered to drive Mohamed to the Tunisian border. Abdul will accompany them. But Mohamed is nervous, the conflict is not over and there are rumours that Gaddafi has been seen in Bani Walid, in Sirte – though no one really knows. Yesterday Gaddafi broadcast one of his speeches through a Syrian channel. 'We will fight against you wherever you are! We will sacrifice our lives and the sand and stones of Libya will become fire!'

And then it is time to leave. If only he did not have to go.

'We've managed without you for three years,' Nafissa says. 'We can manage a little longer. May Allah protect you.'

He hugs Safia. Hugs Nafissa. Promises he will be back.

Nafissa's words ring in his head as the wheels of the truck take him along the coast and up to Djerba. Safia is safe. Now he must get back to Ahmed.

Chapter Thirteen

How incredible it is to be back in Betty's sitting room. No need for that constant state of anxiety, his ears alert for gunfire, for anything that might bring trouble, or worse.

The journey was exhausting, dangerous at times. But he has pulled through. He leans back on the comfortable sofa and closes his eyes. A breeze catches the curtains and sweeps inside, flapping the newspaper on the table. There is none of the fierce summer heat here that is sometimes so exhausting in Libya.

'So, you are returning for good.'

'This is what I plan.' Mohamed opens his eyes. Betty is sitting upright, her right hand clutching the arm of the chair.

'Of course.' Her voice sounds clipped, proper, and her mouth is pursed.

'I hope you will return to Libya one day.'

She nods and smiles but the smile is tight and now her shoulders slump and she looks suddenly frail, although he has never thought of her in that way before.

'Maybe you will come soon,' he adds.

A slight colour stains her cheeks but she sits straight-backed again, continuing to smile in her polite English way. 'I expect everyone will tell me it's terribly dangerous there. Is it?'

He shrugs. 'I think it is OK. Maybe not perfect. I do not think London is always so safe.'

'I rarely go to London these days.' She waves her hand and her bracelets make a tinkling sound like the bells on a herd of goats. 'How is your daughter after her experience? It must have been very frightening for her. For you too.'

'She is all right, I think. Sometimes I blame myself for what happens. Perhaps it was not right for me to leave her in Tripoli, even though she lives with her aunt.' A lump rises into his throat and he coughs and covers his mouth with his hand.

Betty reaches for a small, framed photograph of her daughter. 'You can just imagine what people said about my daughter, can't you?' Her voice has turned brittle like a dry palm leaf. 'They said she was a fool for going to Gaza, that I was a fool to allow her to go. As if I could have stopped her. People must make their own decisions in life and people die everywhere, do they not, and for all sorts of stupid reasons.'

'Die?' he repeats. He does not know what she means. He assumed that her daughter lived far away, that perhaps there was a rift between them that could not be mended.

'Your daughter is a brave young woman. My daughter was too. But being brave is not everything, is it?' She turns to the window. He can see her chest rising and falling; perhaps she is fighting back tears. Yet when she faces him, her expression is as hard as her voice. 'Eva joined a protest against the Occupation. She was arrested by a group of Israeli soldiers, pushed into a van with six others and left in the midday heat.' She clasps her hands together and her gaze moves once more to the window. Mohamed can hear the children's shouts and laughter. 'She suffered a heart attack. It was the heat and the stress. They said that nothing could have been done, that she had a weak heart, but how can anyone believe that? How can I believe that, her own mother?'

'This is a terrible thing, terrible.' If only he had real words of comfort, but he has none. He is shocked too, that she should suddenly speak of this. But times are not usual. 'I am very sorry,' he says, lamely. 'I did not know.'

'How could you know?' Betty says. Her voice wavers. 'Your daughter. Tell me, how is she really? She must have been very frightened.'

'I was worrying for Safia, thinking the men hurt her in that prison. In a bad way. You understand?'

Betty's gaze is unflinching. 'You think she was raped?'

The word catches him off guard. 'Yes, yes. But Safia is not hurt in this way. She is lucky. No men touch her.'

'That is very good news, Mohamed. I am happy to hear this. You and your sister-in-law must be relieved.'

'Yes, but my wife is not so lucky. ' His hands go to his eyes. Now he feels like the boy he once was, caught stealing dates. He cannot look at Betty. He was never going to speak of that matter, especially to a woman he hardly knows, a Western woman, a non-Muslim too. Now the words are spoken he cannot take them back.

Betty is silent. It is her silence that enables him to continue.

'Raped, yes.' He grabs the edge of the chair as his anger rises, almost choking him. 'She is raped by the commander. This is what kills her. He kills her. The regime kills her but I do not understand this at the time because she does not say. Maybe she cannot say. She cannot live with the shame.' He stops. Takes a sip of the tea. It has gone cold. But he must continue. It is like lancing a boil. The needle is already deep in the skin. One cannot withdraw it until the operation is complete. 'One day she takes a bottle of pills – pills to help with sleep. It is Ahmed, he finds her.'

In the silence that follows Mohamed hears a bird sing in the garden and the girl giggling, calling Ahmed's name.

'You must not blame yourself, Mohamed, though of course we do.' Betty's voice has returned to its usual gentle tone. 'I blamed myself for what happened to Eva in Gaza. I've had to live with that all these years. It is a burden, is it not? ' She pauses and breathes in sharply. 'She went to Gaza because she was half-Arab, half-Libyan.' She twists at the bracelets on her arm.

Half-Libyan? It takes a moment for the words to sink in. Betty was married to an Englishman, was she not?

'Her father and I did not keep in touch.' She glances at him briefly, looks away. 'He got married soon after I left Libya. I was married already. I know what you must be thinking and you are right, Mohamed, for I did wrong. But I was a young woman and I fell so much in love.' She turns her head to the window for a third time and next, when her words fall, they are faint like the clouds in the sky outside.

'My husband and I tried for a baby for many years but we had no luck. When Eva was born I knew she was not his but I was very happy. He was happy too. He loved her and we loved each other.' A tear spills down her cheek. 'We have to forgive each other and ourselves, Mohamed, otherwise we are like plants without earth or water.' She leans forward and takes a tissue from the box on the table. 'What a stupid old woman, I am, crying so.'

He rises from the chair and places a hand on her shoulder. She looks at him and he returns the look and perhaps something passes between them, but he is not sure.

⚜ ⚜ ⚜

A grasshopper lands on a stalk of grass. It has a curly tail and tiny feet. What an incredible creature and what a noise it makes for such a small insect – though not so much as the cicadas he used to hear back in Libya. He supposes they will not have a garden in Tripoli; no doubt at first they will all have to squeeze into Aunt Nafissa's small apartment but perhaps one day they will have a garden, though it will never be like this one, so big and wild and green.

'We're going back to Tripoli.'

'I know.' Savannah stares at her bare feet. 'Will I see you after you've gone?' Her voice is so quiet.

'I'll get the internet. And a phone.'

'Oh, right,' she says. 'But it's not the same.' She reaches for her big toe and scratches at the silver varnish there. 'You're a real friend, Ahmed.' She looks at him now, a faint smile on her face. 'I never had a friend who was a boy before.'

He smiles back. If she were older or they had met in Libya, perhaps they could not have been friends in the same way. 'Are you still going to America?'

'I think so.' Savannah sighs and scuffs her bare foot on the grass. 'Will it be all right there?'

'I'm sure it will. It will be different but I'm sure you'll like it.'

'I suppose.' Another sigh, a longer one, like a whistle. 'Have you spoken to your sister again? How is she? What did happen to her? You haven't told me, not properly.'

Ahmed explains and Savannah listens; she doesn't interrupt with questions. When he has finished, she says, 'That's the bravest thing I ever heard. I wish I could meet her.'

'You will, one day. You can come to Libya. Or maybe we'll come to America.'

Now she grins, a big grin. 'Good.' Then she says, 'Was your mother fighting for freedom as well? Is that why she went to prison?'

He knows his mother spoke up against the Colonel but he has never thought of it in that way. 'Yes,' he says. 'She was. But it was the wrong time then. There weren't enough people brave enough.'

'The wrong time,' Savannah echoes. 'Now it's the right time for your country, isn't it?'

A large black bird struts across the lawn. It must be a crow. It begins to peck at something in the long grass. Ahmed wonders what it is eating, ants, or one of Betty's apples. The light is shining on the bird's black feathers and they look like velvet. He would like to draw it but as he turns his head to get a better look, the bird startles and flies away.

Mohamed looks around the apartment that has been theirs for three years; the patterned carpet and scuffed walls, the shabby furniture. Now they must pack everything that is theirs away, or be rid of it. There is much to be organised, before they can finally return home.

He has given notice at work. He will not be returning though he will go back and say goodbye.

They were good to him there. 'This charity shop,' he says to Ahmed. 'What will they take?'

'Books and toys but not electrical.'

'I do not think we have electrical. All that belongs to the apartment.'

'The toaster is ours. And the kettle.'

'Ah yes. But we cannot take those with us.'

'I wonder who will come and live here when we are gone?' Ahmed picks up the heavy glass paperweight Hashim gave him when they first arrived. 'What about this?'

'Yes, that was a present.'

'Was Mother fighting for freedom?' Ahmed asks, turning the paperweight over in his hand. He peers at it. 'This looks like a coral reef, Father.'

'Your mother was fighting for freedom, of course she was. We all were. But it was hard in those days. People were afraid and they had to be extremely careful.'

'Don't you hate what they did to her?'

Mohamed weighs the question in his mind, as if it were that heavy glass paperweight Ahmed still holds in his hand. '*When someone criticises or disagrees with you, a small ant of hatred and antagonism is born in your heart. If you do not squash that ant at once, it may grow into a snake, or even a dragon.* No, I do not hate them. To hate is to give power and I will not give them that.'

Ahmed places the paperweight back on the shelf. 'Why did she leave us?'

He examines his son. Mohamed is sure he has grown taller in the weeks he has been away. But there is something more. He seems less of a child. He has grown in other ways too. 'I think she had to leave,' he says quietly.

'I understand,' Ahmed replies. 'It's OK.' He is still standing by the bookshelf but his eyes are now focused on the floor and he looks suddenly awkward and young once more. How brave he has been these past few years. Perhaps Mohamed has not realised the strength this takes. His mother gone. A new country. A new language. His sister far away. He walks to over to his son and hugs him tight. 'We will be a proper family again, *insha'allah*,' he says.

Ahmed wriggles out of the embrace. 'Will we see Betty before we leave?'

'You call her Betty now? I seem to remember you used to call her Miss Betty.'

His son grins.

'Yes. I am going to invite her for dinner. There is a good place in the town that serves Arab food. The three of us will go. Unless you would also like me to invite your new friend?'

'Yes. I would like that.' Ahmed hesitates. 'I hope she will eat our food. She is quite fussy.'

'Fussy?' Mohamed shakes his head. 'I hope we never get fussy, Ahmed. This is the Western way of eating. All the same, I never believe any food is as good as the food your mother cooked.' That said, he returns his attention to sorting though their belongings.

Chapter Fourteen

The morning is dull and flat, like a dirty piece of paper. Delia has been delayed – some problem with flights Betty cannot now recall – and Betty has taken Savannah into town for a treat.

'I wish Ahmed didn't have to go back to Libya so soon,' Savannah says, slurping her strawberry milkshake.

Betty has taken them to the bookshop café. It has quite the best shakes and cakes in town. She turns to look out of the window. A few spots of rain are falling and a woman passing by is shouting at her toddler. 'Change isn't always easy.'

Savannah shrugs. Betty takes a bite of the lemon drizzle cake and sips her latte. At the next table a mother is trying to keep her two children from running all round the place. Betty catches her eye.

The woman sighs and says, 'Thank goodness, it's almost the end of the holidays. I don't think I could cope another day.'

Betty smiles but she says nothing. She remembers those times, times when she was so exhausted looking after Eva she could hardly think, times she wanted to be elsewhere. To be working. To be back in Libya. To be anywhere but with a small child in a confined space. But then those times were gone, and Eva too.

A nudge and a whisper from Savannah. 'Those children are being very naughty.'

'Aren't you ever naughty?' Betty asks.

Savannah shakes her head and grins. 'What is it like in America?'

'Well,' Betty says, thinking hard. 'They certainly have fantastic ice-creams and shakes there. And deserts and canyons. It's quite an amazing country. One day, perhaps when you're a little older, I'll take you to Libya. When things are more settled there.'

'Can we see the sand dunes? Can we go to the places you went?'

'I expect so.'

'Ahmed says some of the dunes are as big as mountains.'

'Is that so? Dunes can hum. I bet you didn't know that, did you? The sound is extraordinary. It's something to do with the different layers of sand. The noise is very similar to that of a didgeridoo – those long pipes the Australian aborigines have.'

'Like this? Mmmmmmmmmmmmmmmmmmm mmm...'

Betty smiles. 'Yes, just like that.'

⚜ ⚜ ⚜

Savannah is upstairs packing her bag. Betty asked if she wanted any help but she said, no, she could manage. Now Betty is tidying the kitchen and wondering what on earth she will do with her time.

The bell rings. Perhaps it is Mohamed. But it is Annette, an unexpected call.

'You look glum,' Annette says, stepping into the hall. 'Is something wrong?'

'Not wrong, exactly. But Ahmed has already gone and Savannah will be leaving in a couple of hours, and I'll be back to rattling uselessly round this old place.'

Annette hangs her jacket on the hook and follows Betty into the sitting room, the heels on her shoes click-clacking on the tiles. 'Why don't you sell this old place? It's much too big for you.'

Annette has her opinions. But sometimes she is right. 'I don't know. It's been home for so long.' Betty slumps into the sofa and the springs groan as if they no longer wanted her there. 'Too many memories.'

'Memories can hold you back.' Annette fiddles in her ear. 'I went to the audiologist last week. My hearing aid wasn't working properly.' She giggles, like a young girl. 'Now everything is so loud it makes me jump.'

'Yes,' says Betty, staring out of the window. A large black crow is pacing restlessly back and forth across the lawn.

'You're not listening,' Annette scolds. 'Take a trip, a holiday. Go to Libya.'

'Libya? Are you serious? The war isn't over yet. It's not safe.'

Annette kicks off her shoes and settles into the chair. 'When did you ever worry about safety? Goodness me, you don't have many years left, neither of us does, but if you can't, or won't, go to Libya, there are other places. You're mouldering away here. Live a little, for heaven's sake.'

'I'll think about it.'

'Do more than think about it, Betty. Now, you'll never guess what I've been doing.' Annette taps at her nose and gives Betty a sly smile.

'What is it? You've bought another handbag, a pair of those expensive shoes.'

'I don't need another handbag. I'm not that vain.' Annette rolls her eyes in mock horror. 'And no, I have not thrown away large amounts of cash on a pair of Jimmy Choo's.' She holds up a finger. 'I've been speed dating. What do you think of that? It took some doing. I was scared half to death at first.'

'I don't think I could do it. But good for you.' She means it. Annette deserves a little happiness. They all do.

Annette dangles her stockinged feet over the edge of the chair. 'The thing is, Betty, I may have found someone.'

'Really? Well, that was quick work.'

'What of your lovely Mohamed? He's a widow and quite a catch, I should imagine. Didn't you say he used to work as a doctor?'

Betty feels herself stiffen. 'I'm sure Mohamed would wish to marry someone from his own country and his own religion. In any case, I don't think he has any plans in that direction.'

'My, my,' Annette says, with a wave of her hand. 'I have touched a raw nerve. Has he told you that?'

'No,' Betty answers, grumpily.

'Goodness, Betty, you weren't always so buttoned up.' Annette places her feet back on the floor and stands up. She must be about to leave already, Betty thinks, unsure if she is relieved or hurt. Annette only stretches and yawns but, as she does, a button pops off her blouse, exposing the lace edge of her bra.

'Buttoned up,' Betty says, smiling in spite of herself. 'Well you're certainly not buttoned up.'

Annette splutters and giggles, and Betty follows. When Savannah walks in a minute or two later, they are both clutching at their stomachs, laughing hysterically. Like they used to.

'What are you doing?' Savannah asks, her eyebrows shooting up almost to her Alice band. 'You're all crazy.'

'We've got the giggles,' Betty hiccups, 'and we can't stop.'

The knock on the door comes at exactly five o'clock. And Savannah runs down the hall, rushes into her mother's arms.

Five fifteen. Savannah hauls her bag into the hall as the grandfather clock strikes the quarter. 'It will be funny without that clock,' she says. 'I might even miss it.'

Twenty minutes past five. Goodbye hugs.

Twenty-two minutes past. Savannah looks at Betty and waves three times and Betty waves back. Then Savannah jumps in the car and the car drives off, wheels crunching though the gravel.

Half past. Two strikes of the clock. A closed front door. An empty hallway.

Twenty-five minutes to six. A walk down the garden. A single rose in the twilight. A gust of wind in the apple trees. Light falling, fading.

Quarter to six. A walk back to the house.

Now Betty sits alone with the clocks. Tick, tick, tick. No other sound, only her own breathing, slow and steady, and the blood in her ears like the sea. Tick, tick, tick.

An owl hoots. The room grows dark.

A sudden noise, the cat flap opening. Napoleon rubs himself against Betty's leg, purring, purring. She gets up and switches on the light. 'Where's Stealth?' she says, her voice echoing around the empty kitchen. Napoleon stares at her with his yellow eyes and twitches his tail. 'I suppose you want feeding?'

She fills the two cat bowls and pours herself a glass of wine. Then she walks into the sitting room to fetch her sketchbook from the top of the bureau. On impulse she opens the drawer and retrieves her passport. She looks at it thoughtfully, and, leaving it out, returns to the kitchen.

The phone rings. She moves down the hall to answer it.

Acknowledgements

Many people have helped in the writing of this book but I would especially like to thank my close writing buddies, Ros Jones and Lesley Arnold-Hopkins.

Susannah Waters, my writing tutor, gave me good advice and Rebecca El-Kher kindly read through the manuscript for errors on the Libyan side - but any remaining mistakes are mine. My 'virtual' friends on the Libyan blog - some of whom I have now met in the flesh - also fed me vital information on the conflict in Libya and indeed continue to do so.

I thank my family and all my other friends for their continued support. I'm sure you all know who you are!

I would also like to thank Helen Bryant and Yasmin Standen of Three Hares Publishing who believed in my work and made this publication possible.

A number of people and organisations were involved in assisting us leave Libya from the KE Adventure trip in February 2011 but I would especially like to thank our guide, Mohammed, who worked beyond the call of duty and kept us safe.

I would also like to thank all those people across the world who have worked, and continue to work, for freedom from tyranny.

www.threeharespublishing.com

www.threeharespublishing/bookclub.com